P9-BZX-072

Molly was giving him plenty to think about.

He watched in amazement as she slowly, patiently and carefully lured Brianne into a conversation about a group of boys who stood nearby. Beau felt his heart swell with gratitude when she listened to Nicky's convoluted story about something that had happened at school. When the football team rode past in a convoy of pickup trucks, Molly cheered as if she were single-handedly responsible for the team's morale.

By the time the parade had ended, he'd begun to regret that Molly wasn't going to stay around longer. Not for himself, but for his poor confused daughter and for the son who nudged through the crowds and grabbed Molly's hand as if he'd known her forever.

Well...maybe a *little* bit for himself.

Dear Reader,

As a writer, sometimes you stumble across a character who grabs your attention and hangs on. Maybe you're granted a glimpse of certain moments in his life. Maybe not. You only know that you have to find his story and share it.

Beau Julander is one of those characters. He walked into my life and wouldn't leave until I'd done my job. In *The Christmas Wife* we travel back to Serenity, Wyoming, a town I introduced for the first time a few years ago in *That Woman in Wyoming* (Harlequin Superromance #974). Serenity is a quiet town in Wyoming's mountain country, and it has become almost as real to me as the town where I live.

Beau lives there, surrounded by friends and family, the golden boy of his high school graduating class and all the years in between. But people aren't always what they seem on the surface, and there's more to Beau than the image he presents to the world. He meets Molly Shepherd, the quiet girl from high school, who has no family at all and can't even remember their senior year. As Beau struggles just to get from one day to the next, Molly searches for answers about the past...and love follows a plan of its own.

I hope you enjoy getting to know Beau and Molly as much as I did. Please write and let me know what you think of their story. You can send letters to Sherry Lewis, P.O. Box 540010, North Salt Lake, UT 84054. Or e-mail me at sherrylewis@slbwrites.com. Also, visit my Web site at www.slbwrites.com.

Sherry Lewis

The Christmas Wife
Sherry Lewis

HARLEQUIN®

TORONTO • NEW YORK • LONDON
AMSTERDAM • PARIS • SYDNEY • HAMBURG
STOCKHOLM • ATHENS • TOKYO • MILAN • MADRID
PRAGUE • WARSAW • BUDAPEST • AUCKLAND

If you purchased this book without a cover you should be aware
that this book is stolen property. It was reported as "unsold and
destroyed" to the publisher, and neither the author nor the
publisher has received any payment for this "stripped book."

ISBN 0-373-71169-7

THE CHRISTMAS WIFE

Copyright © 2003 by Sherry Lewis.

All rights reserved. Except for use in any review, the reproduction or
utilization of this work in whole or in part in any form by any electronic,
mechanical or other means, now known or hereafter invented, including
xerography, photocopying and recording, or in any information storage
or retrieval system, is forbidden without the written permission of the
publisher, Harlequin Enterprises Limited, 225 Duncan Mill Road,
Don Mills, Ontario, Canada M3B 3K9.

All characters in this book have no existence outside the imagination of
the author and have no relation whatsoever to anyone bearing the same
name or names. They are not even distantly inspired by any individual
known or unknown to the author, and all incidents are pure invention.

This edition published by arrangement with Harlequin Books S.A.

® and TM are trademarks of the publisher. Trademarks indicated with
® are registered in the United States Patent and Trademark Office, the
Canadian Trade Marks Office and in other countries.

Visit us at www.eHarlequin.com

Printed in U.S.A.

For Gene and Vanda Lewis,
the best parents any woman could ask for

Books by Sherry Lewis

HARLEQUIN SUPERROMANCE
628—CALL ME MOM
692—THIS MONTANA HOME
744—KEEPING HER SAFE
816—LET IT SNOW
826—A MAN FOR MOM
883—FOR THE BABY'S SAKE
974—THAT WOMAN IN WYOMING
1072—MR. CONGENIALITY

Don't miss any of our special offers. Write to us at the
following address for information on our newest releases.

Harlequin Reader Service
U.S.: 3010 Walden Ave., P.O. Box 1325, Buffalo, NY 14269
Canadian: P.O. Box 609, Fort Erie, Ont. L2A 5X3

CHAPTER ONE

"HAS ANYBODY SEEN a blue sock?" Beau Julander straightened from the basket filled with clean, unfolded clothes and closed the dryer with his hip. "Anybody?"

Late-autumn sunlight streamed into the renovated kitchen of the old farmhouse he'd inherited from his grandparents, spotlighting last night's dishes stacked by the sink, still waiting to be washed. Leaves from the huge oak trees in the yard fluttered past the window, and the autumn colors on the foothills surrounding Serenity gleamed in the warm Wyoming sunlight.

Beau kicked at the mound of unwashed laundry at his feet and turned toward the table where his twelve-year-old daughter scowled at the pages of an open notebook. "Brianne? Did you hear me?" It was an unnecessary question since he was standing less than ten feet away, but she'd been giving him the silent treatment for days, and he was growing tired of it.

Brianne slowly turned a page in her notebook and rolled her eyes toward the ceiling, where footsteps thundered overhead. Eight-year-old Nicky must still be searching for the missing math worksheet Beau had sent him to find. Brianne let out a sigh weighted with preteen attitude and big-sister irritation, brushed a lock of wheat-blond hair from her forehead and looked back at her father. "When Gram was taking care of us, we always knew where our socks were." One eyebrow arched meaningfully. "That's because they were always clean."

Beau congratulated himself on getting a few words out of her and pretended not to notice the challenge underlying them. Before her mother left, Brianne had chattered at him endlessly, sharing news of her day, talking about her hopes, dreams, joys and disappointments. She'd changed since the divorce, and things had taken another turn for the worse two weeks ago. Now if she wasn't ignoring him, she was starting an argument.

He'd been struggling to hold things together for the past year, after Heather walked out on him. But he'd been sinking fast since the night two weeks ago when he'd decided it was time to do the job on his own. All he wanted was for life to get back to normal. For Brianne to greet him with a smile once in a while. To get through just one morning without an argument.

"These clothes are clean," he pointed out. "At least some of them are. And if each day would just come with three or four more hours attached, they'd be folded and put away, too."

Brianne's only answer was an annoyed sniff, but he supposed that was better than nothing.

Beau was due at the airstrip in less than an hour to begin a charter flight that would keep him in the air most of the day. He'd be home in time for supper and a last-minute meeting of the Homecoming committee, but he didn't have time to spare, and he wasn't in the mood to explain—again—why things had to change.

He bent over the basket and dug until he found two boy-size socks that were similar, if not exact matches. Tossing them on top of the washer, he turned back to the eggs he'd left cooking.

His daughter slid a pointed glance at the stove. "Gram never burned the eggs, either."

"Gram is a better cook than I am," he said as he reached into the cupboard for plates. He flipped the mass of eggs, which had started out as fried and ended up scrambled, and turned off the burner. "But I can learn."

"That's doubtful."

Struggling to hang on to his patience, Beau put the plates on the counter and opened the drawer for the silverware. "Get used to it, Brie. Gram isn't going to be taking care of you anymore."

"Well, she should."

"I know you think so."

Brianne turned a page and shoved a stack of Homecoming flyers out of her way. "You're just being mean."

"No, I'm being practical. Your grandmother was a great help after your mom left. But *I'm* taking care of us now. We have to expect that a few things will be different."

"I don't want things to be different."

"I realize that, too." Beau pulled juice from the refrigerator, found three clean glasses in the dish drainer and carried everything to the table.

"Gram never left dirty dishes around, either," Brianne pointed out needlessly. She brushed a piece of lint from her pink sweater and tossed her hair over her shoulder.

Beau put a glass in front of her and filled it with juice. "Gram's had more experience taking care of a house and kids than I have. I just need to get organized, that's all. Once Homecoming Week is over, I'll have more time."

"You won't have more time," Brianne said sullenly. "As soon as Homecoming's over, you'll start getting ready for WinterFest, and then Christmas."

"Not immediately."

"Almost."

"I might not help with either of them this year."

"Yes, you will, because if you don't, you'll just worry about where they put the banners and whether those wire-deer decorations on Front Street are lit right." She reached for a napkin and wiped her mouth with it. "You *like* doing all that stuff. Mom said so."

He'd heard that accusation more than once. Coming from Heather, it had always made him feel slightly guilty—as if volunteering to help his community was something to be ashamed of. It didn't sound much better coming from Brianne.

"Serenity's a small town," he reminded her. "Without volunteer help, there would be very few things going on around here. But you're not the only one who has to make changes."

Brianne's face twisted in disbelief. "Bet you'll do Christmas. You always do."

"Bet I won't. I already told the mayor to find someone else. And he will." He'd better, anyway. Mayor Biggs hadn't sounded convinced that Beau intended to step down. "I've told him I'm staying just until I can get a replacement up to speed."

A skeptical roll of the eyes met that promise. "I still don't see why Gram can't come back and take care of us. That way you could do stuff like Homecoming and Christmas and you wouldn't have to worry. We wouldn't get in your way, and Nicky wouldn't be so sad anymore."

"You don't get in my way," Beau said evenly, "and

Nicky doesn't seem all that sad to me. And has it ever occurred to you that Gram might have other things to do?''

"Like what?''

He leaned against the counter and crossed one foot over the other. "Okay, fine. Gram would have kept coming over here every day for the rest of her life if I'd let her, but that wouldn't be fair to her.''

"Why not? She likes doing it.''

"I know she does, but taking care of us is *my* job, not hers. Gram's already raised her family—''

"*We're* her family. She says so all the time.''

"Well, of course we're her family.'' At least, the kids were. Beau shifted uncomfortably and tried to find a way to explain the subtle nuances that seemed to be lost on his daughter. Now that the initial shock of Heather's decision had worn off and the divorce had become final in July, it felt more and more wrong to give his ex-wife's mother free rein over his house.

It wasn't that he didn't appreciate Doris's help. What he didn't appreciate was the way she watched and judged every move he made, her belief that Heather would "come to her senses'' one day and return to Serenity, and her repeated insistence that Beau should be waiting for that day with open arms. He didn't like thinking that Doris was filling the kids' heads with unrealistic expectations about their mother, either. But how to explain that to a child who didn't really understand why her mother left?

"Gram's been great to help us,'' he admitted, "and you know how much I appreciate what she's done. But I'm starting to feel like I'm not doing my job.''

"That's dumb.''

Beau sat at the table and filled the other two glasses

with juice. "That from the girl who keeps pointing out everything I don't get done?"

"You're no good at housework, Daddy. That's why Gram has to come back."

Her lack of faith stung, but the "Daddy" took some of the sting away. Beau went after the plates and decided to skip that second cup of coffee. "I'm not saying you can't see Gram, sweetie. You and Nicky can visit her anytime you want."

"Anytime?"

"Within reason. You can't just disappear without asking me, though, and you should make sure Gram's home first. But if you want to stop by after school once in a while, I won't say no."

Brianne kicked the back of her chair rhythmically. "That's not the same as having her here."

"No, it's not. But that's how it has to be." Beau checked his watch and groaned. Once, he'd been a stickler about punctuality. These days, it seemed he was always late. "How about running upstairs to see what's keeping your brother? The school bus will be here in ten minutes."

"I don't think it's fair that *I* have to baby-sit because *you* don't want Gram here."

"That's enough, Brianne. I'm not asking you to baby-sit. I'm asking you to contribute to the family. Now go."

She let out another sigh, rose majestically to her feet and disappeared with one last toss of her hair. Beau spooned cold eggs onto plates with a grimace and made a silent bet with himself about how much the kids would choke down before they ran out the door. He knew exactly how much *he'd* eat.

Brianne was right about one thing, he thought with

a frown. Housework wasn't his strong suit. But that was going to change. He just needed time. A chance to focus. Then the piles of laundry would disappear and the dirty dishes would vanish. His relationship with Brianne would get back to normal, and he'd prove, once and for all, that he was more than capable of raising the kids on his own.

TWENTY MINUTES LATER, Beau stood in his cluttered study and tried to remember where he'd left his car keys. The kids had made it to the school bus on time, but he'd be late if he didn't walk out the door in two minutes. He dug through a stack of old mail, patted the bank statement beside his computer monitor and swore softly under his breath.

He had to get more organized. That was all there was to it.

He'd just lifted a pile of mail that still needed sorting when the telephone rang. He thought about ignoring it, but one glance at the caller ID changed his mind. He snagged the receiver from its cradle. "Gwen? What's wrong?"

"Well, that's a nice greeting," his sister returned. At thirty-one, Gwen was two years his junior, solid and dependable and, lucky for him, willing to take up the slack while he adjusted to the world without his mother-in-law underfoot. "What are you doing home? I've been trying to reach you at the office."

With a frown, Beau cradled the phone against his shoulder. "I have a better question. Why are you calling me?"

"Why shouldn't I?"

"I may be paranoid," he said, "but a call at this hour of the morning isn't a good sign—especially on a day when you've promised to pick up the kids after school.''

Her indrawn breath and soft sigh as she let it out again confirmed his suspicions. Her response cinched it. "Don't kill me, okay?"

"Gwen—"

"It's Riley's mother's birthday. We're supposed to take her to Star Valley to visit her sister. I forgot all about it until five minutes ago."

Beau tossed the mail back onto the desk. "You don't have to pick up the kids until three-thirty."

"We won't be back that early. We're taking Riley's brother and his family with us, and they have the whole day planned. I'm really sorry, but we'll be gone until late."

Beau stared out the window but he barely saw the autumn foliage on the hillside in front of him. "You're leaving me in the lurch because of a birthday party?"

"I have to. We're committed."

"You're committed to me, too, Gwen. What am I supposed to do now? I'll be in Jackson when the kids get out of school."

"I know, but can't they take the bus home just this once?"

"They take the bus home every day, but tonight Brianne has karate and Nicky has soccer practice." Beau turned away from the window and rubbed the back of his neck. "I can't believe you're doing this. I have to take off in just a couple of minutes. People are waiting for me in Grant's Pass—"

"I know, and I'm really, really sorry. Riley feels horrible, too. Usually one of us remembers things like this, but somehow we both spaced it this time."

Beau checked his watch and swore again. "Fine. Whatever. I'll call Mom and see if she can help."

"Don't bother," Gwen said quickly. "I've already called. Lucas says she left for King's Junction half an hour ago."

With a growl of frustration, Beau shoved aside a bunch of magazines and finally spied his keys beneath a picture Nicky had brought home from school the previous afternoon. He stuffed the keys into his pocket so he wouldn't lose them again and carried the cordless phone with him into the kitchen, where the scent of overcooked eggs still hung in the air. "Did you ask Lucas what he's doing?" Their younger brother wasn't nearly as responsible as Gwen, but he'd do all right for a few hours.

"He's scheduled to work until seven."

A tension headache began to pound behind Beau's eyes. He ran quickly through a list of friends close enough to ask a favor on such short notice, but he couldn't think of anyone who'd be home at that hour. "This is one helluva time to leave me hanging," he snarled. "I can't afford to ask another pilot to fly this trip. Property taxes are due in two months, and canceling at the last minute would shoot holes in my reputation."

"Well, of course you can't cancel. I know that. But I can't cancel on Riley's family, either." Gwen's voice trailed away thoughtfully, then brightened again. "How about Doris? I'm sure she'd be glad to watch the kids."

Beau laughed harshly. "I don't think so. She's still upset with me."

"But she's their grandmother."

"A grandmother who's convinced I'm going to fail

with the kids and who's just waiting for me to prove her right."

"This isn't failure," Gwen said reasonably. "This is a scheduling conflict. Besides, you shouldn't let her bother you."

"We're talking about Doris Preston, right? My mother-in-law? The woman who can turn stone to dust with just a glance?"

Gwen laughed. "I'll admit she's a little obsessive, but she's not that bad. Her feelings are hurt, but she'll get over it. Besides, if she knows that you really aren't going to keep the kids away from her, maybe it'll help heal the rift between you."

"I doubt it." Beau tugged open the fridge and pulled out two cans of cola, two apples and a plastic sandwich bag filled with grapes. "I saw her at the gas station yesterday," he said as he stuffed the snacks into his knapsack. "She pretended I didn't exist. She'd like nothing better than to have me begging for help today."

"Oh, please. You're a good father. You were a great husband. Heather's the one who decided she wanted a different life, and Doris feels responsible for some reason. You'll get used to caring for the kids on your own. You just need time."

Beau smiled ruefully. "Thanks, sis. Some days I need a cheerleader."

"Whatever you say. Just be realistic, okay? What other choice do you have?"

Although he tried like hell to think of another solution, Gwen was right. Doris *was* his only option. "Go," he said as he checked to make sure he'd turned off the stove. "Eat cake. Open presents. Have a great time. I'll call Doris and grovel."

"Don't grovel. Just ask."

"Right. I'll ask." He disconnected a few seconds later, but even with the minutes racing past, he couldn't make himself pick up the phone again. He didn't think Doris would turn him down, but asking a favor of her so soon sure felt like he was losing ground.

Beau had never learned how to admit defeat easily—not on the football field in high school, not in his marriage, not in any aspect of his life. Only the balance in his checking account got him to dial Doris's phone number. Only the certain knowledge that Doris adored the kids, and the hope that a visit with her might even soften Brianne's mood, kept him from hanging up when she answered.

"Hey, Doris. It's Beau. Am I catching you at a bad time?"

He sensed a slight tensing on the other end, but that might have been his imagination. "Well, Beau. This is a surprise. What do you need?"

Nope. Not his imagination at all. He kept a smile on his face and hoped it would carry through to his voice. Anything to take the chill off Doris's tone. "I'm in a bind," he forced himself to admit. "I'm calling to ask a favor. If you don't want to or if you have other plans, just say so. I'll understand complete—"

"You need help with the children?"

"Just for this afternoon. I have a charter. Gwen was going to pick them up for me, but she forgot a family obligation."

"And you need *me*."

If the warm sun hadn't been streaming through the dirt on his window, he'd have sworn he'd stepped into one of Wyoming's famous January freezes. "It would help a lot if you could get the kids from school. Brianne has karate and Nicky has soccer—''

''I remember their schedules. It hasn't been that long.''

''Of course you do.'' Beau concentrated on keeping his tone even. ''If you don't mind, I'll pick them up from your house about five.''

''You don't want me to take them to your house?''

And see everything he hadn't done? Not a chance. ''No. Thanks. I don't want to impose, and I'm sure you already have plans around home.'' He kept talking so she couldn't disagree with him. ''I won't be late. You don't even have to worry about giving them supper. I'll be home in plenty of time for that.'' Even if it was just fast food from the Burger Shack.

''I see.''

She sounded so much like Heather, Beau closed his eyes and reminded himself why he was calling Doris in the first place. ''I know it's a lot to ask, but it would really help me out.''

''It's not a lot to ask,'' Doris said firmly. ''That's the whole point. I'm glad to do whatever those children need—and heaven knows, they need plenty. It just seems wrong to me, having to schedule time to spend with them. I don't understand why you're being so stubborn when it's obvious you can't handle them on your own.''

''I *can* handle them. I'm just in a bind this afternoon, that's all.'' He could feel his irritation rising, so he took a couple of deep breaths and watched the neighbors across the street drive away to start their day. ''I need a favor,'' he said when he could trust himself to speak, ''but I'm not going to argue with you. It's time for me to get back on my feet, but that doesn't mean you and the kids can't spend time together. It's not as if I'm trying to separate you from them.''

''Well, it sure feels like it.'' She sighed heavily and he could almost see the scowl on her face. ''Is it all right if I give them an after-school snack?''

When had that ever been an issue? She really was trying to make this difficult. Beau closed his eyes and rubbed his forehead. ''You can give them an afternoon snack,'' he said. ''You can let them watch TV if they don't have schoolwork, just like always. I'll be home by five.'' And then, because he didn't have the patience or the energy for more, he added, ''Thanks a lot, Doris. If you need to reach me, I'll have my cell phone on when it won't interfere with the instruments. If I don't answer, leave a message and I'll get right back to you.''

Before she could argue, he disconnected, letting out a groan that would have frightened small children and animals if there'd been any around. He really had to get his life under control.

He knew he could do it. Like training for football season or learning how to fly. He'd keep distractions to a minimum and focus on the goal. It had worked for him before. He'd just have to make it work again.

MOLLY SHEPHERD absently tapped her fingernails on the rental-car counter at the Jackson airport while she waited for the clerk to locate her reservation on the computer. She was just two hours away now. One hundred and twenty minutes, give or take a few, before she drove into Serenity for the first time since her mother's death. Yet again, she wondered if coming back was a mistake. But after spending most of the day on an airplane, and a significant chunk of money to get here, it was a little late to be having second thoughts.

A soothing feminine voice paged passengers over the public-address system. Soft music underscored the noise of the crowd and should have calmed the nervous energy Molly felt, but every sound only added to the tension in her neck and shoulders.

The card announcing Serenity's Homecoming Week Gala had reached her mailbox at a vulnerable time. One year after her divorce from Ethan, six months after her father's funeral, one month after being downsized out of the job she'd held for five years with a graphic-design firm. For weeks she'd been at loose ends, searching for some way to tie those ends together again. When the invitation arrived, she'd jumped first and saved questions for later.

The man behind her bumped into the trolley holding her luggage. She wheeled it out of his way and glanced out the window at the towering Teton Mountains that created the valley known as Jackson Hole. The rugged peaks already wore a cap of snow, though it was only the first of October. It wasn't that she hadn't wanted to come back to Wyoming before now, just that there had never been a real opportunity. Her father hadn't wanted to return, and Ethan had never been interested in her past. Neither of the men in her life had understood how much the missing pieces of her memory bothered her.

The young man behind the counter clicked his fingers over the keyboard and glanced at her. "We're out of compacts. Midsize okay with you? It'll be the same price."

"Midsize is fine." She forced a smile and tried to shake off her uncertainty. So what if it had been fifteen years since she'd seen or heard from any of her old school friends? So what if she couldn't remember most of her senior year? There were things and people she *could* remember. Most important, she had a chance to find answers to questions that had been haunting her for years.

"Do you want insurance?"

"No," she said, making a conscious effort to stop worrying. "Thank you."

"Are you sure?" A concerned smile quivered across the young man's lips. "You're taking quite a risk. You want to make sure you're fully covered."

Driving without extra insurance felt like a minor risk compared with the others she was taking. "I'm quite sure. Thank you."

"Will there be any other drivers besides yourself?"

"No."

"And you want unlimited mileage?"

"Yes, please." Maybe she'd do some sightseeing while she was here. The butterflies in her stomach made another round, and her hands felt clammy. She silently chanted the mantra she'd been reciting all day. It didn't matter if none of her classmates remembered her. It didn't even matter if she spent the entire Homecoming Week alone. She had to take advantage of this opportunity, or she'd regret it the rest of her life.

"You want the car for how long?" the young man asked without looking away from his screen.

"Two weeks, maybe less. I don't know for sure."

"You don't want the weekly rate?"

He seemed confused, but she didn't want to elaborate. "The weekly rate is fine," she said firmly. "I'll bring it back on the seventeenth."

"Of October."

"Yes."

"You're sure? I can recalculate using the daily rate if you need me to."

The man behind Molly groaned in protest at the delay and she felt a prickle of nervousness. She hated imposing, even on a stranger. "I'm quite sure. Two weeks is perfect. No early return."

The man behind the counter typed a bit more, and Molly turned to glance at the crowd. She became aware of a deep male voice edged with tension coming from the corridor behind her. A heartbeat later, she identified the speaker as a tall blond man wearing jeans and a sage-colored shirt. He maneuvered through the passengers crowding the baggage-claim turnstiles as he set a steady course toward the car-rental area.

"Excuse me." He turned sideways to sidle past a young mother with three children and came up short behind a hefty woman weighted down by several bulging bags. Annoyance pinched his face, and it was easy to see that he was having to work to hang on to his patience. "I'm sorry, ma'am. Would you mind…?"

Molly started to turn away, but something compelled her to look back at him across the crowded area. Maybe she was imagining things, but the voice, the face, even the way he moved seemed hauntingly familiar.

Did she really know him, or was she just jumping to that conclusion now that she was back in Wyoming?

"Okay. I think we're set." The clerk tapped the counter to get her attention. "Here are your keys, and here's your contract. You'll need to keep the contract in your glove box at all times…"

Nodding absently, Molly took another look at the man who towered over most of the people around him. Broad shoulders, narrow hips. The muscular legs of an athlete. He put his hands on an elderly woman's shoulders as he slipped behind her, then pivoted toward the rental counter.

Molly's gaze flew to his face again and the niggling feeling that she knew him took form. This time she was certain it wasn't her imagination. In fact, she couldn't decide why she'd even wondered. His was a face she'd never forgotten, not even for a second.

Beau Julander. High-school jock, senior-class president, every teacher's favorite student, every girl's dream. He was hands down the hottest guy Molly had ever seen in her life—and that list included Ethan when she'd been in love with him.

Her heart raced and her stomach knotted uncomfortably. Fifteen years dropped away as if they'd never been, and she felt young and foolish and hopelessly self-conscious, just like the last time she remembered being in Serenity.

She whirled back toward the clerk and pretended to pay attention to his final instructions as Beau came to a stop at the end of the line. When she tried to swallow, her throat was parched and her mouth dry. She resisted the urge to look back at him and nodded in all the right places as the clerk talked. But even without turning around, Molly was all too aware of Beau.

Time had been good to him. No surprise there. He'd always led a charmed life. He was still tall and solidly muscled, still better-looking than any man had a right to be. She touched one hand to her cheek, then realized how silly she was acting and gave herself a stern mental shake.

So he was Beau Julander. So what? He probably wouldn't even remember her.

She stole one last peek at him. Yes, of course, she'd expected to see him at Homecoming. Homecoming probably couldn't take place without Beau Julander there. But she hadn't expected to see him so soon. Not when she looked as if she'd been sleeping in her clothes. Not when her breath reeked of garlic from lunch on the airplane.

And most important, not alone.

CHAPTER TWO

TRYING DESPERATELY to pull herself together, Molly tucked her credit card into her pocket and turned slowly toward the end of the line. She glanced at the wrinkled linen pantsuit she'd been wearing since early morning, and the blouse that bore faint traces of spilled coffee from her early flight.

"Is there anything else, Ms. Shepherd?"

Molly shook her head at the clerk, apologized to the annoyed man whose path she was blocking and stepped away from the counter. Clutching her purse like a security blanket, she was aware of Beau shifting his weight impatiently from one foot to the other.

Hands propped on his hips, he scowled at the world for having the nerve to keep him waiting. He'd always been Serenity's golden boy, so Molly shouldn't be surprised to discover that he'd grown into the kind of man who thought the world should stand still for him.

She lifted her chin and started back down the long line, dragging her luggage behind her on the rented cart, which suddenly developed steering problems and a hideous squeak in one wheel. But all the determination in the world couldn't keep her from seeking him out once more as she passed.

Like everyone else in line, he was watching her struggle with the cart, but as his gaze settled on her face, recognition flickered in his eyes. Certain her heart had stopped beating, Molly looked away and willed herself not to trip or do anything else clumsy and embarrassing.

"Excuse me." His voice sounded startlingly close to her ear and a hand landed on her shoulder.

She jumped and whipped around quickly. If she'd been wearing heels, she would have twisted an ankle. In flats she teetered just a little and did her best to hide her nervousness. "Yes?"

"Don't I know you?"

Molly's heart thumped against her rib cage, but she managed, somehow, to sound almost normal when she responded. "I don't know. Do you?" Okay. It was a lie. But she was not going to make him think she'd been dewy-eyed over him all this time. Bad enough that he'd once suspected how she felt.

"Yeah. I *do* know you. Aren't you…didn't you go to Serenity High School?"

"Yes, I did." She almost left it at that, but she was thirty-three, not sixteen, so she smiled and held out a hand. "Molly Shepherd. I was Molly Lane back then. But I'm sure you don't—"

"From Mr. Kagle's ceramics class, right?" He took her hand and his lips curved into the grin that had nearly cost Molly a passing grade in Mr. Kagle's class. "Beau Julander."

Molly nearly laughed at the idea of Beau introducing himself, but the feel of his hand around hers froze the sound in her throat. His eyes were still the most incredible shade of blue she'd ever seen. "Beau. Of course." Her voice sounded tight and high, but she prayed he wouldn't notice. "I remember you."

He let go of her and nodded toward the cart she was

clinging to with her other hand. "You're here for a visit?"

As she loosened her death grip on the cart, Molly willed her heart to regulate its rhythm. "I came for Homecoming Week. I got an invitation...in the mail."

He grinned again. "Great. We dug around for a while, but we weren't sure we'd actually found you." His eyes narrowed. "You do know that Homecoming's still a week away?"

"I came early so I could take care of a few things."

"Terrific. So are you headed to Serenity now?"

"I am." She dangled the keys from one finger. "I was just renting a car...obviously."

Beau glanced impatiently toward the front of the line. "Yeah, me, too."

"Oh. Does that mean you don't live in Serenity any longer?"

"I'm still there. I live in my grandparents' old house now, but you probably don't remember it."

Not remember? When she'd spent countless afternoons strolling aimlessly beside the creek and along the dirt road hoping to "accidentally" run into him? She nodded without looking at him. "I think I do, actually. They had that big white farmhouse out on Old Post Road, didn't they?"

"That's the one, but it's not a farm anymore. They sold off most of their land when my dad decided not to go into farming, and Hector Johnson's kids sold his place after he died, so there are houses where many of the fields used to be."

"That's too bad. I remember it being such a pretty place."

"It still is. We're sitting on an acre, so neighbors aren't under our noses."

"And you live there with your grandparents?"

He shook his head. "They both passed away a few years ago. We were there with Grandma for the last six months of her life, but it's just us now. As a matter of fact, I need to get back there in—" he checked his watch "—less than two hours. I should be flying there right now, but I ran into a slight malfunction in the plane and I can't get a mechanic to look at it until tomorrow. My car's back in Serenity, of course, so I'm stuck paying for a way home."

"You have your own airplane?" Of course he did. He was Beau Julander.

"A small one," he said, as if that somehow diminished the accomplishment. "Six seats. Twin-engine." He checked the line's progress once more and returned his attention to her slowly. "I fly charters."

Molly managed a weak smile, praying he wouldn't ask what she did for a living, then reminded herself that she was only temporarily unemployed. "That must be really interesting."

"It is when the airplane works. Not so interesting when the damn thing decides to ruin an already bad day." He shrugged and shifted his weight, then looked at her intently. "You say you're leaving for Serenity now?"

"As soon as I get to the rental car."

"What would you say to taking me with you? I'll split the cost of the car or I'll buy you dinner, whatever you want. I have to pick up my kids by five, and if I stay in this line much longer, I'll never make it."

The question caught her by surprise. "Well, I... The thing is... You have kids?"

"Two."

The line inched forward again and he moved with it, but his gaze implored her to say yes.

Molly couldn't make herself agree yet. Two hours in a car with Beau? *Alone?* She couldn't do it. Of course, children meant that he was probably married. Happily. Because what else would Beau Julander be? But two hours with him? In a car with no one to help with conversation?

She couldn't make herself say yes, but she'd really be mortified if she said no, so she bought herself another minute. "How old are your kids?"

"Brianne's twelve. Nicky's eight."

"And their mother? She's working or something? I mean…well, I mean, she's not home. To pick up the kids. Obviously." Molly let out a jittery laugh and told herself to stop babbling.

"She's not around at all. We're divorced."

"Oh." Molly tried not to look surprised. Or pleased. "I'm sorry." And she was…sort of.

"Don't be. I'm over it, and the kids will be, too, one of these days. As much as kids *can* get over a thing like that. So what do you say? Do you mind if I hitch a ride?"

Molly was barely coherent with people all around them. If they were alone together, she'd probably blather like an idiot. But what kind of person would she be to say no? And what reason could she possibly give if she did? Besides, it wasn't as if she still had a thing for Beau. It was just that seeing him again had caught her off guard. Whatever she'd once felt for him was a thing of the past, and what better way to prove it to herself?

Shaking off the last, lingering bit of childish cowardice, she looked him square in the eye. "Sure. Why not?"

Thirty minutes later, Molly drove out of town and picked up speed on the highway heading south. Though Serenity was less than a hundred miles from Jackson as the crow flew, all but about ten miles of road wound its way through mountains ablaze with autumn color. The brilliant red of oak and sumac, the burnished gold of aspen, the dark green of pine… Molly had forgotten how beautiful it could be.

She watched the passing scenery and willed herself to keep her wits during the drive. As a very young girl, she'd had a tendency to stammer when she was nervous. It had been a long time since she'd worried about that, but now, feeling sixteen again, she wanted to make sure she didn't start acting the part.

Beau leaned forward in the passenger seat and turned on the radio, adjusting the dial until he found an oldies station. When the first strains of "Hey Jude" came through the speakers, he slanted a glance at Molly. "Is this okay with you?"

"Perfect."

He sat back again with a heavy sigh. "I really appreciate this. You have no idea how much."

She shook her head and shifted lanes to pass a slow-moving truck. "It's no big deal. It's not as if I'm going out of my way or anything."

"I suppose not, but I'm still glad we ran into each other. Kind of a bright spot in a bad day." He leaned back in his seat. "So tell me about yourself. Where did we finally find you?"

"St. Louis. I've been there for the past ten years. Before that, I lived with my dad in Urbana, Illinois."

"And what kind of business brings you back to Serenity after all this time?"

The passing lane ended and Molly slowed behind a tractor-trailer. "I told you, Homecoming."

"You also said you had other things to take care of," he reminded her. "Or are they none of my business?"

Molly wasn't sure how to explain the emptiness inside her without sounding maudlin, and that wasn't the impression she wanted to make on Beau. She settled for a partial truth. "While I'm here, I'm hoping to talk to some people who knew my mother. She died near the end of my senior year, and we left town shortly afterward. I guess I need closure, and I'm hoping I'll get that by talking to some of her friends."

Beau nodded. "I remember the night she died. It shook people up pretty badly. But we've had other Homecoming Weeks. Lots of them since we graduated from high school. Why did you wait for this one?"

"The timing was never right before." The truck in front of them turned off the highway and Molly accelerated. "I got divorced last year, my dad died in March, and last month the graphic-design firm where I've been working downsized and I found myself out of a job." She shrugged as if none of those things mattered. "The notice came when I had a little time on my hands, so here I am."

"You've had a rough year," Beau said.

Molly didn't want sympathy. It was hard enough not to cry when she let herself think about her dad. "It hasn't been one of my best," she said, trying to keep her tone light. "But you've obviously hit a few rough patches, too."

"Just a divorce."

"A divorce that left you with two kids to raise."

"Yeah, but they're great kids."

"I'm sure they are. Still, divorce is never easy."

"No." He laughed without humor. "No, it's not."

"So where are your kids?" Molly asked, turning the conversation back to a subject that wasn't quite so difficult. "At some day care that charges you extra when you're late?"

Beau laughed again and shook his head. "I wish that's where they were. No, they're with my mother-in-law. My *ex*-mother-in-law, that is. Doris has been helping out with the kids since Heather left."

Molly flicked a glance at him. "You married Heather Preston?"

"Yep."

Well, that figured. Beau and Heather, a cheerleader, had dated all through high school, so it wasn't a surprise to learn that they'd eventually married. It made her curious about why they'd split up, but not so curious that she'd let herself ask. "That's kind of unusual, isn't it? Your mother-in-law helping, I mean."

"Yes, I guess it is." Beau tapped his fingers on the armrest between them. "Doris has been a big help in a lot of ways, but I'm sure you can imagine how much fun it is to have your ex-wife's mother cooking dinner in your kitchen every night, washing your boxers and making your bed."

An image of Ethan's mother digging around in her underwear drawer flashed through Molly's mind and she shuddered. "I'll take your word for it."

Beau's fingers stopped moving. "Doris is why I can't be late. I'm already on her short list for deciding I can do without her help. My daughter's not too happy with me, either. Brianne doesn't see anything wrong with having her grandma hanging around all the time.''

His candor surprised her, but then, Beau had always been open and easy to read. ''How old did you say she was?''

''Twelve.''

The same age Molly's own child would have been if she hadn't miscarried. But the miscarriage and the news that she'd never conceive again were painful memories she didn't let herself dwell on. ''Almost a teenager.''

''Don't remind me,'' Beau groaned. ''I'm barely hanging on as it is.''

''I'm sure you'll do fine. You're there, and you love her. What more can she ask?''

''You don't know Brianne. She can ask more and she does. It's hard for a girl that age to be without a mother, I guess.'' He sighed softly. ''You haven't mentioned children. Does that mean you don't have any?''

Molly shook her head and pretended that the question didn't bother her. ''No, I don't.''

''Well, at least you knew up front that you didn't want kids. Not that I regret having mine,'' he added quickly, ''but it would have been nice to know Heather was going to resent the kids *before* they got here.''

Molly watched the blur of trees for a few seconds before responding. Maybe she should let him assume what he wanted about her, but that teenage girl who'd been so crazy about him wouldn't let her remain quiet. ''I never said I didn't *want* kids,'' she corrected him after a pause that felt about a year long.

''Oh.'' Beau looked at her. ''I'm sorry. That was a thoughtless thing to say.''

''It's okay,'' Molly assured him. ''It used to be a

painful subject, but I've adjusted. I'll probably have to talk about it a hundred times over the next couple of weeks, so don't worry about it." Still, it seemed unfair that Heather had been blessed with two children she didn't want, when Molly couldn't have any.

"Well, if curiosity bothers you, better think twice about going back to Serenity," Beau said. "The town's full of good people, but you don't get to keep many secrets. I think some of my neighbors know more about my divorce than I do."

Molly was counting on it. How else would she learn about her mother? The radio switched to a Lynyrd Skynyrd song she'd loved as a teenager. She guided the car over the crest of a hill and felt herself relaxing. Beau seemed nice. Easy to talk to. A little more grounded than he'd been as a kid—but who wasn't?

"So tell me about Homecoming," she said, changing the subject. "What can I expect?"

"All the best Serenity has to offer," he said drolly. "Parade on Thursday. Football game on Friday. And, of course, the Homecoming Ball on Saturday. We even got special dispensation from the mayor." He paused. "We don't have to roll up the sidewalks at nine like usual."

She laughed, remembering how often she and her friends had complained about Serenity's lack of decent nightlife. "How long do we get? Until ten?"

"Ten-thirty. First time in Serenity's history. Quite scandalous."

She felt another layer of nervousness drop away. "I hope the police have been notified."

"Of course. We can't have folks running amok. Old Sam Harper would probably sue."

Molly had forgotten how funny Beau could be. She

took her eyes off the road just long enough to glance at his face. The familiar tickle of warmth began to curl right on cue. She had to make sure she didn't let all those old feelings get stirred up again. Not such an easy prospect, considering what was happening to her after just minutes in his company. But the past was behind her and the days of mooning over Beau Julander were long gone.

At least she hoped they were.

BEAU WAS CONVINCED he'd ground his teeth to nubs by the time he finally retrieved his car from the airstrip, where Molly had dropped him, and pulled into Doris's driveway a few minutes after six. He checked the clock on the dash and shifted into Park, as if he could turn back time if he concentrated hard enough. He'd been watching the seconds tick past for nearly two hours now, ever since he and Molly had come upon road construction forty miles outside Serenity, but so far he hadn't regained a single minute.

If he hadn't been so uneasy about being late, and so busy rescheduling the meeting by cell phone, he'd have enjoyed the ride more. He remembered Molly, of course. Their graduating class hadn't been large. But she'd been too quiet to catch his eye, and he'd been too focused on Heather to give other girls more than a passing glance.

She'd certainly grown up nicely. Waves of long, dark hair that fell to the middle of her back. Something in her deep-brown eyes that made a guy think she was ready for anything. More than once during the drive he'd found himself wondering how accurate that impression was, but he'd probably never know. One thing he *was* sure of after three hours in her company—still waters run deep.

He climbed out of his car into the already dark evening, shivering a little in the sharp breeze and hoping the weather would hold until Homecoming was over. The living-room curtain fluttered and he knew that Doris was watching him, assessing, drawing conclusions, making judgments.

Vowing to be quick, he started up the walk. He wouldn't let her engage him in a discussion. Wouldn't let himself get into an argument. It would be in and out. *Hello, Doris, thanks a bunch. Come on kids, let's go.* It didn't have to be more complicated than that. But even as he rehearsed his lines, he knew their conversation would be far more involved. Heather had never done anything quick or easy, and that was just one of the lessons she'd learned at her mother's knee.

He climbed the steps and raised his hand to knock, but the door swung open and revealed Doris. She peered at him, a deep frown pursing her lips and knitting her brows. Though she was much shorter than Heather and at least fifty pounds heavier, the similarities were strong.

"We were getting worried," she said, pushing open the screen door to admit him. "It's *way* past five."

Beau stepped inside and the tangy scents of hot potato salad and bratwurst enveloped him. "Didn't you get my messages? I called from my cell phone three times to let you know about the plane and the construction."

"I got messages, yes. It's too bad you didn't build a little extra time into your schedule." She closed the door and glowered up at him. "But then, maybe you got sidetracked. Things like that happen when you're with someone else.''

"Like I said on the phone, I ran into an old friend at the car rental counter. We decided to ride together, that's all." He sidled toward the kitchen, where he knew Nicky would be watching television and Brianne would be doing some girl thing. "Are the kids ready?"

"They've been ready for nearly an hour. It started getting so late, I made enough supper for everyone."

"That was nice of you," Beau said, keeping his smile in place, "but I told you I'd take care of dinner."

"Yes, you did. But it's already after six, and by the time you get dinner on the table, it will be too late for them to eat. They need time to digest their food before they go to bed."

"I'm sure they'll survive if dinner's a little late one night."

"But will it *be* just one night?" Doris stopped under the arched doorway into the kitchen and folded her arms tightly across her chest. "Who is this old friend you spent the day with, anyway?"

Beau would have liked to tell her that it was none of her business, but he'd opened the door on her interference by accepting her help for so long. If closing it again was difficult, he had only himself to blame. "I didn't spend the *day* with anybody. Only a few hours in the rental car. It's just someone I went to school with who's come back for Homecoming," he said, and slipped past her into the well-lit kitchen.

He found the kids exactly where he'd expected them to be. Nicky lay on the braided rug, shoes at his sides, eyes glued to the television. His hair had grown too long, Beau realized, and he'd changed socks since morning. The pair he had on now actually matched.

Brianne sat at the round wood table with her feet on a chair, one eye on the TV while she swiped lazily at her fingernails with a file.

Nicky glanced up when Beau entered. Brianne pretended not to see him.

Beau didn't want his daughter's aloofness to set the tone for the evening, so he pretended a heartiness he didn't feel. "Hey, you two. Sorry I'm late. The magneto went out on the plane, so I had to leave it in Jackson. If that wasn't bad enough, the road was torn up and it took forever to drive home."

Nicky bolted to his feet and his bright blue eyes filled with an emotion Beau couldn't read. Brianne looked up from her nails, and her expression hit Beau like a kick in the gut. He'd seen that look of bored irritation on Heather's face too often over the years, and he didn't like seeing it on his daughter's.

"You're late," she said. "I thought you weren't coming."

"Of course I was coming. I left three messages on Gram's phone telling you what was happening so you wouldn't worry. Now, why don't you two gather your things and we'll get out of Gram's hair?"

"Out of my hair!" Doris sniffed in disapproval and busied herself stacking Nicky's books. "Don't you dare make these children think I don't want them around. It wasn't my idea to change everything. I was perfectly content the way things were."

Beau's neck and shoulders tensed. "I didn't mean it that way," he assured Doris, but he kept his gaze on Brianne. "Do you want me to help you?"

No hint of a smile relieved his daughter's annoyed expression. "Why can't we stay for supper?"

"Because I already told Gram I'd feed you."

"But it's late and I'm hungry."

"So we'll stop at the Burger Shack." He could almost feel Doris bristle as he retrieved Brianne's backpack from the floor. He zipped it open on the table, but managed to keep himself from gathering her books. "Make sure you get everything. No coming back for forgotten homework or hairbrushes."

Brianne's forehead crunched into an exact replica of her mother's and grandmother's when they were ready to lodge a complaint. "Why do we have to go somewhere else to eat? Dinner is ready, and Gram made enough for all of us."

Because Beau didn't *want* bratwurst and hot potato salad. Because he was tired of feeling manipulated. There were a dozen reasons, dammit, but none that Brianne would understand. "Dinner smells great," he said, "but it's been a long day and I'm tired. I think we should just go home."

"All the more reason to stay," Doris said, looking smug. "Especially since you need to talk to Nicky about his math worksheet."

Beau shot a glance at his son. "What about it?"

"He got a ten on it," Brianne announced with obvious relish.

"A ten, huh?" Beau grinned down at his son and ruffled his fair hair. "Good work, kid."

"*Not* good work," Brianne said, shoving her hairbrush into her pack. "Ten out of forty isn't good."

"Ten out of forty?" Beau's smile faded and Nicky's gaze dropped to the toes of his white socks.

"He can do much better than that," Doris put in before Beau could gather his thoughts and decide how to respond. "You should be disappointed."

"I know he can do better." Beau sat on a chair and

tilted Nicky's chin so the boy had to look at him, but Nicky's eyes were so filled with misery Beau didn't have the heart to make him feel worse.

"Kids let their homework slip if they don't have supervision," Doris warned. "It's only natural."

"They have supervision."

"You know what I mean."

"Yes, I do, Doris. It's hard not to understand what you mean—even when I try not to." She didn't seem to realize that the harder she pushed, the more resistant Beau became. He'd always been that way. He stood and picked up Nicky's backpack, struggling to swallow the words that hovered on the tip of his tongue. He and Doris might not see eye to eye, but she was still his children's grandmother.

He put a hand on Nicky's thin shoulder. "Do you need help with your shoes, buddy?"

Nicky shook his head and managed a shaky smile, but the relief in his eyes made Beau's chest squeeze painfully.

"You really shouldn't let a problem like this go," Doris warned.

"I'll handle it," Beau assured her. "Later." He tempered his sharpness with a tight smile, put an arm around Nicky's shoulders and motioned for Brianne to hurry.

Still frowning, the girl slowly zipped up her backpack and slipped the strap over her shoulder. But for once she didn't argue. Maybe she realized that he'd been pushed far enough for one evening.

He ushered the kids toward the front door, then turned back to Doris, who stood at the table, glowering at him. "Thanks again, Doris."

She crossed her arms high on her chest and nodded, but she didn't say a word. She just watched in stony silence while Beau led the kids out the door.

CHAPTER THREE

MOLLY'S HEAD started pounding the instant she opened her eyes the next morning, and the painful hollow in her stomach convinced her that skipping dinner the day before had been a mistake.

She rolled onto her side in the darkened motel room and took a few seconds to acclimate herself. Serenity. The Wagon Wheel Motel. Nothing had changed in all this time. She could have sworn these were the same curtains that had been here when she'd spent a miserable two months one summer cleaning rooms for the motel owners. They still didn't have coffeemakers in the rooms, and the closest restaurant—the *only* restaurant that would be open so early—was two blocks away.

Her stomach growled loudly and she decided that breakfast had to be the first order of business. She'd just slip into sweats and a T-shirt, eat first, then come back to get ready for the day.

She got out of bed and reached for her suitcase, but one look at her face and hair in the mirror had her moving toward the bathroom shower, after all. Even if she hadn't been in the same town as Beau Julander, she wouldn't have gone out in public with *that* hair.

She showered quickly and finger-combed her hair, then looked out the window to check the weather before she dressed. The sun was just cresting the moun-

tains on the eastern side of the valley, and a web of
gold seemed to hover over the trees on the hillsides.

In this light, the fall colors were jewel-toned, and
Molly forgot about her hunger for a minute. She
opened the window a few inches so she could breathe
the crisp, autumn-scented air. Memories of other mornings rushed her from every side. For a moment she
almost believed that if she closed her eyes, she would
hear her mother urging her to dress for school.

She did close her eyes then, allowing herself to live
that moment for as long as it lasted. She saw her
mother's long, dark hair and wide, dark eyes. The
scents of pine and earth became the sweet, musky scent
of her mother's perfume, and wind chimes dancing in
the breeze somewhere nearby reminded her of the tin-
kle of her favorite jewelry. Ruby Lane hadn't gone
anywhere without her hair done, her makeup on, a
spritz of perfume and jewelry. Always jewelry. Always
original. Always pieces she made herself.

Molly felt the familiar pang of longing for just one
necklace, one bracelet, one set of earrings, but she
pushed it aside. There were things she could change
and things she couldn't. The grief that had driven her
father to get rid of all her mother's belongings was on
the second list, and she wasn't going to waste time
wishing.

The memory faded and Molly let it go, knowing it
was a mistake to hold on too tightly. She wanted the
memories to come and go as they pleased. They would
be more meaningful that way, and maybe, if she was
lucky, she'd eventually remember something about her
mother's final year that she could hold on to.

She reluctantly closed the window and dressed in a
pair of jeans and the oversize Chicago Bears jersey that

had been a present from her dad their last Christmas together. Wearing it gave her confidence, and she needed all the help she could get this morning.

Just as she was putting the finishing touches on her makeup, a knock on the door startled her into dropping the shell-shaped compact that held her powder. It seemed early for housekeeping, but then, Serenity had always functioned at its own pace.

"Just a minute," she sang out. She picked up the compact and crossed the small room to open the door. When she saw Beau standing there with the sun in his hair and a twinkle in his eye, the compact slipped from her fingers again.

Beau bent to retrieve it and handed it to her with a grin. "Good morning. You're all ready, I see. That's good. Obviously my timing is perfect."

As Molly closed her fingers around the compact, her hand brushed Beau's. It was only an instant, but heat traced a pattern up her arm that didn't diminish even when she pulled away. "What timing? What are you doing here? Did you leave something in the car?"

He frowned playfully. "What kind of greeting is that? Let's try it again, shall we? I say good morning, and you say…"

Her cheeks flamed, but the smile in Beau's sky-blue eyes took away the sting. "Good morning," she said apologetically. "*Then* I ask what you're doing here."

"That's much better." He held out a hand as if he expected her to take it. "I'm here to treat you to breakfast."

It was all Molly could do not to gape at him. "Breakfast? Why?"

"Because you did an incredible favor for me yesterday, and I didn't thank you properly." He checked

his watch and glanced behind him. "And don't give
me any excuses, because I know you haven't eaten yet.
The diner won't be open for another ten minutes."

"You're serious?"

He wiped the grin from his face, but his eyes still
danced with laughter. "Don't I look serious?"

"Very." She glanced past him into the parking lot.
A green Cherokee sat in a space near her door, but she
couldn't see anyone waiting inside. "Where are your
kids? Don't tell me you left them home alone."

"No, they're at my sister's. She teaches them piano
on Saturday mornings. Their lessons are forty-five
minutes apiece, which means that we have exactly—"
he tapped the crystal on his watch "—eighty-three
minutes all to ourselves."

A shiver of anticipation shimmied along Molly's
spine, but she ignored it. Beau hadn't meant anything
by that, and she was far too hungry to let insecurities
left over from long ago make her hesitate. "You're
on." She slid the room key into her pocket and stepped
into the cool morning air. "You're talking about your
sister, Gwen?"

"The only one I have."

"I think I remember her. Pretty girl with light-brown
hair and a great smile? The one who played the piano
at WinterFest?"

Beau closed the door behind him. "That's Gwen.
She was a pain when we were kids, but I don't know
what I'd do without her now."

"You're lucky to have her. I used to wish for a
brother or a sister, but it never happened. Being an only
child can get lonely sometimes." She realized she was
becoming too serious and looked pointedly at her
watch. "Technically, we have less than eighty-three

minutes, you know. If it took you seven minutes to get here, it will take seven to get back. That means we have only seventy-six minutes—and I'm *very* hungry."

Beau laughed. "We have as long as we need. Gwen owes me a favor or two." He motioned her toward the street and fell into step beside her. "You don't mind walking, do you? The diner's only two blocks away."

"I don't mind at all. I didn't see much on my way through town last night."

"That's my fault, I'm afraid."

"Not at all. I was too tired to see anything. I'll make up for it today."

Beau stuffed his hands into his pockets and slid a sidelong glance at her. "Need a tour guide?"

"Around Serenity? Has it changed that much?"

"We have a new apartment building by the bowling alley, and ten new houses went up over the summer. Olene Whitefish got married again. She and her new husband put in a food mart at the gas station. If you take off on your own, you're likely to get lost in all the expansion."

Molly's laugh echoed in the early-morning silence. "Thanks. I'll keep that in mind."

When they reached the sidewalk, Beau turned toward the still-dark diner on the next block. "How's your room at the Wagon Wheel?"

"It's fine. The bed's firm and the room is clean. I can't complain."

"And what are your plans for the rest of the day?"

"Nothing set in stone. Why?"

"We have that rescheduled meeting of the Homecoming committee later this morning. I was thinking you might like to come along."

They drew abreast of the diner just as the lights came

on inside, and Molly shook her head quickly. "I don't want to get in the way. Besides, I probably wouldn't know most of the people there."

"You'll know everybody there. It's our year to plan this thing, so the whole committee comes from our graduating class. You know Aaron Clayton and Michelle Reeder?"

"Yes, but—"

"Elaine Gunderson and Kayla Tucker?"

"Elaine was one of my best friends in school."

"Ridge McGraw?"

An image of a bowlegged young man flashed through her mind and she smiled. "Ridge is still here? I thought for sure he'd be riding on the pro rodeo circuit by now."

"He was. Hurt his back a couple of years ago and came home. He's married. Two kids. Nice wife."

Molly hesitated another minute before agreeing. She'd come back to find answers, not to jump into small-town life just because Beau Julander crooked his finger at her.

Then again, she did have two weeks to spend in Serenity. That should give her plenty of time to connect with old friends and still talk to people who knew her mother.

And really, what was so wrong about living out an old fantasy for one day?

THREE HOURS LATER, Beau led Molly up the sidewalk toward Ridge and Cheryl McGraw's tiny frame house on the north end of town. He'd spent a couple of hours with the kids before dropping them off for a brief visit with his mother and rushing back to the motel. His mother had been thrilled to see the kids, but Brianne had been in one of her moods again.

In response to her dour prediction that he *might* make it home in time for dinner, Beau had promised to buy dinner at the Chicken Inn if he was late. He didn't mind paying for the meal, but his daughter's trust was riding on his ability to conduct this meeting and be out of here before noon so he could spend time with the kids.

The McGraws' entire front yard was buried beneath a bed of fallen leaves, and slick spots on the pavement created by old, decaying leaves made the walk a little tricky. Beau had grown so used to Ridge's aversion to yard work, he barely noticed it anymore. But this morning, with Molly behind him, he saw the mess with a fresh set of eyes and wondered what she must think after being away for so long.

He swallowed the apology he felt rising in his throat and pretended not to notice the sagging porch railing and the windows splattered with dirt from the last big storm that had raged through the valley. His own yard and windows weren't much better, and the realization didn't sit well.

He stepped around a piece of broken bicycle frame and turned back to make sure Molly didn't trip. ''You'll like Ridge's wife, I think. They met while he was on the circuit. Pretty girl. Friendly. She likes having the committee meetings here. It lets her keep an eye on him and make sure he doesn't volunteer for something that'll hurt his back again.'' He motioned her toward the short flight of steps leading to the door. ''If Ridge had his way, he'd still be riding bull.''

Molly climbed the steps and moved aside to let him

ring the bell. "I'm sure I'll like her. Does this mean Ridge is the committee chair?"

"I wish." Beau pressed the buzzer and rocked back on his heels to wait. "They voted me head of the committee, but I should have said no. I enjoy being involved. I'm like my dad and grandpa, I guess—kind of a family tradition. But if I'd known how rough things would be with Heather gone, I would have stepped aside, at least for one year."

Molly looked at him oddly. "You miss her a lot, don't you."

"Me?" He let out a sharp laugh. "I wouldn't say that. The kids miss her, though, and that's rough. Brianne's had some tough times with her mother out of the picture, and I'm about as inept as a person can be about things like hair and fingernails and makeup." He shook his head, nostalgic for the days when those were his biggest problems with his unhappy daughter. "But we'll get through this. I'll make sure of it."

He thought Molly was about to say something else, but the door opened, and whatever it was, was lost in the flurry of introductions, shouts of surprise, hugs and chatter as everyone tried to catch up at once. Eventually Cheryl, a tall, blond woman with substantial curves and hair big enough to make any self-respecting rodeo queen proud, herded them all into the kitchen and settled them around the table.

Beau watched Molly covertly as she reconnected with old friends, but when he realized that he was watching her a little too closely, paying a bit too much attention to her hair and eyes, to the curve of her cheek and the sound of her laugh, he forced himself to look away. It wasn't that he was interested in her, he told himself firmly. He just wanted to make sure she was in good hands before he got down to business.

Pulling the list he'd been making for three days from his pocket he spoke loud enough to be heard. "Okay, folks, let's get with the program. Nobody wants this to take all day."

The conversations faded almost immediately, but it still took another fifteen minutes to pass out lemonade to interested parties, decide who wanted coffee, instead, and handle the debate over whether to serve chocolate cookies now or wait until they were ready for a break. No wonder he couldn't get anything done at home. He was stuck in half-day-long meetings that should have taken half an hour at most.

He made a mental note to call Mayor Biggs about his replacement on the planning committee and ignored the flicker of disappointment that came with the thought of stepping down. "Where are we with the parade, Aaron? Did Hinkley Hardware work out whatever the problem was with their float?"

His best friend, Aaron Clayton, leaned back in his chair and linked his hands behind his head. He was as dark as Beau was fair, and the fact that his hairline was receding and Beau's wasn't had become a source of good-natured contention between them. "Everything's fine," he said now. "Betty Hinkley drove into Jackson and found crepe paper in a shade close enough for them to finish making the damn thing, so Alf decided not to withdraw, after all."

"Alf needs a reality check," Kayla Tucker muttered. The faint scent of old cigarette smoke warred with her perfume, and she gestured broadly, putting Ridge's lemonade at risk. "It was *green*. He's never heard of leaves being slightly different colors before?"

Beau met Molly's amused glance across the table, then looked away quickly. "He's happy now," he said. "That's what matters. What about the marching band? Is Mr. Cavalier still upset over that song—whatever it was?"

Ridge moved his lemonade to a safer spot and stroked his thick mustache with a thumb and forefinger. Seeing everyone as Molly must, Beau realized how gray Ridge had grown lately, but it wasn't surprising for a man who'd spent fifteen years being tossed around by livestock.

"He's proposed another compromise," Ridge said. "If we let them play one song by Eminem, they'll add a Sousa march in place of the other one."

"I suppose that's all right," Cheryl put in from the spot she'd taken up near the sink. "It's not as if they're going to be singing, and it's the words people find offensive…isn't it?"

Hoping to avoid another lengthy debate on the evils of rap music, Beau glanced around the table. "Are you okay with this?" he asked Michelle. "More importantly, is Sam Harper okay with it?"

Michelle lifted one shoulder in a gesture of acquiescence. "We talked about it last night and he agreed that as long as nobody sings—and that means all the kids on the sidelines—he won't sue."

"I don't think we can guarantee that," Aaron said. "I'm not even going to try. What's wrong with Sam, anyway?"

"He finds rap music offensive."

"I find the political statements he puts on his shop marquee offensive," Aaron muttered, "but I don't threaten to sue the city over them."

Cheryl rolled her eyes. "That's different. Sam doesn't put profanity on his signs. Just ask him and he'll tell you all about it."

Ridge drained half his lemonade and set the glass down with a thunk. "Some of his opinions sure *feel* profane. The way he's always trying to regulate everything chaps my hide. You can't force people to do what you want them to do."

"Which is all beside the point," Beau said, raising his voice to make sure he stopped the inevitable argument before it got started. "The point is, Drake Cavalier and the marching band are willing to compromise with us, and I think we should adopt the same spirit. All in favor?"

He counted the vote quickly and congratulated himself on the victory, but he had less success in concluding the hour-long debate that followed over whether or not Sally Townsend's homemade sugar cookies constituted a health hazard. Only Molly's quietly offered opinion that Mrs. Townsend's sugar cookies were a necessary tradition and Michelle's grudging compromise to have the food handlers wear latex gloves when serving them brought the discussion to an end.

Thirty minutes to go, and they still had the Homecoming Ball to deal with. Beau wanted to be optimistic about his chances of getting home on time, but he had a sick feeling that he'd not only be shelling out for dinner but paying in other ways for a long time to come.

"Okay, folks, listen up. We have a lot to get through, so let's get to work." He felt the familiar flush of victory as he called for Michelle's report on the decorations and she delivered it quickly and without embellishment. To avoid reneging on his promise to Brianne, he didn't think twice about agreeing to meet with the entire committee on Wednesday evening to finish decorating the school gymnasium.

With only two more areas to cover, Beau began to feel the familiar charge he always got when victory was in sight. Sometimes he thought it was this heady feeling, along with family loyalty, that kept him so heavily involved in the committees. He liked the idea of making a difference in the world—even if it was just in his own little corner of it. "What about the half-time show on Friday night? Any problems there?"

Aaron leaned back in his seat and rested an ankle on his knee. He linked his hands behind his head and set the raised foot jiggling in that peculiar way he had. A stranger might have mistaken his posture for that of a man without a care, but Beau recognized that jiggle and his heart sank.

"We have just one little snag," Aaron announced. "Old Sam Harper has a problem with the fireworks. He thinks we should light them at the other end of the field this year."

Ridge threw himself back in his chair and tossed his pencil onto the table in disgust. "Can't we force that old pain in the shorts to move away?"

"Not in this lifetime." Aaron locked eyes with Beau. "I hate to break it to you, buddy, but he's got Mayor Biggs dancing all over the place. If we want those fireworks, we have to find a way to light them from the north end of the field without setting the scoreboard on fire."

Good thing old Sam wasn't sitting in the room right now, Beau thought. He might not have made it out alive. But Beau wasn't ready to admit defeat yet. "An emergency meeting on Monday, then."

"Nope. Mayor Biggs wants this resolved today or

we can forget the fireworks altogether. Give everybody a five-minute break and then settle in for the long haul, because I got a feelin' none of us are goin' anywhere for a while.''

A LITTLE AFTER five o'clock, Beau climbed the back steps and let himself into his mother's kitchen. The aroma of freshly baked cookies filled the air, and everything from faucet to floor gleamed. He was learning about housework, but the past year had made him realize how hard it was to do those ''simple'' things that kept a house running smoothly. His mom made it look easy, but he wondered if he'd ever get the hang of it.

He tossed his keys onto the little shelf that served as a catchall and closed the door behind him. ''Mom?'' he called out to the silent house. ''Anybody here?''

''We're in the sewing room,'' his mother replied. ''Help yourself to some cookies if you want. They're by the stove.''

Beau didn't have to be told twice. He nabbed three from the cooling rack and polished off one on his way down the hall. He started on his second as he stepped into his mother's favorite room in the house. Years ago, it had been Gwen's bedroom, but the lavender paint had long since been replaced by a more practical off-white, and a quilting frame, sewing machine and chests filled with craft supplies sat where Gwen's bed, dresser and stereo had been.

Vickie Julander, still slim, blond and attractive, sat in front of the sewing machine, piecing a quilt square in bright red, yellow and blue diamonds. For a while Beau had convinced himself that Heather was a lot like his mother, but he couldn't have been more wrong. It wasn't that his mother was a saint, but her natural calm made Heather's personality seem…well, overly excitable was probably the kindest way to put it. He wondered sometimes if she still suffered from the rages that had kept him in the marriage even when he'd been tempted to leave. Hard as it had been to live with her, he'd never once seriously considered leaving the kids to cope on their own with Heather.

He winked at Nicky, who sat beneath the quilting frame, quietly drawing something in one of his grandmother's sketch pads.

Nicky grinned back and popped the last piece of a cookie into his mouth. "Brianne's mad again."

Big surprise. Beau hadn't expected her to be happy. "I guess I'd better talk to her. Where is she?"

His mother glanced up from the quilt square. "You didn't see her when you came in?"

"Should I have?"

"I thought you might. She said she was going to wait outside."

"Great." He finished the second cookie and pushed away from the wall. The look he shared with Nicky convinced Beau he wasn't the only one growing tired of Brianne's sulks. "You want to wait here while I go find your sister?"

Relief filled Nicky's eyes. "Yep. I bet she's out by the rose garden. That's where she was when I went to the bathroom."

His mother glanced up briefly and peered at Beau over the wire rims of her glasses. "Remember, Beau, honesty is always best. Children are no exception."

He nodded, even though he didn't understand why she felt the need to warn him, then made his way back through the house. He was tired and frustrated, but there was no sense putting off the inevitable.

Thanks to Nicky, Beau found his daughter pacing the oval-shaped rose garden his father had planted years ago. The roses had already been pruned and packed for winter, but that didn't seem to matter to Brianne. Her blond hair blowing about in the wind, she was gesticulating and exclaiming as she walked.

Beau knew she was venting. He even dared hope that maybe she'd burned off a little steam already.

He stopped a few feet away and waited for her to notice him, which she did almost immediately. Her nose and cheeks were red from the cold, and she ground to a halt and glared at him. "You're late."

"I know, sweetheart, and I'm sorry."

"You *promised* you wouldn't be."

"I know. The meeting didn't go very smoothly. I tried to finish on time, but I guess I didn't do a very good job of estimating how long it would take."

Her eyes narrowed. "You're late because of the *meeting?*"

"Yes. Of course. That's where I was."

"Nowhere else?"

He considered mentioning his two brief stops at the Wagon Wheel, but decided against it. He'd spent less than ten minutes there, picking Molly up and dropping her off again, and he didn't see any reason to make things more complicated than they already were. "I went to the meeting," he said firmly. "Homecoming Week starts in just a few days, and we had a lot of last-minute details to take care of."

"Oh, poor Daddy." Sarcasm made her voice bitter, and Beau could feel his temper rising. He could have been looking into Heather's eyes, listening to her voice, and he had to struggle to remind himself that he was talking to a child—*his* child.

"I don't know what's bothering you," he said evenly, "but your attitude is getting real old, real fast. It's okay to feel angry sometimes, but it's not okay to treat people as if they just crawled out from under a rock. I'm your dad, not your enemy. I suggest you remember that and start making a few changes."

"Maybe you should make some changes, too," she shot back. "Maybe *you* shouldn't lie to me."

His mother's warning sounded in the back of his mind, but he still didn't understand. "What are you talking about? When have I lied to you?"

"Right now. Why didn't you tell me about the lady you were with?"

"What lady?" So that's what was really bothering Brianne. He wondered how she knew.

"The one I saw you with at the motel."

Beau glanced back at the house. Why hadn't his mother warned him about what he was walking into? "I didn't tell you," he said carefully, "because she's just an old friend who's in town for Homecoming. I picked her up for the meeting and gave her a ride back to her motel afterward, but I wasn't *with* her. We weren't on a date or anything."

Brianne folded her arms and glared at him. "Breakfast wasn't a date?"

Damn grapevine. "Breakfast wasn't a date," he assured his sullen daughter. "She gave me a ride from Jackson yesterday, and I thought it would be a good idea to do something nice to pay her back."

Brianne considered his reply for a moment, then tilted her head to one side. "Do you *want* to date her?"

He shook his head. "I'm not interested in dating anyone right now," he said, ignoring the flicker of guilt that told him he wasn't being entirely honest. "I have too much to do at home. Too many dishes to wash. Too much laundry to do. Even if I wanted to, I don't have time to date.''

"And don't forget Mom."

Beau froze. "Mom?"

"What if she comes back and you're going out with some other woman? She might think you didn't want her to come back and then she might leave again."

Beau took another step closer and weighed his words carefully. "I don't think your mom is coming back, Brianne. And even if she did—"

"But she *is* coming back. Gram said so. She said that Mom's coming back soon. That she's tired of living in Santa Fe and tired of her new friends. Gram *said!*"

"That's what Gram wants, honey, but that's not what's going to happen."

"How do you know? Have you talked to her? Did she tell you she's not coming back?"

Beau couldn't let himself answer that, so he turned the challenge around on her. "Has Gram talked to her? Has she told Gram that she's coming back?"

"Probably."

"I don't think so, sweetheart. And even if she does come to Serenity to be near you and Nicky, she and I won't be getting back together." There was too much heartache, too many angry words and accusations between them. And Heather's one big decision that Beau would never forget. He couldn't understand why Brianne didn't seem to remember the shouting matches, the slamming doors, the nights when he'd slept in the old cabin or on the couch in the family room, the mornings when the coldness between Heather and him had filled the house. Had it not been as bad as he remembered? Or was his daughter living in denial?

He couldn't blame her for that. He'd spent a fair amount of time there himself. There'd been so many things he hadn't wanted to see, so many clues about what the real problems were between Heather and him, but his pride hadn't let him see the truth until the bitter end—not until it had been thrown in his face and there'd been no possible way to dodge it.

CHAPTER FOUR

MOLLY WAS STILL thinking about Beau hours later when she stepped out of her room to get some air. She'd spent the time since the committee meeting cooped up in her room, making a list of people she wanted to talk to and looking up phone numbers and addresses in the small area phone book, but she was ready for a change of pace.

She'd been a little surprised by the reception the committee members had given her. She hadn't expected so many of them to remember her, but their welcome had certainly bolstered her courage.

As she stretched to work out the kinks from sitting in one position for too long, she let her gaze travel along the motel office fronting the street, then to the L-shaped building that housed the individual rooms and on to the tiny playground in the grassy courtyard. The buildings had recently received a fresh coat of paint, but small signs of age and neglect were in evidence, from the pitted sidewalks to the listing porch railings and the potholes in the parking lot.

Making a hasty decision, she reached back into the room for her key and slipped it into her pocket, then crossed the parking lot and climbed the two short steps to the glass door of the office.

This part of the motel hadn't changed in fifteen years, either. The same curtains hung at the windows, the same postcard tray and brochure sleeves sat on the counter. She even thought the same postcards were on sale. Only the computer looked new.

Behind the counter, an open door led to the Grahams' living quarters. Last night it had been the Grahams' daughter Brenda who'd been on duty. Today Phyllis Graham sat on the same old green velvet couch Molly remembered, probably watching the same television programs she'd watched all those years ago.

Molly crossed the room to the counter before the bell over the door stopped tinkling. Mrs. Graham pushed out of her easy chair and hurried toward the counter, patting her gray-streaked hair as she walked. The changes in the older woman left Molly momentarily speechless as the realization sank in that her own mother might have changed as much if she'd lived.

Mrs. Graham had aged and put on weight, but the changes went deeper than that. Her shoulders sagged as if she carried a great weight, and the spark in her eyes had grown dim. Was it just time? Age? Life? Or had something else happened to change her?

"You caught me putting my feet up for a minute," Mrs. Graham said with a self-conscious laugh. "It never fails, does it? Sit down for a minute, and that's when somebody will come through the door. Not that I'm complaining. Don't want to give the wrong idea." She drew closer and her step faltered. "Well, now, *you* look familiar. You're Ruby Lane's girl, aren't you?"

"I am."

"Molly, isn't it?"

"That's right." She extended a hand. "It's Molly Shepherd now. I just arrived last night. It's good to see you again, Mrs. Graham."

"Mrs. Graham?" A hint of that old spark lit her

eyes and she wagged a finger in mock irritation. "None of that, now. We're old friends. Call me Phyllis." She gave Molly a quick once-over and shook her head in wonder. "Just look at you. You're the spitting image of your mother."

The words filled Molly with pride and gratitude. "I knew there was a resemblance, but I didn't realize it was so strong."

"Take one look at a picture of her at your age and you'll know. Gracious, but it's a little startling." She laughed again and sank onto a stool behind the counter. "But don't mind me. I tend to run on when I shouldn't. What can I do for you?"

Molly couldn't bring herself to admit that grief had driven her father to throw out all the pictures of her mother. Much as it had hurt to discover what he'd done, she didn't like the judgment she saw in people's eyes when she told them about it. "Actually I'd like to talk to you for a minute if you don't mind. I'm hoping you can tell me what you remember about my mom's accident."

Something hard and cold flickered in Phyllis's eyes and she drew back sharply. "What is it you want to know?"

Her reaction was completely unexpected, but the coldness in her expression disappeared so quickly Molly told herself she'd only imagined it. "I don't know, really. I don't remember much about that night, so almost anything you could tell me would be helpful."

Phyllis straightened some papers on the edge of the counter, then reached for a stack of mail. "Goodness, Molly, what a thing to ask. That was a long time ago, and a lot has happened since then.'' Her gaze danced across Molly's face, avoiding her eyes. "Especially for someone my age. There are days when I have trouble remembering the names of my grandchildren. Besides, if you ask me, there's nothing to be gained from delving into the past. It's best to keep your attention focused on the future, I always say."

"Normally I'd agree with you," Molly said, "but we're talking about my mother. I really need to fill in a few blanks."

"If you want to know about that night," Phyllis suggested, giving a nonchalant shrug, "wouldn't it be best to ask your dad? I'll bet he remembers things the rest of us don't, and I'm sure he wouldn't appreciate me talking. Unless he's had a life-changing moment somewhere along the way, he doesn't like it when folks talk."

Molly's smile faded. "I can't ask him. He died six months ago."

She couldn't be sure, but she thought Phyllis faltered slightly as she tossed an envelope at the trash can. "Oh?"

"Cardiac arrest. It was very sudden and unexpected."

"Frank's gone?" Phyllis gave a weighted sigh and shook her head. "That seems almost impossible. He was so...full of life." The remark should have been a compliment, but it sure didn't sound like one. Phyllis turned away to reach for something on a shelf behind her. "Family. That's who I'd go to with questions if I were you. Go to the people who'd remember best."

"But that's the problem. I have a stepmother, but she doesn't know anything. Mom was an only child and her parents both died before she did. And I never knew Dad's family. You and Mom's other friends are really my only hope."

Phyllis found whatever she was looking for and carried it back to the counter. "Well, I wish you luck, dear. But as I said, it was all so long ago. I just don't know how successful you'll be. There's been a lot of water under the bridge since then." She flashed an apologetic smile, then swiftly moved on to another topic. "I'm looking at your room portfolio here and I see that Brenda left off your departure date. Why don't we fill that in right now, along with anything else we need?"

It took Molly a second to recover from the abrupt shift. "I'm staying until the seventeenth," she said when Phyllis looked at her expectantly.

"Lovely. But how long are you staying *here?*"

"The entire time of course. Is that a problem?"

Phyllis pursed her lips. "Oh, dear. Yes, I'm afraid it is. You didn't make a reservation?"

"I didn't think I'd need one."

"Well, you wouldn't usually, but Homecoming is a different story. We're full up—or will be in a day or two."

Molly stared at her in disbelief while she tried to process that piece of news. "You don't have *any* rooms?"

"I have one for tonight." Phyllis tapped on her computer keyboard and stared in concentration at the screen. "Looks like I'll have one Sunday and Monday night, too. But nothing after that until Homecoming Week is over."

Molly could have kicked herself for not realizing that lodging might be a problem. "Is there a bed-and-breakfast in town? Or another motel, maybe?"

"Hon, we're the only motel for fifty miles in any direction. Joe Walker rents apartments by the month over on Spring Street, but you probably wouldn't be interested in something that permanent."

"I won't be here that long."

"Well, that's a shame. A real shame. But listen, there's always a chance that someone will cancel at the last minute or just not show at all. Keep the room until we need it, and we'll keep our fingers crossed that something will open up, or someone in town will have a room to spare." She stopped abruptly, sniffed twice and clapped a hand to her bosom. "My applesauce. Can you believe I forgot all about it? You'll forgive me of course. We'll talk later, I'm sure."

And with that, she was gone.

Molly stepped out into the dwindling light and stood for a moment, taking in the shadows stretching across the road, the occasional swish of cars passing on the street, the sounds of dogs barking and muted laughter in the distance. She wrapped her arms around herself and pulled in a deep breath of fall-scented air.

The one thing she *didn't* smell was the distinctive and unmistakable aroma of cooking apples. She had no idea what had made Phyllis so nervous or why she'd lie to avoid discussing the night Molly's mother died...but she intended to find out.

SHORTLY BEFORE NOON the next day, Molly walked quickly along Front Street toward the Chicken Inn. She'd spent the evening trying to find another place to stay in case she had to leave the Wagon Wheel, but everyone she knew had family coming in or homes too small.

Molly refused to be discouraged. There was a solution out there. She just had to find it. And maybe her friend Elaine would have some good news for her at lunch.

A weak storm had moved into the valley overnight. Clouds had turned the sky a heavy, gunmetal gray, and without even the autumn sun to warm it, the air in the valley had become almost frigid. She shivered and hunched more deeply into her favorite sweater, but it didn't help.

She considered going back for the car, but she was almost halfway to the restaurant, so she walked faster, keeping her head down to protect her face from the cold. When she reached an intersection, she looked up long enough to check for traffic, then protected her face again.

As she passed the FoodWay grocery store, she caught sight of a green Cherokee slowly making its way along Front Street toward her.

A chill gust of wind swept around her ankles and sent a shiver up her spine, but she couldn't make herself move. Beau pulled to the curb a few feet away from her and got out. He strode toward her, grinning as if he was really glad to see her. ''Doing a bit of sightseeing?''

She laughed and shook her head. ''Not exactly. I'm on my way to the Chicken Inn. What are you doing out and about on a Sunday? I thought you'd be with your kids.''

''Family dinner at Mom's. She needs whipping cream, and I volunteered to go get it.'' He slid a slow glance along the length of her. ''Do you want to join us? There's plenty.''

''Thanks, but I'm meeting Elaine for lunch.''

''Sounds fun. What are you doing later?''

Molly shrugged. "Hopefully finding someplace to stay."

"I thought you were comfortable at the Wagon Wheel."

"I am, but I didn't exactly think ahead. I have a room through Monday night, and then, if nobody cancels, I'm out on the streets."

Beau glanced down at her. "You didn't have a reservation?"

"I didn't think I'd need one."

"For Homecoming Week? You really have forgotten what things are like around here, haven't you? There are three times of the year when the motel fills up early—all fifteen rooms. You have to plan in advance for Homecoming, Thanksgiving and Christmas. The rest of the year, you're fine to take a chance."

The breeze blew hair into her eyes and she swept it back with one hand. "I wish I'd known. Now that I'm here, I don't want to miss all the fun."

"You *can't* miss it. That's not even an option. I have it on good authority that this is going to be one of the finest Homecoming Weeks Serenity has ever had, no matter what you might think after that meeting yesterday. There has to be someplace you can stay. I'd ask Mom, but my cousins are staying with her, and Gwen's sister-in-law and her family are going to be at Gwen and Riley's."

"That's the story I'm getting from everybody. Jennifer Grant offered me her couch. I can take that if I can't find anything else, but with a husband and four kids in a three-bedroom house, they're bursting at the seams. I hate to impose."

"It's a small house, that's for sure." A car rounded

the corner and he instinctively put an arm around her to pull her farther away from the curb.

Feeling warm beneath his touch, she drew away casually. "I'm not giving up, though. Besides, Phyllis says that someone might cancel."

"I wouldn't count on it. But I'm sure there's another solution. I can make a few calls if you'd like. I have friends in high places...sort of."

Molly caught another wisp of hair and pushed it back from her face. "I've seen how influential you are, and I'd appreciate the help. I've about exhausted my connections. I just hope you have better luck than I've had."

He frowned in mock annoyance. "You *doubt* me?"

She laughed lightly. "Umm...no?"

"Excellent answer." He hooked his thumbs in his back pockets and surveyed the world around him for a long moment. "Tell me how you'd feel about staying in a cabin."

"Does it have a bed?"

"Yep."

"Then I'd feel very happy if it's not too expensive."

"How does 'free' work into your budget?"

"Free?" She eyed him skeptically. "Almost too well. I don't want to take advantage of anyone."

"Right. But that's not a problem. This place has its own kitchen, but you'd have to go to the main house for bathroom privileges and the shower. It's a guest bath, though, so it would be almost like having your own."

"Sounds too good to be true. Do you really think I could get it?"

"Oh, I'm sure of it. The place is a little dusty. It

hasn't been used in a while. But it wouldn't take long to spruce it up.''

''Maybe you should check first,'' Molly suggested. ''I don't want to get my hopes up for nothing. Whose cabin is it?''

''It belongs to a real nice family.'' A strong gust of wind whipped around them, and he took a couple of steps toward the Cherokee, walking backward so he didn't have to break eye contact. ''A single dad with two great kids.''

Molly gaped at him. ''You?''

''It's the original house my grandparents built when they bought the farm. You remember it?''

''I don't want to be rude,'' Molly said, ''but all I remember is a tumbledown old shack behind your house. Is that what you're talking about?''

''It's not so bad. We've done a little work on it since you were here last. I used to sleep there sometimes before Heather and I split up. The only inconvenience is having to cross the yard to use the bathroom, but it's not far.''

Molly didn't know what to say. Surely he didn't expect her to stay in a falling-down old shed, so it must be habitable. She needed a place to stay, but she wasn't sure she'd relax for a second at Beau's. When he didn't break into laughter or wave off the suggestion as a joke, she forced herself to speak. ''I'm not so sure that's such a good idea.''

''Why not?''

''Well, for one thing, what would your kids think?''

''It's just for a couple of weeks. They'd be fine.''

Molly still wasn't sold. ''There'd be gossip,'' she reminded him.

"So? You need a place to stay. I have one. It's no big deal. Don't make it one."

Heat rushed into her cheeks, but he didn't seem to notice. She opened her mouth to argue with him, but the words wouldn't come.

"I thought you wanted to find out about your mom's accident," Beau reminded her. "Isn't that worth staying for?"

"Yes. Of course it is. But—"

"Okay, then. So you'll stay. If you want privacy, you've got it. If you want a friend, you've got that, too. Sound like something you can live with?"

She stared at him, still unable to make herself say yes.

Laughing softly, he swung away. "Think about it as long as you want to," he called back over his shoulder. "You know where to find me when you make up your mind."

She stood frozen, watching him cross the street and stride through the supermarket's parking lot past one car after another. He waved at someone in a pickup truck and stopped to chat with an elderly woman who came outside just as he reached the doors.

Molly couldn't take her eyes off him, but he never once looked back. She told herself that staying in his cabin would be wrong, wrong, wrong. She even argued with herself for a full ten minutes, but there was never any contest. In the end, she did exactly what Beau knew she would do—she crossed the parking lot and stepped into the FoodWay, telling herself that if this turned out badly, she had only herself to blame.

"I *KNEW* IT!" Brianne shouted as Beau cleared away dishes after dinner the next evening. She stood so quickly her chair toppled to the floor behind her. "You lied to me, didn't you?"

"I told you the truth." Beau stashed the plates next to the sink and turned back for more. "It's not what you think."

"Oh, yeah. Like I'm going to believe that." Her cheeks were flushed and her small chest heaved with emotion. "You can't let some stranger stay in the cabin. All Mom's stuff is in there."

Beau glanced at Nicky, who watched his sister closely but didn't seem to share her outrage. "We can move Mom's stuff," Beau said. "There aren't that many boxes. They'll fit in the equipment shed."

"I don't *want* to put Mom's things in the stupid equipment shed!" Brianne shouted. "There're spiders in there."

"I'll spray."

Brianne wrestled with her chair for a moment and finally got it back on its feet. "You want to move Mom's things, don't you? I heard Gram say that you probably wanted to throw everything away."

"Well, Gram's wrong." The muscles in Beau's jaw knotted painfully, but he took a deep breath and picked up the bowls that had held cheese, onion and tomato respectively. "But maybe it's time for us to realize that Mom doesn't want the stuff she left behind."

"She does so want it! There are things I made for her in there. Pictures Nicky drew. The candleholder I gave her for Christmas, even. She'll be really mad if you throw all that away."

Hope and defiance mingled in Brianne's expression, and even Nicky's wide blue eyes filled with worry. Beau turned away so the kids couldn't see the weariness in his own eyes. "You're right, honey. I don't know what I was thinking. We'll keep Mom's things safe and sound for her. Where do you think we should put them?''

"They should stay where they are. In the cabin."

''Then we'll put them back after Molly leaves. She's only staying for a couple of weeks, not forever.''

Brianne dropped heavily into her chair and propped her feet against Beau's empty one, pushing on it until it teetered dangerously on two legs. ''She should stay at the motel. Why can't she do that?''

A wave of exhaustion nearly convinced Beau to leave the dishes, but he forced himself to keep working. ''She can't stay at the motel because she didn't make a reservation. Mrs. Graham doesn't have a room for her after tonight.''

"So?"

''So she came all this way for Homecoming, and it would be mean to make her leave over some simple mistake.''

Brianne pulled her feet away and the empty chair rocked back onto all four legs. ''So what? It was *her* mistake.''

Beau shut off the water and strode over to look his daughter in the eye. ''What's going on with you, Brianne?''

Her gaze swung to his face, then away. ''I don't know what you mean.''

''I mean that you've never been rude or mean to me or to anyone else, but lately that's *all* you are. I know you're unhappy with me for changing the arrangement we had with Gram, and I was willing to give you a little time to adjust. But enough is enough. It's time to get over it.''

She shot to her feet and glared at him, hands on hips

and thunder in her eyes. "You don't get it, do you. I don't *want* to get over it. I don't want everything to change all the time. First Mom left, and then you told Gram to go away, and now you're bringing *that lady* to live here. Well, it's not fair, and it's not right. I don't want to be nice, and you can't make me." She raced from the room, heading for the stairs.

Angry and confused, Beau took off after her. If he lived to be a thousand, he'd never understand females, no matter what age they were. Brianne was already halfway up the stairs by the time he reached the hallway. "Get back here," he demanded. "I'm not through talking to you."

"Well, *I'm* through talking to *you*." She raced up the last few steps and bolted for her room. "Just leave me alone, Daddy. Find somebody else to help you get rid of Mom's stuff because I'm not going to."

Beau took the steps two at a time, but Brianne's door slammed shut before he could reach the top of the staircase. He stopped in his tracks and stood, panting and uncertain, staring at the unyielding slab of wood that separated him from his daughter.

He argued with himself for a moment about what he should do. He didn't want to be too lenient and let Brianne grow into one of *those* teenagers, but he wasn't going to force his way into her room and make her talk to him. Even if he'd been that kind of dad, he had no idea what he'd say to her right now.

As he started back down the stairs, the telephone rang. He was in no mood to talk to anybody, but he had too many irons in the fire to ignore the call. He made it into his study by the third ring and recognized the number of the mechanic in Jackson when he glanced at his caller ID.

Finally some good news—he hoped. Pushing aside his irritation with Brianne, he lifted the cordless phone and punched the talk button. "Smitty? That you?"

"The one and only. I tried you at the airstrip, but I didn't get an answer."

"Not much reason to hang around there when I don't have an airplane." Beau dropped into his chair and nudged open a bottom drawer to use as a footrest. Overhead, music blared to life inside Brianne's sanctuary. "Just tell me you have good news."

"I guess that depends on what you consider 'good.' I'm going to need to replace the magneto on your Cessna. The part's available, but I can't get it here for a couple of days."

Beau ignored the driving bass beat overhead and kneaded his forehead with his fingertips. "Why so long?"

"They have to fly it in from New Mexico."

"Which should take a few hours at most," Beau said sharply. "Certainly not longer than overnight."

"In a perfect world, maybe. They'll ship the part out on Wednesday. We should have it by Thursday or Friday."

"That leaves me out of commission for a full week."

"Sorry. Can't be helped."

Beau leaned back in his chair as the music overhead grew louder and a high-pitched sound track from a video game filtered out from the family room, where Nicky was obviously honing his hand-eye coordination.

He tuned out the slight ache forming behind his eyes and focused on what Smitty was saying. No plane meant no income. No income, no business.

"Just tell me I'll be back in business by Friday."

"That'll depend on the manpower I have when the part gets here. I know you need your plane, but I got two mechanics out with some kind of kick-ass flu and the other one's got a baby due any day now. No tellin' where he'll be when the part arrives."

"What about you, Smitty? Or are you just window dressing these days?"

"I'd make some mighty sorry window dressing," Smitty said with a chuckle. "I could do it for you, and I will if it comes to that, but I've got other jobs ahead of you. First come, first serve. That's always been my policy."

"You'd make an exception if I were one of those celebrity clients of yours. What if I told you I'm supposed to fly Mel Gibson to a location shoot near Yellowstone?"

Smitty laughed again. "I'd say you were a bad liar."

"Yeah? Well, this honesty thing is a real curse sometimes." Brianne turned her music a little higher, and something on the wall began to buzz. "How about if I remind you that we've been friends for about a hundred years?"

"Well, then, I'd buy you a drink if you stop lying to me. But I *still* wouldn't move you ahead of my other clients. We'll get you up and running as soon as we can, Beau. I can't promise you anything more than that."

Beau closed his eyes in frustration, but he was smart enough to recognize a brick wall when he ran into one, and old enough to have learned the futility of going to battle against one. "You'll call me?"

"The very second I can tell you anything."

It wasn't much, but apparently it was all he was

going to get. Even worse, it was the best thing that had happened all night. People had always seen him as lucky, but lately he couldn't seem to catch a break to save his life.

Something had to give—and soon.

CHAPTER FIVE

THE NEXT MORNING at breakfast Beau accidentally charred the toast, broke a plate loading the dishwasher and stepped on a sharp piece of ceramic as he cleaned up. The one piece of good luck that came his way was that the kids had left for school before he put Brianne's favorite blouse through the wash and turned it into a potholder.

He was holding that shriveled scrap of pink in his hands and fighting the urge to let loose some of his favorite curses, when the sound of knocking from behind brought him around. When he recognized his mother looking in through the back door, he was glad he'd kept a little control on his vocabulary.

He tossed the blouse aside and made a mental note to tell Brianne what he'd done before she could discover it for herself. After motioning for his mother to come in, he headed toward the coffeemaker to start a fresh pot. "You're out and about early," he said as he dumped old grounds into the trash. "What's up?"

"I'm on my way to a meeting of the music committee," she said, slipping out of her light jacket and draping it across the back of a chair. "We need to get started on plans for WinterFest, and I came by to get your notes from last year. We don't want to accidentally repeat ourselves."

"Sure. My file's in the study. If you'll finish this,

I'll get it.'' He left her in charge of the coffee and burrowed around in his desk for a few minutes until he found the file he was looking for. When he carried it back into the kitchen, he found his mother holding Brianne's ruined blouse up to the window.

She grimaced as she returned the ruined garment to the top of the washer. ''What are you going to tell Brianne?''

Beau shook his head and handed over the file. ''I have no idea. She was fit to be tied the last time I ruined one of her things. The way she feels about me lately, she'll probably come completely unglued.''

''She's still impossible?''

''Worse than ever.'' He dug two mugs from the cupboard and found two clean spoons in the dishwasher he hadn't yet unloaded. ''I don't know how this happened, Mom. I've tried everything, but she won't listen to reason. Everything I do, everything I say, is wrong.''

His mother sank into a chair and flashed a sympathetic smile. ''She's upset, honey. When Heather left it threw her whole world into disarray. Just when it looked like things were beginning to settle down again, you decided you could do without Doris.'' She glanced at the mounds of laundry and piles of dishes. ''All those changes would throw anyone for a loop. With an emotional child like Brianne, you have to expect a strong reaction.''

''I could handle a reaction,'' Beau growled. ''But what she's been doing goes way beyond that.'' He paced to the other end of the kitchen, scooped up a mound of laundry that had been begging for attention for days and began stuffing it into the washer. ''It's like she's decided I don't deserve any space on the planet.''

His mother laughed softly, then, getting up from her chair and crossing the room, she nudged him out of the way and began layering the clothes into the washer one piece at a time. "Don't overreact, Beau. She's upset, that's all. And you have to admit, she does have reason to be."

Beau's shoulders stiffened and a warning bell went off in the back of his head. He turned away and rubbed his face with one hand. The room was fragrant with the scent of fresh coffee, but unfinished chores loomed everywhere. Floors that needed vacuuming. Windows that needed washing. Phone calls that needed to be returned. Then there were piano lessons, soccer practice and karate on top of committee meetings, town-planning meetings and work. Life was getting away from him, and he wondered for a moment if he could ever catch up.

Even so, he wasn't about to move backward. "What did you want me to do, Mom? Let Doris stay around forever? Do you have any idea how it felt to have her here all the time talking about Heather? Trying to convince me that she's just a little 'confused' and that she'll be coming back? Filling the kids' heads with that garbage? It's hard enough wrapping my brain around what happened and moving on with life, without someone purposely dragging us all backward."

His mother added soap and fabric softener to the washer and closed the lid. "I know it was rough, honey. I'm just thinking about the other things—the more practical things that make up everyday life, like dishes and laundry and dusting."

"All the things I'm not doing. Is that what you're saying?"

"Now *you're* being too sensitive. I didn't say a word about your housekeeping."

Beau laughed. "No, but you were thinking it." He sobered and let out a sigh of frustration. "I know I'm behind. I know I have a lot to learn. But I'll get there."

"There are people willing to help you, Beau, if you'd just let them. I'm sure if you talked to Doris and explained how you're feeling, she'd make a few adjustments. In a strange way I can sympathize with her. She wants what she's saying to be true."

"You don't think I *have* talked to her? She's so convinced she's right she won't listen to anything I say." The coffeemaker stopped and Beau turned away gratefully. He poured a cup for his mother, then one for himself. Gripping his mug in both hands, he returned to the table and sank into a chair.

"It's not just that, anyway," he said when he felt a little more in control. "I need to do this on my own."

She turned toward him with a scowl. "Why?"

"Because it's my job."

"Not all of it."

"My house. My kids. My responsibility."

Shaking her head in exasperation, his mom slipped into the chair across from his. "Haven't you heard that it takes a village to raise a child? Everyone needs help at one time or another. There's no shame in accepting it when it's your turn."

Beau shook his head sharply. "I don't want help and I don't need sympathy. It's just a matter of time until I have everything under control."

"Oh, honey." She eyed him over the rim of her cup. "Are you really going to let stubborn pride get in the way?"

The question stung, and her tone of voice made him

feel like a child again. "I'm just being responsible," he insisted, but his voice came out too harshly. He took a few seconds to compose himself. "I'm taking care of my kids. I'm taking care of my home. I'm pursuing a career."

"But you can't do everything alone, honey. It's too much."

He laughed without humor. "Would you say that if I were a woman?"

His mother's eyes narrowed. "I don't know what you mean."

"I mean that single mothers do it all the time and nobody thinks twice, so why is it such a stretch to believe that a man can do it just as well? Or is it only me who's not quite up to the challenge?"

The smile on his mother's face vanished. "That's not what I meant. I would never question your abilities. You've always excelled at everything you've taken on. But you're not used to doing everything you need to do around here. And the kids—"

"So I can be counted on to toss a football or change a tire, but not to fix a casserole or clean a toilet?"

His mom glanced toward the washer, where Brianne's ruined shirt seemed to take on a special glow.

In spite of his irritation, Beau laughed. "Okay, so I still have a few things to learn. I'll get used to doing what needs to be done, Mom. Just have a little faith in me and support me in this—please. If my own family isn't on my side, what chance do I have?"

Leaning across the table, she cupped his face in her hands. "We are *always* on your side. You must know that."

And he did. His parents' love, trust and support were

three things he'd never had to question. But he wondered for the first time whether his own children would be able to say the same thing about him, and how he'd ever make up for the damage Heather's life-altering decision had done them.

By comparison, a few piles of laundry and some unwashed dishes seemed utterly insignificant, and he couldn't even do those right. He had a sick feeling that if someone tossed him a life preserver now, it would probably hit him in the head and send him under for the third time.

BY TUESDAY MORNING Molly was beginning to have second thoughts about her decision to accept Beau's offer. She'd spent nearly all of Monday with Elaine, meeting old friends, dredging up memories and giggling like schoolgirls over sodas at the Burger Shack. After school let out, reality set in. Dinner with Elaine's family had left her wondering if she'd ever really be able to accept the fact that the miscarriage had left her unable to have children of her own and envying Elaine's relationship with her husband.

To make matters worse, she'd spent entirely too much time thinking about Beau, remembering his laugh, his smile, the sound of his voice and the color of his eyes. She'd been around him for less than a week, but she was as attracted to him as she'd ever been—maybe even more.

Not smart.

Now she was about to move into the cabin he'd offered and spend the next ten days practically living under his roof. Also not smart.

The past year had been hard on her. She didn't need to set herself up for almost certain disappointment. And yet here she was, wedging her last suitcase into the trunk and closing it, as if this was actually a good idea.

And maybe it was.

Spending so much time around him might be for the best. She might find out that he had atrocious habits. Rude table manners. A secret gambling problem. Trouble with alcohol. Maybe he scratched his crotch in public. Belched for sport. With a little luck, maybe she'd finally get over this silly girlhood crush that had resurrected itself without invitation.

She'd told Beau that she'd arrive around noon, but instead, she lingered over a salad at the Burger Shack, then spent some time window-shopping before finally heading toward the farmhouse. His property lay at the west end of town, surrounded by new houses where once there'd been only rolling fields. It was a great piece of land nestled beside a stream. Probably one of the most beautiful lots in town.

She drove across the wooden bridge and a few minutes later pulled into a driveway that led to his sprawling white farmhouse. Rows of trees and a lawn that was easily the size of half a football field separated the house from its neighbors.

Halfway to the house, the drive turned to dirt. She slowed cautiously, aware of the sound of her engine in the stillness and the dust kicked up by her tires. As she pulled to a stop, a curtain in a window twitched, and by the time she opened the car door Beau was striding down the walk to meet her.

Her heart gave a little skip when she saw him coming toward her in snug, well-worn jeans and a black T-shirt that emphasized the muscles in his arms and shoulders. Did he dress that way on purpose, or was he really oblivious to his charms?

A slight breeze lifted a lock of wheat-gold hair from his forehead, and a welcoming smile curved his lips. Her heart skittered again, but she ignored it. If she was going to stay here, she had to start seeing Beau as a friend. A buddy. Just another guy.

Yeah, right.

She got out of the car and rested her arms on the open door, trying to ignore the blue of his eyes and the way the sun lit his hair. "I wasn't sure where to park. Is there somewhere better?"

"This is fine." He nodded toward a copse of trees behind the house. "The cabin's back there by the stream. Walk with me and I'll show you."

Molly fell into step beside him as the kitchen door opened again. This time a young girl with light-blond hair came outside. She wore a frown so fierce Molly could have sworn she felt its weight across the distance. A young boy with hair the same shade as Beau's bounced out the door. The girl sidestepped him, brushing the sleeve of her sweater as if she'd picked up germs simply by standing on the same ground as her brother.

Molly's heart gave an uncomfortable squeeze at the girl's obvious displeasure, but she told herself to push it away. No getting wistful about Beau. No getting soft with his kids. Those were the rules from this moment on.

Beau performed introductions quickly and waved for the kids to join them without ever breaking stride. "Come on, you two. You can help."

"The kids don't have to help me," Molly protested as she struggled to keep up with him. She was pretty sure Brianne would object, and she didn't want to start off on the wrong foot. "I don't have much, and my bags aren't heavy."

"You're a guest."

"I feel like a pest."

Beau's gaze settled on her face and a frown tugged at the corners of his mouth. "I invited you to stay here, and I always take care of my guests."

Molly managed a weak smile and decided not to annoy him by arguing the point.

He nodded toward the willows, their branches still thick with leaves beginning to lose their color. "I hope the cabin's okay. I've had the windows open all morning to air it out, and the kids helped me clean up a bit."

Glancing at the kids, Molly saw that Nicky had already reached the edge of the lawn, but Brianne was taking her time and making no effort to hide her annoyance. Molly could only hope that the girl would relax once she realized that her father's guest wasn't going to be around much.

They rounded the copse of trees, and Molly got her first glimpse of the small log cabin nestled among the willows near the stream.

Far from a run-down old shack, it was utterly charming. Two large windows looked out over a long wooden porch that stretched the cabin's length. Rusted farm equipment, horseshoes and strands of barbed wire twisted into Western shapes decorated the outside walls and porch railings. Two green Adirondack chairs flanked a wide wooden porch swing, and Molly immediately saw herself spending lazy afternoons there while she read or listened to music.

She realized Beau was watching her, waiting for her

reaction with a mixture of pride and vulnerability. "So? What do you think?"

"I think it's wonderful," she said. "I can't believe this is that old run-down shack I remember. You're probably the luckiest guy I've ever met."

Beau's expression changed subtly. "I wouldn't call it luck. My grandparents left the farm to my dad, but he and my mom were settled in town and Mom didn't want to give up her house to move out here. My sister and her husband built a brand-new house on the East Bench about five years ago, and my kid brother was too busy dating and partying to take care of the property. That leaves me here by default."

The East Bench, Molly knew, was a small subdivision of houses mostly built at least forty years earlier. Nice, but nothing compared with this wonderful old home. "It doesn't matter how you got it," she said as she stepped onto the porch. "The point is that you have something that's been in your family for generations. I'd love to have *anything* that had belonged in my family for that long."

Nicky caught up to them and threw his arms around Beau's legs. Beau absently wrapped an arm around the boy's shoulders. "Maybe you will someday."

Molly shook her head and looked away. "It was just my dad and me for the last fifteen years of his life. I don't have anything belonging to my mom, and her folks are gone, so there's no hope of getting something now."

"Your dad didn't keep anything?"

"He was so upset when she died he got rid of all her things." Funny that she could admit that to Beau when she didn't like sharing it with anyone else. "I have one pair of his glasses and one of his sweaters.

My stepmother has the rest. And if we ever had any family heirlooms, they're long gone."

Beau tousled Nicky's hair. "My family is completely opposite from yours, then. I don't think my dad's ever thrown away anything in his life, and my mom's nearly as bad. She still has pictures I drew in first grade and every report card I ever brought home." He grinned at Brianne and seemed not to notice that she didn't smile back. "My kids are going to end up with more mementos from my life than they could possibly want."

He nudged Nicky forward and opened the cabin door for Molly. She stepped inside and took in every detail with a hunger that surprised her. Two matching windows in the back wall let sunlight stream through the room and brought the outdoors inside. A queen-size bed covered with a dark blue comforter and white lacy throw pillows nestled between the windows. A small kitchen took up some of the area in the front, and a living room complete with blue plaid couch and easy chairs in pale blue took up the rest. Dried flower arrangements in varying shades of yellow and ochre added just the right accents.

Beau nodded toward the rock-faced fireplace on the far wall. "Nicky and I will bring some wood for you. Nights can get cool this time of year. There's running water, but unfortunately the sink drain's not hooked up. You'll have to use the washtub and then carry the water outside to dump it. It's more rustic than you're probably used to, but I haven't had time to finish the plumbing yet."

"It won't be any trouble," Molly assured him. "I think this is the most charming place I've ever seen in my life." She put her purse on the wood dining table and let her gaze wander around the rest of the room one more time. "Did you decorate this?"

He laughed and shook his head. "Me? No." He glanced over his shoulder at Brianne, who'd moved into the doorway and stood glowering at the world in general. "Brianne and her mother did most of the decorating, didn't you, Brie?"

"Mom did it, not me." The girl's petulant voice filled the entire cabin like a blast of cold air.

Molly took her cue from Beau and pretended not to notice. "Well, it's beautiful. Your mother always did have a way of putting things together just so."

Brianne's gaze shot to Molly. "You know my mom?"

Molly nodded. "I went to school with her, too."

"Were you friends?"

"Not exactly. Your mom was a cheerleader and your dad was a football player, and I was…kind of a nerd. We didn't hang out with the same crowd."

Brianne's gaze hardened slightly. "Then what are you doing here?"

"I came back for Homecoming Week." She allowed herself a self-mocking smile and added, "Even nerds get invited back."

"Don't let her fool you," Beau put in from somewhere behind her. "She wasn't a nerd."

The ever-so-slight smile on Brianne's lips vaporized. "I didn't think so."

"Oh, but I was," Molly insisted. "At least, I wasn't one of the popular crowd like your mom and dad were. Your dad's just trying to be polite, but he doesn't really know. We weren't friends back then, either."

Hopping on one foot for reasons only an eight-year-old boy can understand, Nicky came in to stand in front of her. "You don't look like a nerd to me," he said after studying her for an uncomfortably long time.

Molly couldn't stop her pleased grin. "Why, thank you, Nicky. I think that's one of the nicest things anyone's ever said to me."

"You're welcome." He tossed a triumphant grin at his sister as he began hopping around the table. "See, Brianne? She *is* nice. You were wrong."

Brianne's face flamed. "I never said she wasn't nice, dummy. I said she was going to be trouble—and she will be, too. Just you wait and see." She spun away and dashed off the porch before Molly could absorb what she'd said.

Beau was after her like a shot, slamming the cabin door behind him. Nicky stopped hopping and stared at Molly with huge blue eyes filled with questions Molly couldn't even begin to answer. "I'd better go," he whispered, and then he was out the door behind his father, leaving Molly staring after him.

The rapid footsteps and Beau's voice faded away. Molly let out her breath in a *whoosh*. "Well," she said to the silent cabin. "I think that went well, don't you?" But the silence that rang in answer convinced her that the less time she spent around Beau and his kids, the better it would be for everyone.

IT WAS NEARLY six o'clock by the time Molly finished settling into the cabin. She'd unpacked her suitcases and spent some time familiarizing herself with the hot plate and refrigerator. She'd tried every chair in the cabin, tested the bed and given the books in the small bookcase near the bed a thorough inspection.

When she finished that, she'd spent a leisurely hour or so on the porch making a list of things to pick up at the FoodWay. But as the afternoon sun slipped behind the western mountains, time and the two large glasses of water she'd downed while she worked combined to force her to make her first trip to the house.

She wasn't eager for another encounter with Brianne, but maybe Beau had calmed her down by now. Besides, it wasn't as if she was going over to visit. She'd slip in quietly, find the bathroom and leave again before Beau and the kids noticed her.

After grabbing her purse and the list, she turned out the cabin lights and began the trek across the deep lawn. The temperature had dropped sharply with the setting sun, and the air had the crisp feel of autumn. She shivered slightly and walked faster toward the old white farmhouse.

Light gleamed in almost every window and she recognized the enticing scents of garlic and oregano on the breeze. Ignoring the rumble in her stomach, she stepped onto the porch and knocked. The door opened almost immediately, and Beau stood before her, framed by light, surrounded by the rich scents of dinner and wearing a shirt liberally spotted with something that looked suspiciously like spaghetti sauce.

Molly held back a grin while her heart did its now familiar tap dance in her chest. While she waited for the sensation to pass, she did her best to find a few faults. But his face was as close to perfect as a face could get, and the splotches of spaghetti sauce added a vulnerable appeal she didn't have the strength to fight.

Beau beamed when he saw her—which didn't help—and pushed open the screen door. "Come on in. I was wondering when you were going to wander over."

Molly stepped into a spacious kitchen that had obviously been recently renovated. Two of the walls, including the one behind the stove, were exposed brick. The other two were painted a shade of blue so soft they were almost white. Just like in the cabin, huge, multipaned windows looked out on Beau Julander's world. A perfect world in Molly's view—if you didn't count one angry daughter, heaps of laundry in the bricked alcove with the washer and dryer, and a stack of dishes by the sink.

She took another look around and realized that—from the laundry to the dishes to the mail stacked on the chopping-block work island—clutter seemed to dominate every surface. Finally! A flaw! Maybe Beau and his world weren't perfect, after all.

When she realized Beau was watching her and waiting for something, she grinned self-consciously. "I thought I should find out where the bathroom is. You know. Just in case."

Beau laughed and tossed a faded kitchen towel over one shoulder. "The guest bath is just down the back hall, second door on your left. And there's no need to knock when you come over. I'll leave the door unlocked while you're here, so just let yourself in when the need arises."

Molly caught another breath of warm garlic bread and her stomach growled again. "What if I need to leave and you're out somewhere? Will it be safe to leave the door unlocked, or would you rather give me a key?"

With a shrug, Beau turned back to the stove. "It'll be fine. This is Serenity, not St. Louis. How's the cabin?"

"It's perfect." She started toward the hallway, stepping over a bright yellow toy bulldozer on her way. "I meant what I said earlier. I think it's the loveliest place I've ever seen."

His pleased smile was almost boyish, and Molly turned away, hurrying down the hall to the guest bath as if she could actually outrun the warmth that curled through her.

Like everything else she'd seen so far, the bathroom was beautifully decorated. White walls were accented with lavender and green accessories, from the shower curtain and towels to the toothbrush holder and the scale on the floor. Heather Preston—Heather *Julander*—had always been perfectly put together as a girl, and obviously marriage and motherhood hadn't changed that.

Time hadn't changed the feelings of inadequacy Molly battled when she compared herself with Heather, either. She caught a glimpse of her reflection in the mirror and turned away quickly. Thick brown hair. Mud-colored eyes. Freckles across her nose and cheeks—even at thirty-three. An unspecified number of extra pounds on her hips and thighs. Molly was about as far from Heather's willowy blondness and subtle grace as a person could get. She probably looked as out of place next to Beau as Raggedy Ann would have looked if she'd started dating a Ken doll.

She had no idea what had brought about the end of Beau and Heather's marriage, but she felt uncomfortable in this big house where Heather and Beau had lived as husband and wife. She wasted no time taking care of business, washing her hands and heading back to the kitchen. She told herself to plow through the clutter and let herself out the door before Beau could sidetrack her with conversation, but the sight of

Brianne and Nicky at the table made her step falter, and Beau spotted her before she could get away.

"Dinner's almost ready," he said as Molly tried to get her feet working in rhythm again. "I know there's nothing to eat at the cabin, so why don't you join us?"

Brianne's head jerked up and color flooded her cheeks. Nicky began to bounce in his chair. "Yeah! Sit right here beside me. We're having s'ketti. It's my favorite."

Molly shook her head and tried to look regretful. "Thanks, but I can't."

"Why not?"

"Well, I...I have things to do." She lifted her purse as if it would prove how busy she was. "I was on my way to the store."

"Now?" Beau picked up a wooden spoon stained red and plunged it into a pot on the stove. "The market closes at seven. You don't have time to go shopping tonight."

"I'd have time to pick up a few things."

"Barely. And why bother?" He stirred carefully and made a face at the pot. "It's not homemade, but I have enough sauce here to feed half of Serenity. There's more than enough for the four of us."

"Yes, but—" Molly looked from Brianne's sour expression to Nicky's eager one "—our deal was that I'd stay in the cabin," she said, turning to Beau. "Not that I'd impose on your family."

"You're not imposing. We'd love you to join us. Meals are always better when they're shared...and we *can* be kind of fun to hang out with." He looked beyond Molly to Brianne. "As a matter of fact, Brianne has something she wants to say—don't you, Brie?"

Brianne looked so unhappy Molly's heart sank, but

she tried not to show any reaction. The girl cleared her throat, shot an impossible-to-miss dagger glance at her father, then swung her gaze to Molly. "I'm sorry."

How was Molly supposed to respond to that? Only a fool would have believed that Brianne was sincere, but Molly wouldn't have said so aloud for anything in the world. Apparently Beau thought that making his daughter say she was sorry would accomplish something. Molly didn't agree. If anything, he'd just made her chances of getting a civil word out of the girl a hundred times harder.

Hoping that *something* would ease the tension, she sent the girl her best smile. "Thank you. That's very nice of you."

Brianne looked away pointedly and focused on the book in front of her. "Okay."

Beau smiled as if something positive had actually happened. "So you'll stay for supper, right?"

Molly could think of a dozen things she'd rather do, but to refuse now would be a slap in the face of Brianne's "apology." And that would be a bad way to repay Beau's generosity.

Like it or not, she was stuck.

CHAPTER SIX

BEAU WATCHED a dozen different emotions filter through Molly's eyes before she finally gave in. "I'll stay," she said, "but only if you'll let me help."

He smiled, hoping she wouldn't guess how relieved he was that she'd accepted. He knew she wasn't fooled by Brianne's apology. Neither was he. But his daughter had been growing more difficult by the day, and he was at his wit's end. He didn't care if she was sincere. He only cared that she'd finally done *one* thing he'd asked her to—although *asked* wasn't exactly the right word to use, either.

"That's a deal I can live with." He ignored the poisonous looks still coming from Brianne and nodded toward the refrigerator. "Salad fixings are in there. Knock yourself out."

Molly looked around for someplace to leave her purse, finally settled on the top of the washer, then pushed up the sleeves of her sweater. "Any particular likes or dislikes I need to be aware of?"

Beau's gaze fell on the softly rounded breasts barely visible beneath the oversize sweater, and the sudden surge of heat he felt caught him by surprise. He looked away and tried to remember what she'd asked. Something about the salad. "Whatever you like," he said, hoping that came close to answering her.

He tried to focus on the spaghetti sauce, but his attention returned to Molly over and over as she pulled vegetables from the fridge and lined them up on the chopping block. She reached into a high cupboard for a bowl, and her sweater hiked up over one hip, accentuating the tuck of her waist and the curve of her bottom, and Beau nearly forgot what the spoon in his hand was for.

It wasn't that he didn't recognize the sensation, but it *had* been a while. He hadn't given women much thought since Heather walked out on him. He hadn't had the time, the energy or the inclination.

He chanced another glance at Molly, who'd moved back to stand at the chopping block while she tore lettuce into the bowl. Those dark eyes and hair combined to make her a strikingly beautiful woman. Her curves were enough to make a man lose his head. But with Brianne going through…whatever she was going through, Homecoming activities the next few nights in a row and an airplane stranded in Jackson, this was a bad time to even think about entanglements.

Besides, Molly wasn't permanent, and he wasn't interested in temporary. Heather had been temporary enough. If he ever got involved with a woman again, it would be someone capable of making and keeping a commitment to him and his kids. Someone who knew who she was and what she wanted. He didn't think Molly fit a single requirement on the list.

He pulled a large pot from a hook on the wall and filled it with water, turning his back on Molly in the process. But he wasn't blind, and by the time he had dinner on the table, Beau knew one thing for certain. Having Molly living in the cabin for the next ten days was going to be a much bigger distraction than he'd anticipated.

AN HOUR LATER, Beau scooted Brianne and Nicky upstairs to do homework while he and Molly cleaned up the kitchen. As if they'd done this a thousand times, Beau carried plates from the table while Molly scraped garbage into the disposal and fit dishes into the dishwasher.

After only a few minutes, he turned on the CD player and the sounds of big-band music filled the kitchen. Molly looked surprised by his choice, but only for a second. She turned back to the dishes and fit the last of the plates into the rack, then straightened and brushed a lock of dark hair from her eyes. "I think that's everything that'll fit tonight. Tell me where to find the dishwashing soap and I'll start the cycle."

Beau glanced at the overloaded dishwasher with a grimace of embarrassment. "I keep it in the cupboard beneath the sink, but you'd never know I even had any, would you. Can I just go on record as saying how embarrassed I am by the mess?"

"You can, but it's not necessary." She opened the cupboard and sent him an understanding smile. "You forget that I lived with a single dad. I know what life is like when one parent has to do everything to hold house and home together." She filled the soap holders and snapped the second one shut, then slid the soap box beneath the sink and closed the door.

Beau gathered the butter, salt and pepper from the table as if he put them away after every meal. "I guess it's too much to hope that you hated your dad for a while, got over it magically and lived together peacefully after that."

Molly shook her head slowly. "I don't think so. Sorry."

"You don't *think* so?"

"I don't actually remember, but Dad never said anything about me being difficult." She reached for a dishcloth and set to work on the stains on the stovetop. "But our circumstances were different from yours. I could hardly blame my dad for Mom's accident." Glancing over at him, she flushed the most charming shade of pink he'd seen in a long time. "Not that I'm saying you're to blame for Heather leaving."

He laughed softly. "I know what you mean. No offense taken."

For a few minutes, only the riffs of clarinet and piano filled the room, then Molly stopped working and looked over at him. Her eyes grew thoughtful and her expression a little distant. "I think the only real argument I ever had with Dad was when I told him that Ethan and I were getting divorced. Even then, I wasn't angry. But *he* was."

Beau wasn't sure what to make of that or how to respond. He only knew he couldn't stand around while Molly cleaned up after him. He grabbed a broom from the closet and tackled a corner that seemed to scream for attention. "Your dad liked Ethan, then?"

Molly let out an abrupt note of laughter. "No. He had no use for Ethan at all, but marriage? That's what he believed in. For better or worse. He couldn't understand anything making life so horrible that we couldn't work through it."

"Yeah? Well, I agree with him—to a point. I thought Heather and I would be together forever. It sounds funny to say that now. Things weren't good between us for a long time before she left, but I still never thought we'd divorce."

"Nobody goes into marriage expecting to get divorced, do they?" Molly said, avoiding his eyes.

"Of course not. But I'm sure some people are smart enough to get a clue when they spend three or four years doing nothing but fighting with their spouse."

Molly's expression sobered and she went back to scrubbing. "Is it possible to be sure you've done everything you can to save the marriage in less time?"

"You're saying that your divorce dragged on for a while, too?"

She looked up at him under bangs that had fallen into her eyes, and Beau had a sudden and unexpected feeling of rightness. As if she belonged there as much as he did. As if this kitchen without her in it would feel wrong.

"Ethan and I fought almost constantly toward the end," she said with a sad smile. "It didn't matter what it was about. By that point, the sound of his breathing irritated me and he hated the way I chewed, but I still thought we were working on the marriage. Living up to our vows. Trying to stay together."

"Sounds familiar," Beau admitted. "What happened?"

Molly sighed. "He found someone else. Someone more like him. Someone who came from money and who understood all the nuances of being a rich man's daughter-in-law, which he'd decided I would never learn."

"Ah. Nice. So your husband came from money?"

"I think he was made out of it." She laughed. "I, most definitely, am not."

The urge to put his arm around her came upon Beau without warning. He gripped the broom handle to keep his hands where they belonged. "There are worse things than being regular folk."

"Not according to the Shepherds." Molly glanced

at the dishcloth in her hand with wry amusement. "Finding out about Bambi was a shock at first, but it only hurt for a little while."

"That's her name? Bambi?"

Molly laughed and shook her head. "It's Emily, but I think Bambi fits better." She sobered again and glanced toward the stairs. "Of course, I didn't have children who were hurting and who needed me to help them understand why their world had just been tossed upside down. Only a father who thought I should fight the divorce and stand by a man who didn't want me."

"So you're telling me this Ethan Shepherd guy is a total idiot?"

The corners of Molly's mouth curved with pleasure.

Beau could tell that he'd caught her off guard. He'd also strayed into territory he'd be smart to avoid. He changed the subject before he could go any further. "I'm afraid I haven't done a very good job of helping my kids understand what happened. It's…complicated. I was too numb at first, and I let their grandmother step in and take over. It seemed great for a while. The house was always clean and the kids knew just what to expect. But then the other problems got too big to ignore. I'm afraid I let Doris influence the kids too long as it was."

"Doris sounds like my dad. And you and Heather *were* together a long time. A lot longer than Ethan and I were."

"Yeah, but time doesn't count for much when one person decides they want something else." He didn't know how to explain that his relationship with Heather had become habit long before they'd gotten married, or that he'd wondered for years if he'd ever actually loved her. Everyone else had thought it romantic for high-school sweethearts to get married and they'd both been swept up by other people's expectations. But saying that part aloud made him sound like a jerk, and he still wasn't ready to admit the truth. He could barely admit it to himself.

He concentrated on creating a nice mound of dirt with the broom. "I just want Brianne to forgive me for taking her grandmother out of our daily lives."

"She will. Eventually." Molly leaned against the stove and watched him. "You're her whole world now, and she loves you."

"She has a funny way of showing it."

Molly's lips curved in a smile again. "Cheer up. She'll come around. She's just trying to make a point in the only way she knows how. She's twelve, not twenty. She's still learning how to discuss things calmly."

"I hope you're right." Beau switched gears again. "The Homecoming committee is getting together tomorrow night to decorate the gym. You're planning to come along, aren't you? We could use an extra hand."

"Are you sure I wouldn't be in the way?"

"Are you kidding? You heard how much we have to get done this week. Trust me. Everyone will welcome you with open arms."

She grinned shyly. "Okay, then. I think I'd like that."

"Great. Plan on having dinner here with us before we go."

Her smile faded and she glanced toward the stairs again. "Thanks, but that's not necessary. I've already intruded enough."

"You haven't intruded. The salad was great, you saved me some work by making it, and I enjoyed having another adult to talk to. You'll be doing me a favor. Besides, it might do Brianne good to have a woman around. Someone without an agenda—that is, if you can stand her attitude.''

Molly hesitated, but only for a heartbeat. "All right, then. I guess it would be okay for one more night.''

One more night. Beau felt a ridiculous grin stretching his face, but he didn't even try to hide it. It had been a long time since he'd felt like a winner. Too damn long, in fact.

THE NEXT MORNING Molly made herself wait to take a shower and use Beau's phone until she was certain he and the kids had gone for the day. Last night's conversation had left her tossing and turning for hours after she'd said good night—not because of their discussion, but because she'd realized that it would take almost nothing to convince her that she was head over heels in love with him.

Again.

But that wasn't why she'd come to Serenity, and she wasn't going to let herself get sidetracked—especially since she didn't trust her feelings. It wasn't just Beau, she'd realized around midnight. She couldn't trust her feelings for *any* man right now. She might downplay the devastation of her marriage to Ethan when she spoke of it aloud, but his betrayal had ravaged her emotionally. Her self-esteem had taken a direct hit when he'd decided to replace her with someone his family would approve of, and she wasn't about to use Beau to soothe her hurt feelings.

She was far too vulnerable, but at least she knew it. Imagine the trouble she could get into if she didn't.

There was fresh coffee in the kitchen, along with a

note from Beau to help herself. She ignored both and hurried down the hall to the guest bath. She'd watched Beau drive away, but she couldn't shake the feeling that he might return at any moment. Only after she'd dressed again did she allow herself to pour a cup while she studied the list of people she wanted to contact about her mother.

She had no clear idea what she wanted to ask them, but she hadn't come all this way to let uncertainty stop her. Biting down on her bottom lip, she found Beau's cordless phone and dialed the first number on her list.

Louise Duncan had been her mother's closest friend, and Molly had vivid memories of spending time as a little girl in Louise's big, sunny kitchen while the two women laughed and chatted. She held her breath while the phone rang and felt the flutter of nervous excitement in her stomach when a familiar voice came on the line a few seconds later.

Molly's heart was thumping, but she forced herself to remain calm. "I don't know if you remember me," she said when she'd verified that she was talking with Louise. "You used to be friends with my mother, Ruby Lane."

"Molly?" Louise's voice rose in excitement. "My word, child, is it really you?"

Unexpected tears stung Molly's eyes. "You remember?"

"Well, of course I remember." Louise gave a soft laugh and the years fell away. "My, but it's good to hear your voice. Where are you calling from?"

Her obvious delight made Molly feel young again, and cradled by familiar things. "Actually I'm here in Serenity. I came back for Homecoming Week."

"And you thought to call me while you're here? Aren't you sweet!"

Molly battled a twinge of guilt. Would she have called if she hadn't wanted something? "I'd love to see you while I'm here. Is there any chance the two of us can get together?"

"What a question! Of course we'll get together. I'm tied up today, but you'll come to my place tomorrow. No excuses."

"No excuses." Molly laughed and felt herself relaxing. "I'd love to come. It'll be great to see you again."

"And you. Do you remember how to get here?"

"You'd better give me your address and directions," Molly said. "I don't think I could find it without help." She glanced around for paper and something to write with, then added, "I really do appreciate this. I have so many questions about my mother, and the two of you were so close I'm sure you're the best person to ask."

There was a brief pause before Louise's voice came again, and this time she sounded slightly less enthusiastic. "Questions?"

"I hope you don't mind. It's just that I don't remember anything about that night." Molly dug into the stack of papers beneath the phone until she found a spiral notebook and the nub of a pencil. She carried everything back to the table and sat. "I don't know why it's a blank, but for about six months on either side of the accident, I don't remember anything. Dad never talked about Mom much, and now that he's gone, it's too late to find out what he remembered. I don't know anything except that she went off the road somewhere. I don't even know where it happened."

"Your father's gone?" This time there was no mistaking the change in Louise's tone.

But Molly still couldn't think of any reason for it. "He died of a heart attack six months ago."

"Oh." A brief pause, then, "I'm sorry to hear that. I wish I'd known. I'd have sent a card or flowers."

Molly cradled the phone between her shoulder and ear. "I probably should have let someone here in Serenity know about his death, but I honestly didn't think of it."

"Well, of course you didn't, and no one could have expected you to. It wasn't as if we ever saw you after you left, and Frank never bothered to let us know where you were." Louise paused briefly, then sighed. "But listen to me going on. You don't want to hear about all that. Let me tell you how to find me, and tomorrow we'll talk about happier things."

While Louise gave directions, Molly scribbled notes. The edge in Louise's voice had disappeared, and Molly wondered if she'd only imagined it.

"I'll expect you around eleven," Louise said. "If that's okay with you, that is."

"It sounds perfect. I really appreciate this, Louise. I have so many things to ask you."

"Don't be silly," Louise said after another brief pause. "But I hope you don't expect too much. It's been a long time, and I'm not sure how much I'll be able to tell you."

She rang off before Molly had a chance to ask what she meant by that. She stared at her notes for a long moment, telling herself one more time that she'd only imagined the wariness in Louise's voice. But this was the second friend of her mother's who seemed unwilling to talk about the accident, and she didn't believe for a second it was merely coincidence.

MOLLY'S NEXT FEW CALLS were even less satisfying than her first one. Eleanor Peck's phone rang at least eight times before Molly conceded that no one was home. Charmaine Wilkinson's went to voice mail, and the number she had for Belinda Hunter had been disconnected.

Frustrated, she drove to the grocery store and wandered up and down every aisle, picking up everything on her list and a few impulse items, as well. She spent a few minutes in the pharmacy talking with Mrs. Dooley, whose daughter Katelynn had been a school friend of Molly's. According to her mother, Katelynn had moved to Tulsa with her husband nearly ten years earlier, and she wasn't planning to come back to Serenity for Homecoming Week.

Molly was a little disappointed to learn that, but she was even more discouraged by Mrs. Dooley's insistence that she hadn't known Molly's mother well, and that she didn't remember any details about the night Ruby Lane died.

Was there *anyone* who remembered her mother? Anyone who'd admit to remembering? Serenity was a small town. Too small for a fatal accident to go unnoticed. People *must* remember…

So why wouldn't they talk about it?

She thought about trying to find the spot where her mom had gone off the road, but she wouldn't even know where to look. And even if she went to the effort to find out, she was pretty sure that going there alone wasn't a good idea.

Back at the cabin she put her groceries away, pretending that the place was really hers and that it mattered where she put the tuna, bread and mayonnaise. By the time she saw Brianne and Nicky getting off the school bus at half-past three, Molly was so eager for company she convinced herself that her previous encounters with Brianne hadn't been that bad. Molly was an adult, after all, and Brianne was a hurt child. She could make more of an effort to get along with the girl.

Armed with fresh determination, she closed up the cabin, crossed the lawn to the house and knocked on the door. She hadn't forgotten Beau's instructions, but she wanted to make sure the kids knew what he'd told her before she barged in on them.

Through the glass in the door, she could see Brianne enter the kitchen. She wore a pair of jeans and a pale blue sweater, and her hair skimmed her shoulders when she walked. She recognized Molly and her step faltered, but she came to the door, threw it wide and turned toward the refrigerator. "You don't have to knock, you know. I thought my dad told you that."

"He did." Molly stepped inside and closed the door behind her. "I just didn't want to come barging in and frighten you."

Brianne pulled a can of soda from the fridge, opened it and drank deeply. "We're not babies," she said when she paused for a breath. "We wouldn't get frightened just because you came into the house."

"I know you're not," Molly assured her. "That's not what I meant. I saw you and Nicky get off the bus. Are you here alone very long before your dad gets home?"

Brianne shrugged. "A little while. Why do you care?"

The question caught Molly by surprise, but if Brianne wanted direct, Molly was happy to oblige. "I don't, really," she said with a shrug and a smile. "I'm just trying to make conversation."

Brianne's eyes widened almost imperceptibly, then immediately narrowed again. "Why?"

"Because you and I are standing in the same room, and it would be rude to ignore you."

"It's not rude to ignore somebody you don't like," Brianne said with a smirk. "And it's worse to pretend to like somebody when you really don't."

"Does that mean you don't like me, or that you think I don't like you?"

Beau's daughter leaned against the fridge and folded her arms. "What do you think?"

"Well, since I have no reason not to like you, I think I know the answer. Are you going to tell me why? Or do I have to guess?"

Brianne's shoulder rose in a nonchalant shrug. "My dad might not know what you want, but I do."

"Oh? And what do you think I want?"

"I don't think, I *know*." Brianne met Molly's gaze with a challenging glare. "You're after my dad, aren't you?"

Molly gaped at her. "Ex*cuse* me?"

"I said, you're after my dad and you think you can make him like you. That's why you're here. That's why you're staying in the cabin. And that's why you had dinner with us last night."

The girl looked so sure of herself Molly knew she'd have to choose her words with great care. "That's not true," she said. "I do like your dad, but we're friends, that's all. I've never even thought about making him like me." *Not since high school, anyway.* "I'm here for Homecoming, and to talk to people who used to know my mother. I'm staying in the cabin because the motel is full and I didn't make a reservation. And I was planning on taking care of my own dinner last night, but your dad invited me to stay.''

Brianne tilted her head and looked at her from behind a curtain of pale-blond hair. "Why should I believe you?''

"Because I understand how important your dad is to you and I wouldn't insult you by lying.''

"Then why do you look at him that way?'' Brianne asked, flipping the pull-tab on her can with an annoying pinging sound.

A denial rose to Molly's lips, but Brianne would never believe it. "I'm not sure how I look at him,'' Molly said with a sheepish smile, "but you have to admit that he *is* a pretty good-looking guy. He always has been.''

"So you're in love with him.''

"Not at all.'' Molly moved to stand beside the counter. "There's a difference between appreciating a good-looking man and being in love. I don't know your dad well enough to be in love with him.''

"But you could fall in love with him, couldn't you?''

Molly laughed uneasily. "I'm not sure what to say, Brianne. If I say no, you'll think I'm insulting your dad. If I say yes, you'll think I'm lying about the rest. I don't think there is a good answer to that question.''

Brianne's lips actually curved into a semblance of a smile, but the challenge still burned in her eyes. "I won't think you're insulting him if you say no. Why should I? You're not his type at all.''

Ouch! But it wasn't exactly news. "So we agree that it's highly unlikely that I'm going to fall in love with your dad. What do you say the two of us try to get along while I'm here?''

''That's not a real no.''

Shaking her head, Molly laughed in disbelief. ''You drive a hard bargain, kid. But I'm old enough to know better than to say 'never.' You're going to have to be content with highly unlikely, extremely remote, and it would take a miracle.''

With another shrug, Brianne pushed away from the refrigerator. ''That's what my dad said, too,'' she announced as she headed down the hall toward the front of the house. She stopped at an open doorway and glanced back at Molly. ''You can have a soda if you want one,'' she said, then disappeared, leaving Molly staring at the empty hallway and trying not to admit how much Brianne's offhand comments hurt.

CHAPTER SEVEN

SICK TO DEATH of blue and gold crepe paper, Beau followed Aaron out of the gymnasium and into the darkened corridor that led to the school's cafeteria. They'd been working for hours, tying banners and stringing streamers until Beau's fingers were stained with the school colors.

But his attention had only been partially on the job.

Every time he climbed the ladder, his eyes sought Molly across the cavernous room. Every time he went down, he caught himself straining to hear what she was saying. Her laugh intrigued him. Her walk fascinated him. He was acting like a man who hadn't had sex in years. Three. And a half. But who was counting?

He was having a hard time staying focused on anything but Molly, and his inability to think was starting to annoy him, so he'd jumped at Aaron's suggestion that they pay a visit to the snack machines outside the cafeteria. Maybe a short break would help him clear his head and put his fascination with Molly in perspective.

Music from Ridge's portable CD player trailed after them as they walked through scraps of crepe paper trimmed from streamers.

"Tell you what," Aaron said with an old man's groan. "If I never see another roll of that damn stuff again in my life, I'll die a happy man."

"You're not the only one." Beau caught a fluttering bit of blue and stuffed it into his pocket to throw away later. "I'll be glad when this is over. I need a few nights at home."

Aaron trailed his fingers along the lockers as they passed. "You won't get many. Mayor Biggs has already called a meeting of the WinterFest planning committee for next week."

Beau moaned in protest. "I hope he finds my replacement soon. I need a break."

"You don't really think he's going to replace you?"

"He has no choice. I've already told him that I have to resign."

"So? There's always been a Julander on the WinterFest committee. The town's entire Christmas is inside that thick head of yours." Aaron snorted a laugh and palmed his thinning hair. "You know what? I'll believe it when it happens."

Before Beau could argue, they drew to a stop in front of the darkened cafeteria and Aaron pulled a handful of change from his pocket. "So what's the story on Molly?" Aaron asked, as Beau dropped quarters into the vending machine.

Beau's first instinct was to punch Aaron for bringing the subject up. They'd been friends as long as he could remember and gotten into more scrapes together than he could count. They'd played on the same teams from Little League to their trophy-winning, high-school football squad, and each had been best man at the other's wedding. He trusted Aaron like no one else—but he had no idea how to answer his question.

He shrugged and culled a few quarters from the change in his own pockets. "No story." He fed four quarters into the coin slot and made a selection. ''Why do you ask?''

Aaron snagged his bag of corn chips and tore it open. ''No reason. Just curious. How did the two of you hook up, anyway?''

Beau dropped more coins into the slot and punched the buttons for another bag of chips. ''We didn't hook up. She's staying in the cabin for a few days, that's all. No big deal, okay?''

''Whoa, buddy!'' Aaron froze with a chip halfway to his mouth. ''It was just a question. I didn't mean anything by it.''

''Yeah? Well, then, don't say it like that. You could give somebody the wrong impression.''

''Okay. Whatever.'' Aaron glanced over his shoulder toward the gym. ''Is it just me, or is she a lot prettier than she was in school?''

Beau didn't want to think about pretty. He moved to the soft-drink machine and held out an impatient hand for some financial input from Aaron. ''Not everyone reaches their peak at seventeen.''

''You saying *I* did?''

''You? No. But there are times when I wonder about myself.''

The laughter in Aaron's eyes faded almost immediately. ''You're serious?''

Beau gave up trying to figure out what he wanted to drink and leaned against the cool brick wall. ''Tell me what you think of me.''

''What I *think* of you?''

''Yeah. You know. What do you think of me? If you had to sum me up in a few words, what would they be?''

"You're my friend. A pain in the neck sometimes, but still my friend. Why?"

A distant burst of laughter echoed through the empty hallways, and Beau could have sworn he could tell Molly's laughter from the others'. He just couldn't understand why, when he'd been perfectly content to be alone and get his life together, he had to start letting things become complicated. He raked his fingers through his hair and told himself—again—to stop thinking about her.

"It's just…well, Molly said something the other day that's been bugging me. She has this image of me as lucky, and I know she's not the only one who feels that way."

Aaron quirked an eyebrow. "You? Lucky?"

Beau smiled halfheartedly. "I didn't say it, she did. But when I put that together with some of the things Heather used to say, it makes me wonder if *everyone* sees me that way."

"Well, *I* don't."

"I'm not sure you count," Beau said grudgingly. "You know me too well. You know what I've screwed up and you know where I've failed. But what about other people?"

Laughing, Aaron dumped the last of his chips into his hand and crumpled the empty wrapper. "Did Molly give you a reason for this assessment of hers?"

Beau thought back for a moment. "Well, she thinks I'm lucky for inheriting the house and the farm."

"And you are."

"Yeah, and I'm the first one to admit it," he said, though the instant the words left his mouth, he realized they weren't quite true. "My lousy marriage wasn't lucky. My divorce wasn't lucky. Having an ex-mother-in-law who still wants to run my life isn't lucky.''

"So you're an unlucky SOB instead. What do you care what Molly Lane thinks?"

"I *don't*." Beau pushed away from the wall and tried once more to figure out what kind of soda he wanted. He punched a big flat green button with his fist. "I was curious, that's all. It's no big deal."

"Get me one of those, wouldja?" Aaron fished a bill from his pocket and handed it to Beau. "You had a great run in high school. Senior-class president. Captain of the football team…and whatever else you were. You got good grades. Girls were all over you. You could have dated anybody you wanted."

"And you think I lucked out in all that? All the hours I spent working on my game and hitting the books meant nothing?"

"No. But what's the big deal?"

"It's not a big deal," Beau said. "But if you work hard for something, it's nice to know your efforts are appreciated. Nobody wants people to write off their skill and hard work as dumb luck."

"And you think that's what people do with you?"

"I don't know."

"Well, hell. You've had some bad luck, too, and everybody knows it. So even if some folks did think that when we were kids, they don't now."

Beau handed over change and a cold can of root beer to his friend, and started back toward the gymnasium. "Then there *are* people who feel that way?"

"No. No!" Dumbfounded, Aaron ran a hand along the back of his neck. "I don't know. Nobody ever said anything to me. I said *if* they'd felt that way. But even if they do, what does it really matter? You know who you are, so what does somebody else's opinion matter?''

Beau had no answer for that. These days, it seemed that there were a whole bunch of questions he couldn't answer. When they reached the gymnasium again, he glanced through the open doors and his gaze flew to Molly. She stood in the center of the crowd, smiling broadly, basking in the attention of her former classmates. Even from a distance, he could see the glow in her eyes, and his heart turned over twice before he could pull himself together.

It had been too long since he'd been with a woman, he told himself. That was all. He was reacting the way any man would react to the sight of a particularly beautiful woman. Hell, if circumstances were different, he might be tempted to let nature take its course.

But circumstances *weren't* different. Molly would be here for just ten more days. Then she'd go back to her life and Beau would stay in his. Another man might have taken advantage of the situation, anyway, but marriage to Heather had cured him of any interest in a superficial relationship, and temporary just didn't cut it.

He *did* care what Molly thought of him, even if he wasn't ready to admit how much.

''I STILL CAN'T believe you're really here,'' Jennifer Grant said from atop a ladder a few hours later. She'd been another of Molly's friends when they were girls, and it had taken only a few minutes to rediscover their former closeness.

''To be honest, I can't, either,'' Molly admitted. She stretched high to hand Jennifer one end of the soft blue netting they'd been assigned to drape over the plain walls of the gymnasium. Only about ten people had showed up for tonight's work party, so there hadn't been much time to chat, but they were nearly finished and the mood was beginning to lighten.

Even Beau, who'd been working nonstop all evening, had disappeared. She glanced over one shoulder to see if he'd come back, but there was still no sign of him. "You can't imagine how glad I am you've all been so welcoming," she said, turning her attention back to Jennifer. "I was a little worried about coming back. I was afraid that you'd have all forgotten me."

"You're one of us, Molly. Always have been. Moving away didn't alter that."

Unlike some of the others in their class, Jennifer hadn't changed much since high school. She'd put on a few pounds, but she still had tons of energy and wore too much makeup and flirted outrageously with every man in sight. But the flirting had always been harmless, and her husband—a good-looking guy Molly remembered only vaguely—didn't seem to mind.

Jennifer secured the netting in place and started down the ladder again. "The only thing I can't figure out is why you're suddenly so…insecure."

The comment threw Molly and she nearly missed Jennifer's cue to pick up her end of the ladder. "Insecure?" she asked when they were finally in sync again and moving toward the next patch of bare wall. "Is that how I strike you?"

"A little." Jennifer set her end of the ladder on the floor and headed back for the bolt of netting. "You're less confident than you used to be. But you're still smart. Funny. Lots of fun to hang out with. Don't you realize that?"

Molly shook her head. "It's been a while since I had

any close friends,'' she admitted numbly. ''Dad was a bit of a loner, and I'm probably a lot like him—but not because that's what I want. I like being with people and I'm having a great time tonight.''

''I'm glad.'' Jennifer carried the netting over to the ladder and wedged it against a folded stack of bleachers. ''I guess losing your mom didn't help—especially not the way it happened.''

For the second time in less than a minute, Molly felt as if she'd been hit hard. She picked up the basket holding scissors, tape and string, and walked over to join Jennifer. ''You remember the accident?'' she asked, setting the basket on the floor

''Of course I do.'' Jennifer seemed oblivious to the fact that she was discussing something that everyone else had decreed off-limits. ''It shook everybody up practically forever.''

Or maybe Molly had misinterpreted everyone else's reticence. ''Would you mind telling me what you remember?''

''Sure.'' Jennifer shrugged. ''But you must remember more than I do.''

''Actually, I don't remember anything at all. The year around my mom's accident is a blank.''

''Seriously?''

''I'm afraid so.''

''You don't remember anything?''

''Not a thing. The only things I know are what my dad told me, but he didn't like to talk about it. Now that he's gone, the people here in Serenity are the only ones who can tell me about that night.''

Jennifer reached into the basket for the scissors and tape, tucking them into the waistband of her jeans. ''Well, that stinks.''

Lanie Byers interrupted long enough to get the keys to Jennifer's Suburban so they could bring in the disco ball. When they were alone again, Jennifer's expression grew thoughtful. "I remember that night really well. It was cold. Sometime in January, I think."

"April tenth." That much Molly did know.

Jennifer looked confused. "Yeah, but we had a storm. A blizzard. A white-out. That's why she went off the road, wasn't it? That and the ice?" She paused. "I guess you could be right. It was probably one of those freak spring storms we sometimes have. I just remember the phone ringing and someone telling my mom about the accident. It happened out past the Trego ranch, I think. The car hit a patch of ice and went through the guardrail. They figured Ruby died on impact. I know it's not much, but at least you can feel better knowing that she didn't suffer."

Molly nodded slowly, letting those few details filter in to mingle with what she could remember about the town. "The Trego ranch…" she said after a few seconds. "Isn't that way out on the East Bench?"

Jennifer nodded. "Past the houses out there, on the way to Beaver Creek."

Molly could picture the road—a narrow, winding strip of asphalt barely wide enough for two lanes of traffic and usually closed during bad weather. "Did they ever say what she was doing out there?"

"Not that I heard." Jennifer tilted her head to one side. "It does seem like an odd place to be in the middle of a bad storm, doesn't it?"

"Very. I thought that stretch of road was closed when the weather was bad, so how did she get out there in the first place?"

"It is closed—usually. They lock the gates in late

October and don't open them again until almost Memorial Day, except in mild winters.''

Molly nodded thoughtfully. She didn't know what to think, but she didn't want to be guilty of blowing things out of proportion. Still, her dad's refusal to discuss the accident had never seemed so unfair or so wrong. She should already know the details of her mother's accident. She shouldn't have to beg people to tell her about it.

"I wonder if anyone knows what she was doing out there," she said, more to herself than Jennifer.

"One of her friends might."

"I've talked to a couple of her friends," Molly said, "but nobody seems willing to say much. What about your mom? Do you think she might know?"

"I don't know." Jennifer fished a piece of gum from a pocket. "I'll ask. She still wears the jewelry she bought from your mom."

Molly realized they'd slacked off with the decorating and grabbed the bolt of netting to unwind a length of it. "Really?"

"Yeah. She's got some really great stuff." Jennifer pulled out the scissors and waited for Molly to stop. "I keep trying to convince her to give me those turquoise earrings your mom made when we were seniors, but she won't even consider it." Molly stopped unwinding and Jennifer cut the netting to the proper length. "I'll tell you what I really wanted—that beaded choker she made for you that Christmas. That's still the most elegant piece of jewelry I've ever seen. Do you still have it?"

Although she struggled to remember something—anything—about a choker, Molly's mind was a blank. "I wish I did, but Dad gave away all her jewelry and clothes to charity after she died. By the time I realized what he'd done, it was too late.''

''But that choker was yours,'' Jennifer protested.

''Dad must have given it away with all the rest.'' Molly tried not to feel the cold spikes of anger that bumped around inside her, but they were getting harder and harder to ignore. She understood her father's grief. She knew how painful it must have been to see reminders of his beloved wife, but why hadn't he realized that Molly might feel differently? That she might *need* the reminders? Or had he just not cared?

A faint wisp of memory stirred—a shadowy image surrounded by anger and shouting, though she couldn't make out the words. A vague sense of uneasiness ran through her, but she didn't know why. Had she been angry, or had she been frightened by someone else?

Frightened?

Yes. There was anger all around her, but she was frightened and nearly overwhelmed by sadness. Just as quickly as the image came, it was gone. She let out a shaky breath and rubbed her temples with her fingertips. ''I don't *think* I remember, but I'm not sure. It's like there's something right outside my line of vision. I see this shadow, but then I turn to find out what it is and it's gone.''

Jennifer grabbed one end of the netting and climbed the ladder. ''Maybe it would help you remember if you could see some of the jewelry your mom made.''

''I'd love to. You can't imagine how much.''

''Okay. I'll talk to my mom and let you know. And who knows? Maybe Mom will be able to tell you something about the accident.''

A faint spark of hope stirred in Molly's chest, but she tried not to let it grow too large. Jennifer's mother probably did know something. The real question was, would she be willing to talk about it?

Molly was almost afraid to hope.

SHE WAS ASLEEP the second her head touched the pillow and slept straight through until eight the next morning, something she hadn't done since her father's heart attack. She awoke slowly, stretching beneath the light blanket and reveling in the autumn sunlight that streamed into the cabin through the windows.

Other than a few brief moments during her conversation with Jennifer, she'd had a wonderful time at the school, and even that conversation seemed less sinister in the daylight. The possibility of seeing her mother's jewelry after all this time got her up and out of bed, but she tried not to let herself get too excited or hopeful. After all, Jennifer's mother might be as reticent as the rest of Serenity when it came to Ruby Lane.

Almost without thinking, she crossed to the front windows and looked at the main house, remembering the drive home with Beau well after midnight. Had she really seen a spark of something different in his eyes last night, or had exhaustion and excitement made her imagine it?

She yawned and started to turn away, then realized that the Cherokee wasn't in the driveway. The kids would be at school and Beau was gone. Maybe she could save herself a few steps. She crossed the lawn wearing her robe, pajamas and slippers, and carried shoes and clean clothes with her so she could dress after her shower.

Weak sunlight filtered down on her, and the sounds of Serenity coming to life surrounded her. It was such a lovely morning, maybe she'd even have coffee on the porch. But when she let herself into the kitchen, she saw Beau standing in front of the washing machine. She came to an abrupt halt and one of her shoes dropped to the floor with a thud.

He wore a pair of faded jeans slung low on his hips. No shirt. No socks. He turned as Molly entered, and the sight of his bare chest, whisker-shadowed cheeks and lopsided smile sent her heart into overdrive. Her mouth went dry and she clutched her clothes in front of her like a shield, but she couldn't do anything about her makeup-less face or the hair poking out from her head at all angles.

His gaze swept her from head to toe, but his expression gave no clue as to what he thought. "Morning," he greeted her, as if disheveled women wearing pajamas burst into his kitchen every day of the week. "Coffee's on. Toast and jam's on the table. I can fix a couple of eggs if you're not particular, or I saved you two of my mom's peach muffins. They're on a plate near the microwave."

"Muffins are fine," Molly croaked out around the lump of pure mortification lodged in her throat. She tore her gaze away from his flat stomach and made herself meet his eyes, but that wasn't a whole lot safer, since they seemed exceptionally blue this morning. "I didn't see your Jeep in the driveway. I thought you were gone."

Beau checked the pockets of a Nicky-size pair of jeans and tossed them into the washer. "I had to leave for a while. The kids missed the bus. By the time I got back, Mom was here with muffins so I parked on the street." He pulled a pair of Brianne's jeans from the mound at his feet and checked the pockets. "Guess I'm finally getting that chance I've been wanting to catch up around here."

Molly poured herself a cup of coffee and leaned against the counter. She made herself look at the swollen mound of laundry, instead of Beau. "I'm not a very good houseguest. I should offer to help with something."

"With what? My dirty laundry?" Beau laughed and shook his head. "Even if you did offer, I'd turn you down. The kids and I made this mess. We'll clean it up."

"Your laundry wasn't exactly what I had in mind." When she realized she was staring at a pair of men's boxers, she looked away from the clothes. "You keep feeding me, though, so maybe I should pay you back by cooking dinner one night."

Beau dropped a sweatshirt into the washer and fixed her with a skeptical look. "You know how to cook?"

It had been a long time since anyone had teased her, and she'd forgotten how it felt to view life as something to be enjoyed rather than simply endured. She managed to keep a serious expression on her face and shook her head. "No. Is that a problem?"

"Not if you can keep from giving us all food poisoning."

"I can certainly try."

He grinned and turned back to his laundry. "Well, what more could a guy ask? When do you want to fix us this feast?"

"How about tonight?"

"Tonight's the parade and I need to be there early. I'm afraid you'll have to join us for a quick bite at the Burger Shack."

"Tomorrow, then."

"Football game. Pizza. And Saturday's the Home-coming Ball. The kids will be at my parents' house, and I don't think you should have to toil over a hot stove before you need to get dressed. I thought we could have dinner at the Chicken Inn on our way to the school." His gaze shot to hers and she saw a glimmer of uncertainty in his eyes. "If that's okay with you of course."

Somewhere way in the back of her mind a voice whispered caution, but she ignored it and nodded. "It's fine. So I'll fix dinner on Monday, then. What do the kids like?"

"Oh, they're pretty fussy. They insist that the food be at least semiedible."

"Don't you think that's a bit demanding?"

"Well, yes, as a matter of fact." He dumped laundry soap into the washer and closed the lid. "I've tried talking to them about their extreme demands—three meals a day, clean clothes, a roof over their heads…" He shook his head in mock exasperation. "It's this younger generation. They think they're entitled to things we never had."

Molly chuckled. "How about chicken? I have a great recipe. It has to be marinated overnight, but it makes the meat so tender you won't believe it."

Beau crossed to the coffeemaker and poured a fresh cup. "Sounds great, but you don't have to get fancy. We're just small-town folk here."

"It's not fancy," Molly assured him. She carried the plate of muffins to the table and made herself comfortable. "It takes hardly any time at all. And living in a small town doesn't mean you can't gussy up from time to time, does it?"

Beau pretended to consider that for a moment. "No,

I suppose not. We gussy occasionally. We just don't gussy our chickens.''

"Cute." She broke off a piece of muffin and popped it into her mouth. "Well, Monday's chicken *is* going to be gussied, and I promise you it's semiedible. I'll just have to remember to stop at the FoodWay for garlic and oranges.''

"You should find 'em there. We're small, but we do have produce.'' He looked at her over the rim of his cup and her heart took off at a gallup. She knew she was playing with fire, but she couldn't make herself look away. He was still the best-looking man on the planet, bar none.

CHAPTER EIGHT

AFTER WHAT SEEMED like hours, Beau finally broke eye contact and took up the conversation as if the moment had never been. "So now that you've been here for a few days, what do you think? Disappointed?"

Molly drew a breath and tried to follow his lead. "In the town? Of course not. I'd forgotten how much I like it here."

"It's not too unsophisticated for you?"

"Not at all. Did you really think it would be?"

Beau shrugged and joined her at the table. "Lots of people have gone in search of something bigger and better since we graduated."

"Yes, but I didn't leave by choice. I left because my dad left. I didn't go out to look for something better, and I came back to find what I lost." She ate another bite of muffin and made a mental note to ask for his mother's recipe. "What about you? Do you ever regret staying?"

Beau lowered his cup to the table and nodded. "Once in a while."

"Really? I didn't know you'd ever thought of leaving."

"Of course I did. I thought about it all the time when I was a kid. Not that I don't love it here. I do. And I love my family. I don't really regret my choices, but there are times when I look at some of the other guys in our class and wonder what might have been.''

''Like who?''

''Dave Marbury, for one. He's on the coaching staff at the University of Wyoming. Hank Hilton writes for the *Denver Post*. Steve Cummings just bought a summer house on an island off the coast of Maine. And here I am, living in my grandparents' old house and flying my little airplane from one place to another.''

''Yeah, but most of those guys would have given a limb to be you back in school.''

Beau's lips curved into a wistful smile. ''That was a long time ago, Molly. It's a little disheartening sometimes to realize that the best thing you'll ever do in life happened before you were twenty.''

''But I thought…''

''You thought an achievement or two during high school should be enough to carry a guy through life?''

She laughed uneasily. ''I guess not.''

Beau spread butter on a piece of toast and followed it with blackberry jam. ''Don't get me wrong. I do love my life. I have great kids and a terrific career, and I'm following in the traditions that mean so much to my family. It might not be what I originally wanted to do, but it's close. Still, every once in a while—usually around Homecoming when the guys come back—I think about what might have been and I feel a twinge of envy.''

''What did you want to do?''

''I was going to be a commercial airline pilot,'' he said. ''I had dreams of traveling all over the world, seeing everything, soaking up different cultures.''

''So why didn't you?''

''Life got in the way.'' He took a bite of toast and

washed it down with coffee. "Heather and I took a few wrong turns and weren't as careful as we should have been. She got pregnant before the end of high school, so we got married and settled into life here in Serenity, and that was that."

Had Molly known that at the time? Was that another thing she'd forgotten? She shook her head in confusion. "But Brianne isn't old enough—"

"No, she's not. The baby was stillborn." Old heart-ache flickered across his face, but he went on quickly, "I think some folks expected us to split up after that, but losing the baby after everything we'd been through was almost too much for Heather. I couldn't walk out on her. I loved her. I wouldn't have married her if I hadn't."

Molly finished her muffin and wrapped her hands around her coffee mug just to have something to hold on to. "I'm so sorry. I had no idea."

He shrugged away her concern. "How could you? You were gone."

"Well, yes, but—"

"It was rough," he said, "but we got through it. We gave up one set of dreams and worked on another. That's life." He finished his toast, then stood and stacked plates and silverware. "Like I said, I don't even think about it much except when Homecoming rolls around."

His thoughts must be especially poignant this year after Heather walked out and left him holding that new set of dreams by himself. Molly bit her lip to keep from asking if Heather had run off to chase her old dreams, and if he resented her for leaving him to raise the kids alone. She knew the answer, anyway. Even if he har-bored some mild resentment, he clearly adored his children, and would have been heartbroken if Heather had taken them with her to Santa Fe.

She drained the rest of her coffee and carried her mug to the sink, where Beau had started scraping dishes and loading the dishwasher. "It's a funny thing about comparisons," she said. "I've been thinking how lucky you are and what a great life you have, and here you are comparing yourself to other guys. I wonder why we can't ever just be happy with the life we have."

Beau shot a glance at her. "I *am* happy."

"I wish *I* could say that and mean it."

He shut off the water and turned to face her. "You're in the middle of a rough year. I couldn't have said I was happy when the baby was stillborn. I'm not sure I could have said it when I stopped working for my dad and opened the charter company. And I sure as hell couldn't say it last year when Heather walked out. But I *wanted* to be happy, and sometimes that's enough."

Molly smiled slowly. "I can say *that* and mean it."

"So there you go."

She shook off the slight melancholy that had taken hold and turned back to the table for the rest of their dishes. "I'm a happy person most of the time. It'll take a while to get over Dad's death. I know that and I'm prepared for it. Losing my job bothers me in a different way—probably because it's the one thing I should have been able to control. There are so many people out of work now that it's not easy finding something else."

"You've been looking?"

"Since the day I was let go." Molly sighed. "I've probably sent out seventy résumés, and I've only been called in for two interviews—and both of those were disastrous. One was for a different position from the one they advertised—at about half the pay. The other was for a company that declared bankruptcy a week later.''

''Are you trying to stay in the same field, or would you consider branching out?''

''I'd love to stay in graphic design, but I'm not sure if that's because I enjoy it or because it's all I know. I'm pretty good at crafts, but there's not much money in popsicle-stick birdhouses. But the graphic-design field is glutted right now, so I don't know what I'll do. I'm just lucky I have a little time to get on my feet again. My dad had a couple of life insurance policies. My stepmother was the beneficiary on one, but I was named on the other, so I don't have to take the first minimum-wage job that comes along.''

''Well, at least you're not destitute.''

''No, or I wouldn't be here. But I don't want to live off the insurance money indefinitely. I know Dad would want me to use that money for something big and wonderful. He wouldn't want me to fritter it away month by month on rent and utilities.''

''Then we'll both keep our fingers crossed that you won't have to.'' Beau shut the dishwasher and looked over the kitchen with a satisfied smile. ''And that the perfect opportunity will come knocking soon.''

''I hope so, but with the job market the way it is right now, I'm not going to hold my breath.''

''So maybe you should think about doing something else. Make your own opportunity.''

Molly laughed. ''If only it were that easy.''

''Maybe it could be. What do you know how to do?''

''Not a whole lot, that's the trouble.''

"And the crafts? No possibilities there?"

She crossed to the trash can and tossed in their napkins. "I need more than a little pocket money. I don't think a hobby is the answer."

"Depends on the hobby, doesn't it? Look at your mom. She did all right for herself with her jewelry business. I'll bet every woman in town bought stuff from her, and I'll bet most of them still have it. If she'd been able to launch a business on the Internet, Ruby Lane would probably be a household name by now."

Molly started to shake her head, but something stopped her and a tiny seed of excitement took root. "I do know how to make jewelry," she said, testing the idea as she said it aloud. "At least I used to. It's been a while, but I helped my mom a lot when I was younger."

Beau held out both arms and grinned. "You see?"

"There's just one problem," she said, trying to be practical. "My mom's jewelry was special. Unique. She was a genius at design, but I'm not. I might be able to do all right if I had her sketches, but I'm sure my dad threw them out along with everything else."

Beau waved off her argument with one hand. "You could copy your mom's designs, couldn't you?"

"Maybe."

"So we just find everybody in town who has your mom's jewelry and you go from there. You've got a little capital of your own, and I'll bet Pete Gratz over at the bank would be willing to talk to you about a loan if you need one."

Molly was having trouble keeping up. "But I'm not staying here, and I—"

"At least think about it," he urged. "It's an option,

and five minutes ago you didn't have one. You're already ahead.''

His optimism was contagious, but Molly wasn't Beau. Life didn't go the way she wanted it to simply because she wanted it.

''At least think about it,'' he urged again.

And Molly nodded. Because she *would* think about it, even if she knew that it was too much to hope for.

MOLLY SET OFF for her appointment with Louise Duncan at a little before eleven. She tried to put Beau's suggestion out of her mind, but the possibility of resurrecting her mother's jewelry designs was awfully appealing, even if she couldn't make a living at it.

She considered various possibilities as she drove through town and into East Bench subdivision. Even though the homes there were aging now, they still sported manicured front lawns and wide driveways filled with boats, snowmobiles on trailers and recreational vehicles.

Once she'd found Louise's sprawling rambler, she pulled up to the curb and sat for a moment, remembering. The house hadn't changed much since she'd last seen it. The trees in the front yard were taller, and there were more flower beds along the sidewalk, but memories of time spent here with her mother swirled all around her.

Only a few fallen leaves littered the carefully tended lawn; someone had gathered the rest into orange trash bags, which now formed a neat stack at the end of the driveway. Those bright pumpkin-shaped bags forced her to acknowledge something she'd been holding at arm's length for months—the holidays were just around the corner.

She'd been dreading Thanksgiving and Christmas
ever since the funeral, but she couldn't ignore them
much longer. She was going to have to find some way
to get through them alone.

With an effort she shook off the melancholy and
smiled at the leaf bags. Unlike most of the folks around
Serenity, Louise had always turned up her nose at the
practice of burning leaves in the fall.

Ruby had teased her relentlessly, but nothing she'd
said had changed her friend's mind. Molly could almost hear the two women bantering now, and she
smiled as she imagined the sound of her mother's delighted laughter.

Her father had grown to hate Serenity, but Ruby had
loved living here. She'd been artistic and passionate,
ruled by her heart rather than her head, and she'd loved
the volatile springs, the hostile winters, the heat of the
summer and the glorious autumns. She'd found joy in
everything, from the first buds of leaves in the spring
to the sting of sleet on her face in the winter. But she'd
found that joy because she'd looked for the best in
every situation and always expected to find it.

A whole lot like Beau.

Molly wished suddenly that she'd inherited more of
her mother's ability to find the good and less of her
father's tendency to expect the worst. Ruby wouldn't
have balked at the idea of embarking on a journey into
the unknown. She'd never been the careful, cautious
type.

Then again, if she'd been more cautious, maybe
she'd have stayed off the road to Beaver Creek and
would be here still.

That possibility made Molly's heart ache, but she
didn't want to spend the day filled with regrets over

things she was powerless to change, so she resolutely pushed everything out of her mind and took a few deep breaths of crisp, autumn-scented air. She wanted to find out about her mother's accident, but maybe not today, after all, despite the fact that it was her main reason for visiting Louise. Today, she wanted to spend the time celebrating her mother's life, remembering her spirit and talking about the things that had made her happy.

She climbed out of the car and started up the curving sidewalk to the front door, but she'd only gone a few steps when someone called out to her.

"Molly? Molly Lane, is that you?"

She wheeled back around and found a blond woman in her late fifties striding across the road toward her. It took only a second for Molly to recognize Joyce Whalen, a friend of her mother's she hadn't yet tried to call.

With a glance at Louise's still-closed front door, she changed direction and walked back toward the street. Joyce looked exactly the same as she had the last time Molly saw her. Trim. Athletic. Full of energy. She wore a pale-blue warm-up suit and new tennis shoes, and she still had a spring in her step.

She swept Molly into a hug and released her again just as quickly. "I heard that you were back in town. When did you get here?"

Molly frowned slightly when she realized how many days had slipped away already. "I've been here nearly a week."

"You've been here all this time and I haven't seen you? Where are you staying?"

"Believe it or not, I'm staying in the cabin on Beau Julander's property."

"Oh?" Joyce's eyes flickered with interest. "That's a nice place, if I do say so myself. I worked with Heather on some of the decorating."

"Did you really? I had no idea you were a decorator."

Joyce laughed and shielded her eyes against the glare of the sun. "Well, I wouldn't go *that* far, but I do like to dabble from time to time. Ruby used to encourage me to take a risk, and I finally got my courage up. But what about you? Are you married?"

"Divorced."

"How many little ones?"

Molly shook her head. "None."

Joyce didn't so much as blink, just motioned at a white brick house across the street where a tennis racket and a tube of bright yellow balls sat on the driveway beside a dark-colored Buick. "I just got back from a match, but I'd love to visit with you for a while. Would you like to come over? I was just going to make a pot of coffee. I even have some of that lemon poppyseed cake you used to like so much."

Another wave of memory swamped Molly. "It's been years since I've had that cake," she said with regret, "and I'd love to take you up on your offer. But I made arrangements to spend some time with Louise this morning, so I'm going to have to say no. I'd love to come by another time, if that's all right."

Joyce squinted toward Louise's house. "Louise is expecting you?"

"At eleven." Molly glanced at her watch and realized that she was already a few minutes late. "I should hurry. I don't want to keep her waiting. Are you in the book? Do you mind if I call you tomorrow?"

"I don't mind at all," Joyce said. "But are you sure

Louise is expecting you? I saw her getting ready to leave early this morning. She said she wouldn't be back until Sunday tonight.''

"Oh, but that can't be," Molly said. "I talked to her just yesterday." But the words were a token protest and a sick feeling settled in her stomach. She knew that Joyce wasn't lying, just as she knew that Louise had skipped town to avoid talking to her.

"Well, then, I must be wrong." Joyce's eyes filled with sympathy, but that only made Molly feel worse. "Or maybe something came up at the last minute," she said, trying to sound as if she actually believed it. "You know how that can happen." She squeezed Molly's arm and smiled encouragement. "Tell you what—you run over and check, but if Louise isn't there for some reason, just come to my place and let yourself in. Tom's out of town this week and I could use some company—and I'd love to hear what's been happening in your life since I saw you last."

Molly nodded, almost too numb to think. She turned away and started up the sidewalk again, but the joy she'd felt earlier was crushed beneath a wall of doubt and fear. When she reached the front door, she lifted her hand to knock, but a piece of paper taped inside the screen door caught her eye. And when she realized that her name was scrawled across the note, the disbelief and anger she'd been fighting got the upper hand.

She jerked open the door and tore the note from the glass, read Louise's half-baked explanation for taking off without a word of warning and crumpled the paper in her fist. For a long time she stood there, trying to decide whether to cross the street and take a chance that Joyce might actually talk to her when she found out what Molly wanted.

She couldn't bear to set herself up for more disappointment, but what if Joyce *was* willing to talk?

With one last glance at Louise's empty house, she crossed the street to Joyce's front door. But she refused to get her hopes up. Ruby hadn't been as close to Joyce as she was to Louise. If Joyce had any ideas about why her neighbor left town, she'd have said so already. The idea of company was appealing, however, and it might be a good thing to spend some time talking about her mother's life, instead of always worrying about her death.

"OKAY, BUDDY, do you have them all?" Beau settled a jacket on top of the load he'd already piled on Nicky's outstretched arms. "Are you sure you can carry all that?"

Nicky scowled up at him from beneath a too-long sheaf of hair. "Of course I can. I'm not a baby." He pivoted away, eager to help, but still a little young to handle much responsibility. A jacket sleeve dangled from the pile and nearly tripped him on his way out the door. Beau watched until he was certain Nicky wouldn't fall down the stairs and called after him, "If your sister's out there, tell her it's time to leave."

He'd spent the day getting ready for the parade—roping off prime viewing areas, making sure the banners were draped on the cars of local dignitaries, shuffling the order of parade entrants to allow Melvin Greenspan more time to fix the brakes on the float entered by the high-school science department.... He'd been running on high for hours, and he was ready for the part that made all the work worthwhile.

If any problems arose now, they were Ridge's responsibility. For the rest of the evening, Beau was just another spectator, and he was determined to enjoy every minute.

Whistling softly, he turned back to the list of last-minute details he'd made that morning and checked off another item. A shadow passed in front of him and he glanced up to find Molly standing in the open doorway.

She wore a pair of jeans and a shape-hugging white sweater, but she seemed completely unaware of how incredible she looked. "Rope and jackets delivered safely, sir. Two blankets tucked into the back seat as ordered. What next?"

He grinned, marked off the items on his checklist and patted his pockets, searching for his keys. "Next, we head out—unless there's something else you need." When she shook her head, he checked the stove one last time to make sure he'd turned off all the burners. "Did you happen to notice if Brianne is out there?"

Molly nodded. "I saw her coming around from the front as I came back here. But are you sure she's going to be okay with this? I mean, I don't need to stay with you all evening. I'd be happy to meet up with Elaine or Jennifer if that would make things easier."

"Absolutely not!" He spied his keys near the phone and crossed the room to get them. "I invited you and I'll be insulted if you don't come. It's time Brianne realized that she doesn't get to call all the shots around here."

"O-kay," Molly said hesitantly.

Beau laughed at her obvious lack of enthusiasm. "It's going to be okay. We'll have a great time, I promise. Just relax. Brianne's a great kid, and once she realizes that she can't run you off with a tantrum or two, she'll give up and you'll get to see the good parts of her personality."

Molly still didn't look entirely convinced, but Beau appreciated her willingness to give Brianne another chance. He followed her out and locked the door, then fell into step at her side as they strode across the lawn toward the Cherokee.

"How did your meeting with Louise Duncan go?"

"It didn't." She slanted a glance at him. "But let's not talk about that, okay? I just want to have a good time tonight."

"Okay. Sure." As they approached the car, Beau realized that Brianne had already buckled herself into the front seat. He scowled and swore under his breath. What was *wrong* with this kid of his, anyway? It wasn't like her to be so rude.

Not wanting to start the evening on the wrong foot, he pasted on a smile and opened the car door. "Hey, funny face, how about sitting in back with your brother so Molly can sit up here?"

Brianne smirked at him. "Why should I?"

"Because I asked you to." He kept the smile but put a little heat into his voice so she wouldn't misunderstand.

Either she didn't understand, or she just didn't care. "I don't want to sit back there. I want to sit up here. With you. There's lots of room in the back seat—" she looked at Molly with all the haughty disdain Heather had shown toward the end of their marriage "—unless she's too big to fit."

Beau's smile vaporized. He shot a glance at Nicky and jerked his head, and his son jumped out of the back seat without hesitation. Brianne folded her arms and stared straight ahead through the windshield.

Still determined to save the evening, Beau leaned into the car and lowered his voice so that the others couldn't hear him. "This is completely uncalled-for, young lady. Molly is my friend and my guest. I want her here even if you don't, and I won't tolerate rudeness. Is that clear?"

Brianne's glare was hostile. "Well, I *don't* want her here. Don't I count for anything?"

"Of course you do. And when you behave like the young lady I raised you to be, you'll get a voice in the way things are done around here. If you're going to behave like a baby, you don't get a vote. Now get in the back seat and sit with your brother, and if I hear one more rude comment or see one more dirty look directed at Molly, you and I are going to have some real trouble."

A muscle in Brianne's jaw twitched, and for a minute Beau thought she was going to refuse again. Finally she sighed and released the lock on the seat belt. "I thought you didn't like us to lie."

"I'm not asking you to lie. I'm telling you to be civil."

She climbed into the back through the space between the front seats. "What's Mom going to say when she comes home and finds her here?"

"Mom's not coming home," Beau snapped. He regretted it immediately and tried to soften his tone when he spoke again. "I know you want her to come back, but wanting it won't make it happen. You're going to have to accept that, because it's how things are."

"Gram says—"

"Well, Gram's wrong," Beau cut her off before she could spout more of Doris's delusions. He leaned farther into the car and gripped the seat as if hanging on to it might help him keep a grip on his temper. "Gram wants your mom to come back because she's unhappy with the choices your mom made and she feels guilty. It's not Gram's fault. It's nobody's fault. Your mom is who she is. But I think Gram blames herself for what your mom did. She thinks that if Mom will just come back to live with us again, it'll prove that Gram was a good mother.''

The anger in Brianne's eyes seemed to break apart, and whatever had been holding her so stiff and unwieldy for weeks crumbled. In a flash, she was young and frightened and vulnerable again. ''But what if Mom's wrong? What if she isn't really…like that?''

Her inability to say the word *lesbian* aloud filled Beau with a mixture of sympathy for her and outrage at Heather. He understood only too well how hard it was to say the word aloud. The realization that Heather had never been sexually attracted to him had bruised his ego badly, but he would eventually learn to live with that. What he couldn't understand—what he would never be able to forgive—was the hell she was putting their children through.

''Your mom isn't going to change her mind,'' he said gently. ''It isn't easy for me to admit it, but she was never happy with me. The life we lived wasn't right for her. She's much happier in Santa Fe with Dawn, and I hope they have a great life together.''

''Then you're not angry with her anymore?''

If she walked back into his life this second, swearing she'd been wrong and begging for his forgiveness, he wouldn't have been able to grant it. But he shook his head and forgave himself the lie for his daughter's peace of mind. ''I'm not angry with her. In fact,'' he said, switching to the truth, ''I'm grateful to her. If she hadn't married me, I wouldn't have you and Nicky, would I?''

"I guess not." Brianne dragged her gaze away from his and settled it on Molly, who'd moved to stand on the lawn near Nicky. "Are you going to marry her?"

"Who? Molly?" Beau laughed, but there was no humor in it. "No. We're friends. I think she's kind of pretty, and it makes me happy to have a pretty woman to spend time with, but she's only going to stick around for another week, so I think you're safe."

"But you'll marry somebody, won't you?"

"I might someday. But not yet, Brie. I'm still trying to figure out which way is up, and I don't plan to turn our lives upside down again until I know where my feet are."

Brianne smiled sadly and Beau reached through the seats to brush her cheek with his fingertips. He wasn't naive enough to think they were out of the woods, but for the first time in weeks, he actually believed they might make it through this.

And that was enough—for now.

CHAPTER NINE

BEAU TRIED HARD to maintain his equilibrium during the parade, but it wasn't easy. Now that Brianne's hostilities were on hold, he had plenty of time to think about Molly. And Molly was giving him plenty to think about.

He watched in amazement as she slowly, patiently and carefully lured Brianne into a conversation about a group of boys who stood nearby. He felt his heart swell with gratitude when she listened to Nicky's convoluted story about something that had happened at school. When the football team rode past in a convoy of pickup trucks, Molly cheered as if she was single-handedly responsible for the team's morale, and even Brianne started getting into the spirit.

By the time the parade ended, he'd begun to regret that Molly wasn't going to stay around longer. Not for himself, but for his poor, confused daughter and for the son who held Molly's hand as if he'd known her forever.

Well...maybe a little bit for himself.

Just after dark, the marching band rounded the corner and the last strains of the school's fight song faded away. Beau picked up an empty French-fry holder and tossed it into the trash, followed it with two half-empty cups someone had left leaning against a lamppost and tried to figure out what had happened this afternoon.

He turned back to the three people who waited for him near the curb. Brianne stood a little apart from Molly, but the high level of hostility was gone. Nicky walked the curb like a tightrope, carefully placing one foot in front of the other and using his arms for balance. Molly stood to one side, watching him with an expression he couldn't read and looking nothing short of stunning.

Overhead, the stars began to show in the gathering darkness, and a surprisingly warm breeze stirred the air. Laughter faded as people began to move off toward whatever they had planned next, but Beau was frozen in place by a longing for something he could never have.

He shook off the feeling and forced a smile as he walked toward them. He'd been feeling a little strange since his conversation with Brianne, and it wasn't surprising that the desire to be part of something real and right would be hovering around after that. He could pretend all he wanted, but Heather's bombshell had done some damage. Yet even if Molly had been planning to stick around, he wouldn't have rushed into a relationship with her. It wouldn't have been fair to any of them.

"Well," he said as he stopped in front of Molly. "What did you think? Impressive, wasn't it?"

Her lips curved into a smile. "You think I'm going to say no, don't you?"

"Come on, admit it. It was a little small-town compared with what you're used to."

She made a face at him. "I'm not admitting any such thing. I haven't been to a parade since I left Serenity, Mr. Know-it-all, so this is *exactly* what I'm used to. And I think it was wonderful. A perfect size, too. Not so many entries that you get bored watching. Not so many people in the crowd that you can't see. Just perfect."

Beau laughed softly and called for Nicky to follow, then turned toward the Burger Shack. Brianne fell into step beside him, and he decided to take a risk and actually touch Molly's arm to help guide her through the crowd. "So we lived up to your expectations?"

"As a matter of fact, you did. It really was fun, Beau. Thank you for inviting me to come along."

Brianne plucked at his shirtsleeve. "You need to walk faster, Dad, or we won't get a table."

They were less than a block from the Burger Shack, and a lot of people appeared to be heading in the same direction, but Beau wasn't quite ready to start battling crowds for a place in line or position at a table. "So we'll wait a few minutes. It won't be the end of the world."

"But I'm hungry."

"Okay, then, why don't you and Nicky go on ahead and get your food? We'll be along shortly."

Brianne needed a minute to think about that, but she finally held out her hand. "Okay. Fine."

Beau gave her a few bills from his pocket. "Off you go, then. Keep an eye on Nicky. And save us a place!"

His daughter set off running with Nicky right behind. Now he was alone with Molly. As alone as they were going to get in Serenity on a night when the entire town and everyone in the outlying areas were crammed into the center of town.

She smiled up at him, and the light in her eyes made the breath catch in his throat and desire flame deep in his belly. He shrugged and tried to toss off a casual response. "I'm glad you liked it, and I'm glad you came with us. I think there's a law about watching a parade alone.''

"And you were simply trying to save me from spending time in jail?"

"What can I say? I'm just that kind of guy.'' To keep from wanting to kiss her, he glanced away. But he caught their reflections in the window of a store they passed, and that brought up a whole new set of emotions. They looked good together, and his fingers tightened on her arm.

Her gaze shifted toward him and their eyes met for only a second, but it was enough. He saw recognition dawn quickly, followed by a glimmer of shared yearning, and he knew she wasn't completely immune to him, either.

Well, well, well. That was going to be hard to forget. He wasn't even sure he wanted to.

His shoulder collided with something solid and jerked him back to reality. He looked up sharply and found himself face-to-face with Eve Donaldson. Eve had graduated the year before Beau had, and she'd been Heather's closest friend for years. She was one of the few people in Serenity who knew the truth about his divorce. She'd never breathed a word, but the chip on her shoulder when she was around Beau was the size of a bull moose. He had no idea why she resented him. He wasn't the one who'd lied about who he was. He hadn't forced Heather into the life they'd created. But in Eve's eyes he was still somehow to blame for Heather's misery.

Tall and willowy, with pale-brown hair and disconcerting gray eyes, she laughed and put out a hand to steady herself. "Goodness, Beau. You nearly broke my shoulder running into me like that." Her curious eyes lingered a moment on Molly, then returned to Beau's. If it hadn't been for the glint in their depths, he might have believed her friendly smile was sincere. "I looked for you in our usual place, but I didn't see you. Doris was looking for you everywhere. We didn't think you'd come."

He merely smiled as if there were no undercurrents. "Well, as you can see, we're here."

The glint grew a little sharper as she turned to Molly. "You look familiar. It's Molly Lane, isn't it?"

Molly must have felt the chill emanating from Eve. It was impossible to miss, and Molly wasn't naive. But she smiled as if she'd just been invited to dinner. "Thanks. It's Molly Shepherd now."

"Oh? You're married?"

"Divorced."

"Oh." As if Eve cared. "So much of that going around these days." She shot a look at Beau as if he'd been the one to walk out on Heather. "It seems like nobody wants to stay for the long haul."

"Isn't that the truth?" Molly's smile never slipped, but her voice dropped a few degrees. "One person decides to walk away, and the one who *was* in for the long haul is left to pick up the pieces. It's definitely not right."

Beau was torn between irritation with Eve and admiration for Molly. He didn't need her to defend him, but he couldn't deny that he liked knowing she would do it. He gave her arm a gentle squeeze of support and changed the subject. "Where's Cal?" he asked Eve.

"With the kids, getting the car. When did you two start seeing each other?"

"Oh, we're not—" Molly began.

"Molly's been staying with us for nearly a week.

You don't have any objections to that, do you?'' The night and the mood worked together to make Beau a little reckless.

Eve's eyes narrowed dangerously. ''Why would I object?''

''Well, I don't know. I guess you wouldn't.'' He grinned and slipped his hand from Molly's arm to her back and urged her to start walking—which she did in spite of the stunned expression on her face. ''My best to Cal,'' he called over his shoulder as they walked away.

''Why did you do that?'' Molly asked when they'd put a few feet behind them.

''Do what?''

''You know what. Why did you leave her with the impression that you and I were an item?''

''Do you mind?''

She blushed. He could see it even in the dim light spilling onto the sidewalk from the small businesses they passed. ''That's not the point, Beau. You deliberately misled her, and now there's going to be talk.''

He stopped walking and took her by the shoulders, pulling her gently around to face him. ''I'm sorry. I shouldn't have done it. I don't care if there's talk, but it obviously bothers you.''

Her eyes shuttered. ''I don't think you and I are the issue here, do you? I can survive the talk. I won't be around. But what about Brianne and Nicky?''

Her question brought about the strangest reaction. On the one hand, Beau knew she was right. He'd let his irritation with Eve get the best of him. On the other, Molly's worry about Brianne and Nicky almost made him glad he'd done it. Heather had been so consumed by her own identity crisis for so long, she'd barely noticed the kids. Doris loved them, but she was also soothing her own battered conscience through them. Beau tried to put them first, but he sometimes wondered just how well he succeeded. And here was Molly, who had no reason to care, and yet she did.

Without thinking, he pulled her close and lowered his mouth to hers. It lasted no longer than the space of a heartbeat and probably didn't even qualify as a kiss, but it ignited a fire inside him, and judging from the look on Molly's face when he released her, it did the same to her.

Someone behind them let out a whistle and someone else howled, and Molly's face turned redder than ever with embarrassment. Without saying a word, Beau found her hand and laced his fingers through hers, then set off walking toward the Burger Shack, feeling better than he had felt in years.

MOLLY PACED restlessly around the cabin, still buzzing from that half-second kiss on the way to dinner a few hours ago. Somehow—she didn't know how—she'd managed to follow the conversation over burgers and fries and had made arrangements to meet Jennifer in the morning so they could talk with Jennifer's mother. She'd even answered Nicky's nonstop questions on the way home.

But now that she was alone again, she couldn't stop thinking. She couldn't read because of it, and she couldn't sleep, either. And her heart seemed to beat just one message over and over again.

Beau Julander had kissed her.

The teenager that still resided somewhere inside her was jubilant. The adult was numb and a little worried. Had he meant anything by it, or had it simply been an impulse? Did he feel something for her, or had he put it out of his mind as soon as it happened?

Did she care?

She could have just asked him, but she didn't trust herself to discuss it. She was quite sure she couldn't talk to him without giving away her feelings. And what if he *didn't* feel an attraction for her? What would she do then?

More than a little confused, she microwaved water in a mug, stirred in powdered cocoa and made a mental note to buy marshmallows next time she was in town. After pulling on a sweatshirt over her pajamas, she carried her cocoa and a blanket to the porch. She settled into one of the Adirondack chairs and let her gaze drift across the lawn, the neighboring houses, then finally to the sky with its full moon and an endless field of stars.

Except for one lone porch light, Beau's house was dark. That ought to tell her something, shouldn't it? Obviously Beau wasn't losing sleep over her.

She leaned back in the chair and searched her heart for clues to what she was really feeling. When she was a girl, she'd spent endless hours dreaming about sharing a kiss with Beau. But instead of contentment over a dream realized, she found herself wanting the kiss to be the beginning of something new and wonderful.

Sighing softly, she cradled the mug in her hands and turned her thoughts, instead, to people's huge reluctance to tell her the details of her mother's accident. Like in her conversation with Joyce, which had been pleasant, but certainly not informative. Half her time in Serenity was gone, and she was no closer to learning the truth than she'd been a week ago. Now she wondered what had possessed her to think that coming back to Serenity after so long would be the solution—to anything?

Just as she was about to set her cup aside, the sound of a footstep on gravel reached her ears. A second later she saw the glint of moonlight on Beau's hair as he came around the trees and started toward the cabin. He disappeared into the shadows, but not before her heart began to race and her hands to tremble.

He was walking so slowly she'd have had plenty of time to gather her things and disappear inside. But she didn't want to disappear. She wanted to make sense of where she was and what she was doing. She wanted to figure out what she wanted from life and how she was going to get it. And she couldn't do that by running.

She pulled the blanket up to her chin and waited till Beau reappeared. In seconds he did, and she saw he was still wearing the jeans and leather jacket he'd had on at the parade. When he reached the patch of lawn in front of the cabin, he paused for an instant before starting toward her. Her breath caught in her lungs and all her senses were on high alert by the time he reached the bottom of the steps.

His eyes met hers and held. "You're awake."

She nodded, but the intensity of his gaze took her voice away. When at last she felt she could speak, the world's most inane response came from her lips: "So are you."

He propped one hand against a post, still without looking away. "I tried sleeping, but I couldn't get comfortable. Must have been the excitement of the parade."

"And the stress of being in charge," Molly suggested. "Stress can do strange things to a person."

Beau's eyes danced with amusement. "That was a joke, Molly. The parade had nothing to do with it."

Heat rushed into her cheeks, and her gaze faltered. "Oh."

Laughing softly, he motioned toward the chair beside hers. "Mind some company?"

"Of course not." She sat a little straighter and slipped one hand from under the blanket. "Please...sit down." He closed the space between them and spent a few seconds getting comfortable. Every cell in her body felt as if it was on fire, but she tried not to let that warp her perception or cloud her judgment. "So, if it wasn't excitement over the parade that kept you awake, what was it?"

Beau leaned back in his chair and stared up into the sky. "A little bit of everything, I guess. Brianne. Nicky. Laundry. Nosy neighbors. Wondering when I'll be able to work again." He rolled his head to the side and looked straight at her. "You."

The blanket Molly held slipped from her grip and puddled around her waist. Even wearing a sweatshirt over her pajamas, she felt exposed and vulnerable, but she didn't let herself reach for the blanket again. "Me?"

"You."

"I don't understand." She sounded foolish. He was being clear enough, but how could she let herself believe after wanting this for so long?

Beau covered her hand with one of his and heat spread up her arm. "You're a beautiful woman, Molly. Surely you realize that. You're intelligent and funny. You're easy to talk to and great to hang around with. And you're a whole lot more of a distraction than I ever thought you'd be."

He looked sincere, but she still wouldn't let herself believe him. "Do you want me to leave?"

"No, Molly. I want you to stay." He reached out and gently ran one finger along her cheek. The touch robbed her of the ability to speak again, but she wouldn't have known what to say, anyway. "It's been a long time since I tried to make a move on a woman," he said, still holding her gaze. "I'm really rusty and I could use some help."

The confession astonished her. "What kind of help?"

"Well, you could say something to help calm the butterflies in my stomach. Tell me if I have a chance or stop me if I don't."

If he hadn't sounded so sincere, Molly might have laughed. "You're asking if *you* have a chance with *me?*" Was he nuts?

He drew his hand away slowly. "I don't know what I'm asking. I mean, it's not as if you're going to be around after next week, so it's not like there's a chance that we could become anything permanent, and yet…"

Molly swallowed convulsively and her gaze traveled slowly across his features. Her heart stuttered with heightened awareness. She noticed everything from the curve of his brow to the tone of his skin, from the slight indentation beneath one ear caused by a long-forgotten scar to the faded scent of aftershave.

His gaze left her eyes and followed the line of her chin, locking on her lips and remaining there for so long she was afraid she'd never breathe again. She wondered what he'd say if he knew how many times she'd dreamed of this, but she didn't want to find out. So much had gone wrong in her life lately that she couldn't resist the pull of having just one dream come true—even if she knew it couldn't last.

He trailed a finger along her jaw and tilted her chin, then edged forward oh, so slowly and touched his lips to hers. The chill disappeared and sensations flamed to life inside. Molly drew in a ragged breath as his lips brushed hers tentatively, uncertainly, as if asking permission for more.

He leaned back and searched her eyes. She tried to hang on to her reason, but the moon and stars seemed to work together to create a magic that made rational thought impossible. He moved in close again, and this time when he kissed her, all that had been tentative before vanished.

He claimed her with an energy and passion she couldn't have resisted if she'd wanted to—and God help her, she did *not* want to. She gave herself over to the moment and let the sensation envelop her. His lips were soft and warm…so very warm. He pulled her close and caressed her with hands that were at once gentle and demanding. His tongue brushed her mouth and she parted her lips to offer him entry.

It was more than a dream, and she never wanted it to end. His hands seemed possessed by a need that matched her own. His mouth spoke silently of longing deep as the night and endless as the sky, and she knew that whatever was passing between them in this moment was larger than them both.

Too soon, the kiss ended and he pulled away. Their eyes met again and he smiled almost sheepishly. "Too much?"

Too much? Not enough!

Molly shook her head and whispered, "I have no complaints."

His smile grew and he briefly kissed her lips once more. "You have no idea how good that is for my poor, battered ego."

"Your ego?" Molly laughed softly. "I don't think your ego needs rescuing by me."

He cupped her face in his hands. "You might be surprised."

Somewhere nearby a lone cricket that hadn't noticed the colder weather began to sing. The sound and the touch of Beau's hands soothed her, and she pressed her cheek into his palm. "I think you're probably the last person around who should be worried about your ego. There wasn't a girl in our high school who wouldn't have sold her soul to go out with you, and I have a hard time believing that anything's changed."

Something flickered in his eyes, and she felt a sudden *ping* as she realized there was another Beau hidden behind the mask he presented to the world. She studied his expression carefully and the sensation grew. "You could have anything or anyone you want just for the asking," she said softly, "but you really don't know that, do you?"

He crooked a smile and drew his hands away. "That might be the way it looks to you, but that's not how it was in school, and it sure isn't how things are now. I'm a castoff, Molly. An old shoe that Heather grew tired of wearing."

She started to protest, but the look in his eyes stopped her.

"I'm just trying to find my way through life again, that's all." He sighed heavily. "There are a million other guys out there just like me, walking around in a daze and wondering if we'll ever figure out what the hell happened."

His voice had changed, and a shadow drifted across his expression. Molly didn't want to pry, but something stronger than her normal reticence made her ask, "What did happen between you and Heather?"

"She left me..." He took a deep breath and let it out slowly, and the agony on his face kept Molly from interrupting while he worked out what came next. After a long time, he stood and walked to the edge of the porch. He stood there, bathed in shadow and obviously struggling for a long time.

Molly wished she could take back the question.

"It's been a year," he said at last. "You'd think I'd have adjusted to this by now."

"Please don't feel like you have to answer me," Molly said quickly. "I shouldn't have asked."

He waved away the offer with one hand, but tempered the gesture with a thin smile. "It's all right. Like I said, it's just my poor bruised pride that's hurting." He ran a hand along the back of his neck and looked her in the eye. "She left me for a woman," he said at last. "After seventeen years together and the birth of three children, she suddenly realized that she preferred women."

Somehow Molly managed not to gasp, but her mind had trouble processing the bombshell. "Heather Preston?"

Beau actually grinned. "Yes, ma'am."

"But how... Why..." She stopped and tried to pull her thoughts together. "I would never have guessed. She seemed so interested in boys...in you."

"If it's hard for you to believe, imagine how I feel." He leaned against the post with one shoulder. "She wasn't exactly reluctant when we were dating, and I always figured we created the mess we made together. Now I wonder if I just wasn't paying attention.''

Molly stood, still shaken, but needing to do something more than stare at him. ''I don't think you can blame yourself. If it's true that Heather felt that way, she had a responsibility to tell you.''

His laugh held no humor. ''Well, I kinda thought so, too, but I have it on good authority that I never paid attention to her, never listened to anything she said and didn't give a damn about anything that was important to her. I'd like to think that if a woman finds sex with her husband repellent, it might be a good idea to give a stronger clue than 'Not tonight.' But apparently I'm wrong about that, too.''

Molly still couldn't completely wrap her mind around the news, but the numbness was beginning to wear off a little. ''So she's living somewhere. With…''

''Dawn.'' He made a face and added, ''That's D-a-w-n, not D-o-n.''

''And the kids? Do they know?''

''Brianne does. Nicky knows as much as he can comprehend—which isn't everything.''

So many things about Brianne came clear to her all at once. The girl obviously felt betrayed and lied to on top of being deserted, and it was no wonder she had so much anger inside her. Molly's heart ached when she thought of someone so young carrying such a heavy burden. ''How are you dealing with it?''

''That depends on the day, and sometimes on the minute.''

''Have you considered getting counseling?''

He nodded and looked at the tops of the trees. ''I considered it, but the counselor at the county mental-health department is a good friend of Heather's, and I don't think she's the right person to be talking to the kids right now.''

''There's no one else?''

''No one close enough to do any good. Rural Wyoming isn't exactly bursting with options.''

He looked so lost, so confused and so angry all at the same time that something in Molly shifted. She'd carried around an image of him for so long that she'd practically turned him into an icon. Now, for the first time in her life, she saw clearly beneath the surface to the man inside, and she liked what she saw even more than the image she'd created. ''You're a good dad, Beau. You'll figure out what the kids need. I have no doubt of that. You're open with them, and that's very important.''

''It's funny,'' he said, moving close again. ''You don't even know my kids, but you've shown more concern for them in the few days you've been here than Heather did in years. She walked out on us a year ago, but she was gone a long time before then. Thank you for that.''

He brushed a kiss on her cheek and let his gaze linger on her for a long moment before turning a regretful glance toward the house. ''I'd love to stay longer, but I should get back. Nicky doesn't always sleep through the night, and I swear Brianne has some kind of internal radar that goes off when I'm not there.''

Molly nodded quickly. ''Of course. You need to be there with them.''

''Thanks for that, too.'' He started down the steps, but he paused at the bottom and looked back. ''I'll see you tomorrow?''

''Of course,'' she said again, and the sudden smile

on his face did the strangest thing to her heart. She watched him walk away, waiting until he disappeared again into the shadows before she went back into the cabin. But as she closed the door on the night, she wondered how easy it would be to walk away from him in a week.

CHAPTER TEN

THE PHONE RANG promptly at six-thirty the next morning—before Beau's eyes were completely open, before he had coffee on, and long before he was ready for trouble. He'd slept like a log after his late-night visit with Molly, and he had a feeling it was going to be a very good day. He'd much rather start by sneaking a few kisses before the kids woke up than talking to someone who thought six-thirty was an acceptable hour for phone calls, but kickoff was just twelve hours away and there were bound to be problems. Smitty might even be calling to tell him the Cessna was ready.

He rolled onto his side and picked up the phone a split second before his sleep-blurred eyes registered the name and number on the caller ID. Holding in a groan, he flopped onto his back and draped one arm across his eyes. "Hello, Doris."

"You're awake?"

Her voice was harsh and cold, but Beau tried not to respond in kind. "I am."

"I realize it's a bit early," she said, "but I didn't want to miss you. I looked for you at the parade."

"We were there."

"Not in our usual place *or* at the Chicken Inn afterward."

He resisted the urge to explain and said only, "You're right. Is that why you're calling so early?"

"Not exactly. I heard something last night that upset me so much I barely slept a wink."

Still groggy, Beau sat on the edge of his bed. "Let me guess—this thing you heard has something to do with me?"

"Eve called after the parade. You know what she told me."

Beau stood, stretched and started toward the stairs. He kept his voice low so he wouldn't wake the kids. "I have a pretty good idea what she told you, but Eve needs to mind her own damn business."

"She's concerned."

"She's trying to make trouble."

"That's not true. She sees smoke and she's worried about fire."

Beau wasn't wide enough awake for this argument. "It's nothing. She's overreacting."

"Is she? You're over there with a woman who isn't your wife. Parading all over town with her—and right in front of the kids. What on earth are you thinking? What's gotten into you, letting some other woman stay in my daughter's house with my grandchildren under the same roof?"

The fog of sleep evaporated by the time he reached the bottom of the stairs, and a slow anger began to burn. He pulled a fresh filter from the cupboard and scooped coffee from the can, hoping the everyday actions would help him hang on to his self-control. "There are a couple of things wrong with your argument, Doris. This isn't your daughter's house, and Molly isn't in the house, she's staying in the cabin. It's all perfectly safe and harmless, and the kids aren't being exposed to anything sinful."

Doris snorted in disbelief. "Harmless? Please, Beau,

you're not exactly a naive young boy. You know how these things work. You're there with this woman, making a spectacle of yourself and completely disregarding the children.''

''The kids,'' he interrupted sharply, ''are the *only* thing I think about. I would never do anything to hurt them.''

''So you say, but what's going to happen when their mother comes back?''

''If you're concerned about the kids, I suggest you talk to Heather. She's the one who's completely disregarded them, not me.''

''We're not talking about Heather. We're talking about you. Even if what you say is true, you're only confusing those poor children needlessly.''

Why was the woman so determined to settle the blame for this mess on his shoulders? He filled the coffee-machine reservoir with water and flipped the switch. ''Heather isn't coming back, Doris. It's time you accepted that.''

''Of course she is. You've known her all your life. You know what she's like. You know what she wants. She's going through a phase, that's all.''

''Well, it's one helluva phase.''

''One of these days she's going to wake up and realize what she's lost, and then she'll be back. What will she think if you've been dating other women— setting them up in the cabin—while she's gone?''

Beau leaned on the counter and looked outside at the rising sun, the glory of autumn, the mountains uncluttered by human mistakes and heartbreak, and he wondered how long he had to drag this heartache around with him. ''So it's a phase when Heather finds a new girlfriend, but it's a sin if I do?''

"Don't be smart."

He closed his eyes in frustration. He didn't want to throw up walls between them, but he couldn't keep letting Doris back him into a corner. "Even if you're right and she does come back, it's over between us. I can learn to forgive her if this really is something she can't change. But if it's a phase, if this is a choice she made, I don't think I can."

"You're trying to divert me," Doris snapped. "The point is you and that woman."

"She's a friend. I'm not 'setting her up' in the cabin, but I'm enjoying her company. And I know you won't like hearing this, but who I date and what I do isn't any concern of yours."

"I don't believe this! You've been in love with Heather since you were a boy."

"Things change."

"Love doesn't just die like that, Beau. After all the years you've been together?"

"She *left* us, Doris. And you know why she left. She doesn't want me and apparently she doesn't want the kids, either. Love *does* die, and so does trust."

"You make her sound like a horrible person. Don't you understand that she's just confused?"

"If that's the case, then I'm sorry for her, but it doesn't change the way I feel."

"The two of you married so young, and then losing the baby... I don't think she ever recovered from that. All her hopes and dreams were gone. All the things she once wanted to do."

He didn't know how to answer Doris's desperate need to clear Heather of responsibility. Apparently she couldn't release herself of blame until she'd lifted the burden from her daughter. "My dreams didn't survive, either,'' he reminded her, ''but I didn't spend a lifetime lying about who I was or take off and leave my wife and kids in the lurch.''

''You're stronger than she is,'' Doris wailed. ''You always were. You're the rock in the family, I won't deny that. But you and Heather are family, and you'll always be family. You need to be there for her when she comes to her senses.''

Beau sank into a chair and chose his next words carefully. ''Listen to me, Doris. I want you to really hear me this time. I know she's your daughter and you love her, but what we had died a long time ago. I don't love her anymore, and you're going to have to accept that it's over between us. Heather and I will never be together again, and I don't want you filling the kids' heads with the idea that we might be. It's not going to happen and I'm not going to discuss it with you again. Heather will get on with her life and I'll get on with mine, but we won't do it together.''

''Beau—''

''No, Doris. I want Heather to be part of the kids' lives, but only if she can give them security and stability. Those are two commodities that have been in short supply around here for the past few years. But frankly, I'm not sure she's capable of providing those things, and until I'm convinced, I'll do whatever it takes to keep her away from the kids.''

''She's a good mother.''

''Not right now she's not.'' He kneaded his forehead where a dull ache was forming above his eyes. ''I meant what I said before. I'm not going to keep rehashing this. I'm sorry you're upset, but this conversation is pointless and I'm hanging up.''

He disconnected and tossed the phone onto the table.

Lowering his head into his hands, he tried to put the call out of his mind. A soft noise behind him brought his head back up, and he turned to find Brianne standing in the kitchen door, feet bare and hair still tousled from sleep.

Nicky stood just behind her, his eyes wide with shock. He said something Beau couldn't hear, and Brianne rounded on him. "Don't you get it, Nicky? He doesn't love Mom anymore, and he doesn't *want* her to come back."

She jerked her sweatshirt from its hook by the door before Beau could get up, then slipped her feet into an old pair of shoes and raced outside.

The door banged shut, but Beau took off after her. He threw it open again and shouted for her to come back, but she was halfway across the lawn and it was clear she had no intention of listening to him.

"Dad?"

Nicky's trembling voice stopped him in his tracks. He whirled back to find the boy leaning against the wall. The look of misery and disbelief on his face twisted Beau's gut. He didn't know whether to follow Brianne or stay and comfort Nicky. Both kids needed him, but he'd been giving Brianne more than her share of attention lately, and he had to trust that she'd do what she'd done a hundred times before when he and Heather fought. She'd head into the field and run off steam, but she'd be fine. Right now, the stricken look on Nicky's face worried him a whole lot more than Brianne's volatile anger.

He hunkered down in front of his son and touched the boy's shoulder gently. "Nicky? Are you okay?"

The boy's blue eyes lifted to meet his slowly, and

the fear in them made Beau feel about two inches high. "Is it true, Daddy? Do you hate Mom?"

"I don't hate her, son." And he didn't when he was thinking clearly. "But Mom and I aren't going to live together again."

"Because you hate her?"

"No. No, son. Because Mom and I don't love each other anymore. Sometimes that happens with parents." He picked up his little boy, straightened to his full height and winked in a lame effort to lighten the moment. "But we're doing okay on our own, aren't we? I got some laundry done yesterday, so you'll even have matching socks today."

Nicky smiled slightly, but his eyes still looked sad. "It's okay, Dad. I don't mind if my socks don't match."

"Well, I appreciate that, but every kid deserves to wear matching socks to school."

"Okay. But Brianne says I shouldn't bug you. She says maybe you'll stop loving us."

Beau felt as if someone had punched him in the gut. "She said what?"

"She says we were a pain for Mom and that's why she stopped loving us. She said maybe if we're a pain to you, maybe you'll stop loving us, too."

A searing pain tore through Beau's heart. If that's what Brianne thought, why did she constantly push his buttons? To see how much she could get away with? How much he'd take before he broke? He felt broken now. "I could *never* stop loving either of you," he assured Nicky. "You're my kids, made right from a piece of my heart."

"But you stopped loving Mom."

Beau could have kicked himself for ever saying that

aloud. "Well, now, that's not entirely true," he back-tracked. "I still love Mom, just in a different way than I used to." He kissed his son's cheek soundly and tried to smile. "How could I stop loving the woman who gave me you and Brianne? You two are the very best thing that's ever happened to me."

Some of the clouds cleared from Nicky's eyes, but he still wore a worried frown. "Then why did Mom stop loving us?"

"She didn't stop," Beau said with a heartiness he didn't feel. "She loves you as much as I do. You're the greatest kids in the world. How could anyone *not* love you?"

"But she left."

"Yes, she did." Still carrying Nicky, Beau started into the kitchen. He wanted to buy a few seconds to think, but the only thoughts he could put together were how small his young son was and how much he wanted to wring Heather's neck for making their children doubt their worth, even for a second.

After a quick glance out the window for Brianne, he settled Nicky at the table and poured him a glass of orange juice and a coffee for himself. "I want you to listen to me, Nicky," he said as he carried both to the table. "Your mother did not leave here because she doesn't love you and Brianne. She left because she has some things to work out. You know how Brianne runs outside when she gets mad and walks around the field until she stops being angry with me?"

Nicky nodded solemnly.

"Well, Mom's doing the same thing."

There was a moment's silence while Nicky took a swallow of juice and wiped his mouth with his pajama sleeve. "Is Mom mad at you, too?" he asked at last.

Beau smiled sadly. "I don't know, son. I think she's just confused. But she loves you. And one of these days she'll come back to see you. I guarantee it."

Nicky grinned as if Beau's word was good enough for him. After another drink of juice, he began to hum softly. But Beau had a sick feeling that he'd just lied to his son. He only hoped Nicky would eventually forgive him for it.

MOLLY WAS ON PINS and needles the next afternoon as she sat in the gleaming kitchen that belonged to Jennifer's mother. She'd spent many hours here as a kid, and even more as a teenager. From this very chair, she'd giggled with Jennifer and Elaine over boys and downed more tortilla chips and sodas than anybody should ever consume. Today she felt an odd mixture of strangeness and familiarity as she watched Jennifer and her mother working together.

Like everyone else, April Dilello had aged since Molly had seen her last. Her hair had once been a rich shade of auburn; now it was a shade of red that could only have come from a bottle, and even that color had faded. But her eyes were still filled with the same caring that had drawn the girls to her kitchen in the first place. And she could still carry on two conversations at once.

"I just can't get over how wonderful it is to see you again, Molly. You look... No, Jennifer, the other box. Lemon cookies will be better, don't you think? You really do look beautiful, Molly. Stunning, in fact." She brushed her hands on the plaid apron she wore and wagged a hand toward a door near the refrigerator. "Napkins are in the pantry. Will you grab them, dear?"

Molly was halfway to her feet when April gasped and motioned for her to sit again. "You stay put, Molly. Jennifer will get them. Tea will be ready in a minute, and I know you're eager to get down to business. I understand you're interested in your mother's jewelry."

Sinking back into her chair, Molly nodded. "Yes, I am. Jen says you still have a few of the pieces she made."

"Not just a few. I still have everything I ever bought from Ruby. I wouldn't dream of parting with them. They're the nicest jewelry I own."

"And you don't mind if I look at them?"

"Mind? Oh, heavens no." April patted Molly's shoulder and turned away with a wave toward the stove. "Just keep an eye on that kettle and I'll be back in a minute."

"I'd be glad to help," Molly called as she disappeared through the door.

April laughed and stuck her head back into the kitchen. "Not on your life. My bedroom is a disaster area, and it'll destroy my reputation if you see it."

She disappeared again and Molly shared a grin with Jennifer. "She hasn't changed a bit, has she?"

"Not much." Jennifer finished arranging cookies on a plate, took two more from the box and handed one to Molly as she joined her at the table. "So how's it going over at Beau's? Anything fun and exciting to report?"

Memories of those knock-your-socks-off kisses swept through her mind, but Molly laughed them away. "Yeah," she said. "We were up half the night making out."

Jennifer stuck out her tongue and broke off a piece

of cookie. "Nothing, huh? Figures. You have a golden opportunity and you're throwing it away."

"I'm not here for Beau," Molly reminded her. "I'm here to find out about my mom. I keep telling myself that Mrs. Duncan had a good reason for standing me up yesterday, but I know she's hiding something."

Jennifer slid down on her tailbone, just as she used to do when she was a teenager. "I wouldn't worry about it. It's probably because you've showed up suddenly after such a long time. Nobody expected you, and in a town like Serenity, people tend to circle the wagons to protect each other."

"But I'm from Serenity, too," Molly said. "And who are they protecting? My mother? From *me?*"

Her friend tried to look reassuring. "Don't read too much into it. It's just the idea of answering questions about a friend that gets them nervous. They'll soon think it through and change their minds. Meanwhile, *you* should relax. Try to have a good time." She leaned close and waggled her eyebrows suggestively. "Now, tell me what's really going on with you and Beau."

The abrupt change of subject made Molly laugh. But after what she'd learned last night, she didn't want to stir up gossip Beau would have to deal with once she'd left. She shrugged and glanced at the kettle on the stove. "There's nothing going on with me and Beau. He offered me a place to stay because I didn't think about making reservations and the motel was full."

"Oh. Right." Jennifer leaned back in her chair again and wagged a hand between them. "Beau's always inviting women to stay in his cabin. He has a new one there at least once a week. Come on, Moll. You can tell me."

Friendship pulled at her, but the wounded expression

on Beau's face was stronger. "There's nothing to tell. Honest."

"The two of you went to the parade together. You went to the committee meeting with him. You've been seen all over town together, *and* you're staying in his cabin."

"All of which means absolutely nothing."

Jennifer popped another piece of cookie into her mouth. "Everybody was blown away when Heather left, but nobody expected Beau to stay single as long as he has. I swear you're the first woman he's looked at in all this time—and he *is* looking. Everyone's noticed."

Molly's cheeks burned, but the rush of pleasure inside her more than made up for it. "He's only been single since July," she pointed out. "That's not very long."

"But Heather's been gone for nearly a year."

"I know that, but…" Molly shook her head. "Beau and I are friends. That's all."

Tucking a leg beneath her, Jennifer settled in more comfortably, as if she still expected a story. "Everyone knows how much you liked him in high school—" She broke off as if she realized she'd said the wrong thing, then grinned sheepishly. "At least, you know, the old gang knows. Not everyone."

Molly laughed. "Sorry to disappoint, but that's as exciting as it gets."

"Okay. But there's nothing that says you can't make it more exciting, right?"

Molly stared at her friend in amazement. "And how do you think I should do that?"

"Figure it out. You've been in love with Beau for your entire life."

"With a short fifteen-year hiatus during which we both married other people."

"Whatever." Jennifer waved an impatient hand at her. "The point is, you're there right under his nose, and he's certainly available. You have the chance of a lifetime. I want to know what you're going to do about it."

"Absolutely nothing."

"Nothing? Are you crazy?"

A loud thud sounded from the bedroom and Molly thought she had a reprieve, but a laugh from April and her call that she was fine put a quick end to it. "He has kids," Molly said when she realized Jennifer was waiting for an answer. "Have you forgotten that?"

"Well, I wasn't suggesting that you jump him at breakfast. You can wait until the kids are safely asleep in the house and then lure him to the cabin."

"*Lure* him?"

"Put on something sexy and offer him a glass of wine."

A wave of nostalgia swept over Molly. She hadn't had a close girlfriend in years, and she'd missed this kind of teasing banter. "I didn't bring anything sexy with me, and I don't have wine at the cabin." She tapped her cheek and pretended to consider. "But maybe I could lure him with my sweats and T-shirt, and seal the deal with a straight shot of root beer."

Jennifer bobbed her head enthusiastically. "I say, if it works, go for it."

What would Beau do if she took Jennifer's advice? Molly wondered. It made a nice fantasy, but letting herself get carried away would be a big mistake. "I can't seduce him. Not only am I a little rusty at the fine art of seduction, but I don't want a one-night stand—and that's all Beau and I could ever be. It wouldn't be worth the trouble it would cause.''

Jennifer opened her mouth to argue, but her mother chose that moment to burst into the kitchen, talking as if they'd all been carrying on a conversation the entire time. ''I *knew* that pair of garnet earrings was behind the dresser, but do you think Jim would pull it out and find them for me? Sometimes that man is enough to try the patience of a saint—though heaven knows I'm no saint.'' She held out her hand and showed Molly a pair of earrings so delicate the stones seemed to be suspended on strands of spun silk. ''Do you remember these? I think they're my favorites.''

Molly gasped and reached for the earrings, then instinctively pulled back her hand and looked to April for permission.

April moved them closer. ''Go ahead. Take them. Your mother did exquisite work, didn't she?''

Molly nodded and carefully picked up one of the earrings. They'd been made for pierced ears, and two thin strands of wire curved away from either side of the hook, then swept downward and met to form a delicate cradle for the gemstone. ''They're so beautiful. It's hard to believe my mother made these.''

''She had a real gift,'' April said wistfully.

''I used to help her when I was younger, but I know I disappointed her when I got into high school.'' Molly returned the earring and battled a stab of guilt. ''I was too caught up in my own little world. School and friends and boys.''

''And that made you a typical teenager, so don't you feel bad.'' April lowered a small jewelry box to the table and lifted the lid. ''Take your time. Look them over. You don't find craftsmanship like this every day." The kettle began to hum, but she didn't turn away. "I hope looking at them will help."

"I've been thinking about taking up where she left off," Molly admitted aloud for the first time. "I'd like to sketch these before I go, if you don't mind."

"Well, of course I don't mind. In fact, why don't you take them with you for a day or two? I think I can survive that—as long as I get them back."

"Thank you." Molly couldn't believe her luck. She lifted an intricate bracelet made of tiny seed pearls and turned it over in her hand. "I don't know if Jennifer told you, but I don't remember Mom's accident or the last six months she was alive. That's really why I'm here."

Jennifer took charge of the kettle. April pulled several pieces of jewelry from the box and took what felt like forever to spread them on the table for Molly's inspection. Molly held her breath, afraid to do anything that might disturb her.

"Your dad never told you?"

"He wouldn't talk about it."

"No." April smiled sadly. "I suppose he wouldn't. That time probably wasn't something he liked to think about."

Something in her tone left Molly oddly unsettled, but she told herself it was only her imagination. "I'd be happy if I could just remember what happened the day she died. I don't even remember the last conversation we had. I'd love to know the last thing I said to her." Her voice cracked, but she made herself go on. "Or the last thing she said to me."

Jennifer started back with the tea tray and Alice made room for it on the table. "I suppose there's nobody left who can really tell you those things, is there."

Molly's throat tightened, but she managed to speak. "No. And maybe I'll just have to accept that there are some things I'll never know."

April set out three small plates and put the cookies in the center of the table. "The only two people who know what happened in your parents' marriage is the two of them. The most anyone else can do is speculate about why things happened the way they did."

Molly's heartbeat slowed ominously. "If you know something, won't you please tell me?"

April seemed surprised by the question. "But I don't really know anything at all. There was a lot of talk at the time, but it was mostly just guessing. I don't suppose any of us will ever know for sure what came between them."

For a moment Molly could have sworn that time stopped. "Are you saying that my parents were having trouble in their marriage?"

"She didn't know?" April shot a confused glance at Jennifer.

"*I* don't know," Jennifer said, and at her mother's expression of outraged disbelief, added, "I was a teenager. I didn't care about things like other people's marriages. I was completely freaked out by the idea that somebody's mom could actually die. I didn't want to even hear about it."

"You must be wrong," Molly said to April, her head beginning to pound. "My dad would have told me if they'd been having trouble in their marriage. And besides, surely I'd remember something like that."

Jennifer nudged the cookies toward Molly. "Not necessarily. Remember Stacy Edwards? She married this guy from over in Star Valley who turned out to be an alcoholic and abusive. Things were really bad for several years before she left him. Even after all this time, there are things she doesn't remember about the years she was married. It's like her mind went into self-protective mode or something.''

Molly shook her head sharply. "That's not the same thing at all.''

"Your mind has shut out those months for some reason.''

Before Molly could protest, April continued, "Honey, I know this must upset you, and if I knew anything more for certain, I'd tell you. But all I can tell you is gossip and hearsay, and that won't help. I'll tell you who you ought to talk to, and that's Clay Julander.''

Although Molly scoured her memory, she came up blank. "*Clay* Julander?''

"Beau's uncle," Jennifer explained. "You remember him, don't you? Big guy. Worked for the police department for years. He's retired now, but he used to drive around town in that old blue truck with his dog in the back.''

Molly nodded slowly. "He used to say the dog was his deputy, didn't he?''

"That's right. You remember him, then?''

"Yes, but…'' Way in the back of her mind, a horrible possibility tried to reach her, but she ignored it. "I don't understand why you think I should talk to him.''

April's eyes filled with sympathy and Molly knew what her response was going to be. She battled the urge to leave, to run, to plug her ears and scream so April's words couldn't reach her. But maybe for the first time in her life, the need to know was greater than the need to forget. She forced herself to sit in her chair and hold on to a teacup covered with delicate yellow roses, while April said what she must always have known.

"Sweetheart, Clay's the one who responded to the calls every time your parents had one of their disagreements. You talk to him. If anyone knows what went on at your house the night your mother died, he will."

CHAPTER ELEVEN

MOLLY DROVE BACK to Beau's house in a daze. A sense of unreality and inevitability left her shaken and uncertain. She'd have to talk with Beau's uncle soon, but she didn't want to face it just yet. She needed time to adjust to what April had told her, and she wasn't sure she could face Clay alone.

The sudden need to have someone with her seemed odd. She'd spent so much of her life alone. Without family, except her dad. Without close friends. Without emotional support. Before she came back to Serenity, she'd felt strong enough to handle anything on her own.

Now, even with April's small jewelry box on the seat beside her, she felt weak and shaky. She wanted to talk to Beau before she did anything else. She just didn't understand why. She could have turned to Elaine. She'd have found a willing shoulder and a listening ear if she had. But whether or not it made sense, whether or not it was smart, she *wanted* to talk to Beau.

He had his hands full with Homecoming, with his kids, his house and his job. He didn't need Molly's problems on top of his own.

She pulled into the driveway a few minutes before three o'clock, and when she realized that his Cherokee was gone, her bleak mood grew even bleaker. Already, afternoon shadows stretched across the lawn and clouds had begun to gather on the horizon. The temperature had dropped sharply while she'd been with Jennifer and April, and the chill she felt now matched her mood exactly.

Still hoping that Beau might be home, she climbed out of the car and started toward the house. She'd only gone about halfway up the long walk when a movement caught her attention. She looked more closely and realized that someone was sitting on the corner of the back porch. Brianne.

The girl's feet dangled off the edge of the porch and she was leaning forward, elbows propped on her knees, and holding a small black box in both hands. Molly spotted a toy car turning circles on the sidewalk and realized that Brianne was playing with one of Nicky's toys. Even so, the set of her small shoulders and the look on her face didn't belong to a happy child.

Molly wasn't sure she could handle one of Brianne's moods, but the girl had already seen her, and her obvious unhappiness jerked Molly out of her own misery. She might be nursing old pain, but Brianne's crisis was happening right now.

As she stepped onto the walk, the toy car stopped spinning circles and began to race down the sidewalk toward her. Brianne's lips curved into a sly smile, but Molly dodged the car easily and kept walking toward the house.

The high-pitched whine of toy tires on cement told her that the car was on her tail. She glanced over her shoulder just in time to avoid a second near-collision and sidestepped the car once more before she reached the porch.

One look into Brianne's pain-filled eyes wiped away her irritation. Brianne was a child. Hurt and confused and, judging from the expression on her face, extremely upset about something. Molly had no idea what to do for her, but her own longing for someone to talk to was too strong, and Brianne's distress too evident to ignore.

For the first time in years, she didn't run away from the questions about the child she'd lost. Would she have been like Brianne? If her child had lived, Molly would have learned how to handle the sadness, joy, misery and pain that came along with adolescence, but her child hadn't survived, and she felt completely out of her element now.

To avoid future car attacks, she stood on the bottom step. "You're home early, aren't you? Didn't you have school today?"

Brianne met her gaze slowly, and the disdain on her face made it clear that she found Molly's presence offensive. "Why do you care?"

So they were back to square one. Molly shrugged and let her gaze trail away so the girl wouldn't feel challenged. "I don't, really. I'm just talkin'."

From the corner of her eye she saw Brianne register surprise, but the sullenness quickly returned and she brought her attention back to the box in her hand. "You don't have to pretend to like me just to impress my dad."

Molly felt a stab of pain at the girl's unhappiness and a flash of anger with Heather for walking away from her children and leaving them to work through all the issues her departure had created. She lowered her purse to the step and slipped her keys into her pocket. "Is that what you think I'm doing?"

"Isn't it?"

"Actually, no, it isn't." Molly moved a few inches

closer to where the girl was sitting. "I don't pretend to like people, Brianne. That's dishonest." The girl cast her a skeptical look and Molly smiled. "I was always taught to tell the truth, and I'm not going to change that now."

For a heartbeat Molly thought she'd made an impression. But Brianne looked away again and gave a snort. "You really expect me to believe that you like me?"

Molly's heart twisted. How was a child supposed to believe in herself when her mother didn't appear to care? At least Molly had never had to experience that kind of rejection, and she wished she could take it from Brianne. She sat on the edge of the porch, almost close enough to touch the girl, but far enough away to leave her space. She let her legs dangle over the side and kicked her feet gently.

"The truth is, I don't know whether I like you or not. We really haven't had a chance to figure that out yet, have we?"

Brianne raked her gaze over Molly before looking away again. "I know that I don't like *you*."

"You don't know me, either. I think what you do know is that you don't *want* to like me." Molly watched the toy car circle on the walk while Brianne pretended to ignore her. When she figured the girl had had time to absorb what she'd said, she pressed on. "I understand a little of how you feel. My mom died when I was a bit older than you, so it was just my dad and me for a long time. Then one day, he brought home this lady."

Brianne's eyes flickered toward her, then darted away again.

"She was very nice," Molly went on, "but it took

me a while to figure that out. I did just what you're doing. I decided that I wasn't going to like her, and I made sure she knew it.''

''That's not what I'm doing,'' Brianne said, but her protest didn't hold much conviction.

''I didn't have a remote-control car,'' Molly said with a conspiratorial grin, ''but I think I might have used it on her if I'd thought I could get away with it.''

The car stopped spinning and silence stretched between them for a long time. ''What did you do to her?'' Brianne asked at last. Her voice sounded slightly less hostile—at least, Molly thought it did.

''Well, I was older than you are when she came along, so I couldn't put too much salt in her dinner or food coloring in her shampoo, but I thought I could talk my dad out of falling in love with her in other ways.'' She grinned sheepishly. ''Dad liked to jog, and staying in shape was really important to him, so I thought he might not fall in love with Cassandra if I helped him notice that she ate too much. And he really hated owing people money, so I made sure he realized that she liked to shop, and every time I saw her wearing something new, I told him.''

Brianne's lip curled into something resembling a smile. ''Did it work?''

''No. He married her, anyway. And now she's the only family I have in the world.''

''That's too bad.''

''No, I'm very lucky, really. At first, the only thing we had in common was the fact that we both loved my dad, but we became friends eventually. She's a nice lady, and without her I'd be completely alone. My dad's gone, I'm divorced, and I don't have kids of my own. The holidays are right around the corner, and I *really* don't want to be alone. With Cassandra around, I might have somewhere to go for Thanksgiving and Christmas, and there's still someone in the world who'll call on my birthday. I'm awfully glad I didn't manage to run her off.''

Brianne didn't say anything, but she swept Molly's face with a slow, assessing glance.

And that was enough. For now.

Molly stood and dusted the backside of her jeans. ''It's okay if you don't like me, Brianne. I'm not here to stay. But one of these days, your dad might bring home somebody new, and I hope that you'll give who-ever she is a chance before you start attacking her. She might turn out to be pretty cool once you get to know her.'' Molly turned away, then decided to take another gamble. ''If it's okay with you, I've decided that I re-ally do like you, and I'd like to be friends. You can think about it and let me know.''

Brianne still didn't speak, but Molly didn't expect her to.

It didn't occur to her until she'd closed the door behind her that while she'd been talking to Brianne, she'd forgotten all about her own worries for a few minutes.

THE NEXT MORNING, Molly pushed a cart filled with groceries across the nearly empty parking lot at the FoodWay. A handful of cars and two mud-splattered pickup trucks were parked close to the store. She didn't recognize any of them, but the instinctive expectation that she might surprised her a little. She'd only been in town a week, but in her unguarded moments she was already beginning to feel as if she belonged here.

Like coming home.

Beau had been so busy the night before during the game, she'd only seen him for a minute. Just long enough to learn that he was bringing his plane back to Serenity later this morning. Aaron would be picking him up in just an hour, and Molly wanted to do something to make the day easier for him.

He was on the go so much it was no wonder he got a little behind on the laundry and dishes. Overnight, Molly had come up with a plan to surprise him with breakfast, and she'd slipped away early to buy what she needed for the stuffed French toast she wanted to make.

Now, with everything in her cart, she stopped behind her rental car and began to load bags into the trunk. She worked quickly, enjoying the morning and softly humming a tune that had been playing on the PA system in the store. When she picked up the small bag holding the needle-nose pliers she'd found in the hardware aisle, a rush of pleasure made the whole day seem brighter.

She'd spent hours after the game making rough sketches of her mother's jewelry and wondering if she really could re-create some of the designs. Finding those pliers on the rack had felt like an omen. Buying them had been much more than impulse. Even standing in the parking lot with them in her hand felt like a life-changing commitment.

But maybe she was just being fanciful again.

"Excuse me?"

The voice so close behind her startled her. She turned quickly and found herself face-to-face with a stout woman of about sixty, whose disapproving expression wiped the smile from her face.

"Molly Lane, isn't it?"

She bobbed her head once and tried to chip the years away so she could remember the woman. She looked familiar, but Molly had met so many people the past week she couldn't place her. "Yes, but it's Molly Shepherd now."

The woman surveyed Molly critically from the tip of her head to the toes of her shoes. "Well, you certainly do look like your mother, don't you?"

Molly had lost track of the number of times she'd heard that since she'd arrived in town, but this time it was *not* a compliment. The woman's hostility confused her, but she wasn't going to be the first to look away. "I've been told that a few times. Were you a friend of my mom's?"

She knew what the answer was even before it came. "Not exactly. But I certainly knew her."

Trying not to let the woman unnerve her, Molly put the bag she was carrying into the trunk and reached for another. "Do I know you?"

"You should. Doris Preston. Heather Julander's mother." Her eyes narrowed and a direct challenge glimmered in them. "I *know* you must remember Heather."

Molly froze with a bag halfway from the cart, and she had to force herself to keep moving. "Of course I remember Heather. How is she?"

"She's doing well." Doris lifted her chin as if she dared Molly to argue with her. "She's living in Santa Fe...for the time being. Of course, she'll be coming home again soon. To her children. And her husband. Just in case you had any idea that she might not be."

The woman's intensity was hard to meet straight on. Molly couldn't imagine how Beau had lasted a full year with her peering over his shoulder. She knew she should stay calm for Beau's sake and for the kids, but the past few days were beginning to take a toll and she'd had just about all she could bear of hints and innuendo. "Why would I have any ideas about Heather's plans?"

"Are you saying you don't?"

Molly felt another wave of sympathy for Beau and a rush of understanding for poor, confused Brianne. She straightened and looked hard into the older woman's eyes. "It's pretty obvious that you're trying to make a point, but it's been a long week and I'm not in the mood for games. Why don't you make this easier on both of us and just say what you mean?"

"I think you already know what I have to say. You're interfering with my daughter's family. I want you to stop."

"I see." Molly shut the trunk carefully. "I think you're under the wrong impression, Mrs. Preston. Beau has been kind enough to let me stay in the cabin for a few days. There's nothing more to it than that." To signal that the conversation was over, she pushed the empty cart toward the collection point near the front of the store.

Doris trailed behind her. "You think I don't know what's going on over there? You think the whole town doesn't know?"

Molly shoved the cart into the metal cage and turned back. "Even if there were something going on between us, it wouldn't be your concern."

"Heather only left because she needed time and space to find herself," Doris insisted, grabbing Molly's arm to keep her from walking away. "She has always intended to come back."

"Beau told me why she left, Mrs. Preston. But out

of respect for him and the kids, I'm not going to discuss it with you in the parking lot of the grocery store."

Haughtiness gave way to desperation in Doris's eyes. "He told you? Everything?"

"Everything. But I have no intention of telling anyone else, if that's what you're worried about."

The older woman seemed to sag. "I don't know why she wants to hurt everyone this way. It's just not like her. But she'll come to her senses one of these days. She wasn't raised to walk out on her responsibilities."

The change in Doris cut through Molly's irritation and she almost felt sorry for the poor woman. Molly had never known Doris well. Unlike April, the woman had been a little aloof around the kids her daughter's age. But it wasn't hard to see that she was hurt and afraid. Obviously Beau and the kids weren't the only ones having trouble accepting Heather's decisions.

Molly wasn't sure of the right thing to do under the circumstances, but it seemed mean to let the poor woman worry about something that wasn't an issue. A kiss or two didn't make a commitment, and nothing had changed because of them. "I'm not here to stay," she assured Doris. "And I'm sorry if you've worried about my relationship with Beau, because we simply don't have one beyond friendship. If he ever wants to patch things up with Heather, I certainly won't come between them."

She started toward the car again, but Doris put out a hand to stop her. "Then you won't object to finding another place to stay while you're in Serenity?"

Molly turned back slowly, trying to recapture some of the sympathy she'd been feeling just seconds before. "The motel is full until the middle of next week, and there *is* no other place to stay."

"I understand that, but you're giving people the wrong impression. There will be talk. Folks will think there's something going on between you, even if there's not. And what about Brianne and Nicky? The two of you are setting a bad example for them. I just can't allow that."

Molly was the first person to admit that she knew very little about how families worked, but this much interference seemed way over the top. No wonder poor Brianne had such a suspicious nature.

"The kids aren't in any danger from me. They're not seeing anything they shouldn't. And they couldn't have a better father than Beau. I understand that you're upset, but that doesn't give you the right to toss around accusations without any regard for the truth."

"I call it like I see it."

Molly struggled to remain patient. "Well, you're wrong, and you're being terribly unfair to Beau."

"I don't blame Beau. I know you've always had a thing for him, and I'm not at all surprised that you'd go to such lengths to get what you want. You're obviously just like your mother."

Everything inside Molly turned to ice. Her heartbeat suddenly seemed way too loud and she wasn't absolutely sure she was still breathing. "If you're unhappy with the way things are," she said, speaking slowly to make sure Doris understood her, "talk to Heather. She's the one who walked out on her husband and children, not me, so don't blame me for her mess."

Molly pivoted and walked back to the car, keeping her gait slow and firm when what she really wanted to do was run. Her heart thundered in her chest, and her throat was dry. Her hands trembled and tears filled her eyes, but she refused to let them fall.

Even after she'd driven away, the accusation against her mother rang in her ears. She tried to tell herself that Doris was mistaken, but she could feel something stirring deep within her, far beneath the shock and the outrage.

Like a stick in a muddy pond, her return to Serenity had stirred things up. It was only a matter of time before the truth rose to the surface.

HOURS LATER, Molly stood on the sidelines of the dance floor, trying to catch her breath. She was determined not to let anything ruin the dance, so she hadn't mentioned her conversation with Doris to Beau. She'd done her best not to think about it herself.

For the first time in her life, she'd danced nearly every dance since the music began—first with Beau, then with a succession of other partners, half of whom she hadn't recognized. She'd be dancing even now if she wasn't in such desperate need of fresh air.

Smiling with remembered pleasure, she scanned the crowd for Beau without success. It had been several minutes since she'd last seen him, but she was also making a conscious effort to keep some space between them. She didn't want to think about Doris's accusations, but she couldn't forget them, and she wasn't going to make things worse for Beau and the kids.

She turned toward the outside doors, humming as she walked. Someone had done a good job picking out the music, she thought idly. The selection spanned several decades, but every song was familiar and easy to sing along with. From older couples to teenagers, everyone could dance to tunes they knew. Molly wouldn't have been surprised to learn that Beau was responsible. It seemed like the kind of touch he'd bring to the job.

Funny, but when she'd imagined herself in love with him all those years ago, she hadn't had a clue just how great he really was. She learned something new about him every day, and she liked him more all the time. Despite her assurances to Doris, she was close to losing her heart completely—and this time she wouldn't be able to get over it so quickly.

Dancing with him had been heaven on earth. The touch of his hand. The feel of his arm around her waist. The scent of his aftershave and the rhythm of his breathing. It had all been so intimate and wonderful. But it had also been an illusion, the product of her own imagination. What she felt for him wasn't real. What he felt for her...

What he felt for her was probably just a reaction to Heather's leaving. No matter how much Molly might want things to be different, that was the unvarnished truth. Beau's ego had suffered a tremendous blow when Heather walked out on him. He'd said so more times than she could count. And she'd be a fool to let herself believe that he was doing anything more than bandaging his pride by sharing a few kisses with a willing woman. She might have been insulted, but she'd started out doing the same thing, and she still had no illusions about creating a lasting relationship.

She pushed open the outside door and stepped into the evening air. The temperature had dropped sharply after the sun went down, and she realized immediately that it had been a mistake to wear the dress she'd chosen. The fabric felt paper-thin in the mountain breeze, and with only thin straps and a light shawl to cover her shoulders, she might as well have been naked.

That would teach her to choose fashion over function.

Vowing to stay outside for only a minute, she took a deep breath and caught the scent of a cigarette somewhere nearby. She glanced around and saw a red-tipped glow hovering near the corner of the building. The shadow moved, and the shape of a man came into view.

He stepped into the beam of light from a security lamp, and Molly recognized Whit Sharp from her graduating class. He'd grown tall and broad in the years since she'd seen him, and his once-thick brown hair had receded. But his eyes were still filled with laughter, and the hesitant smile she remembered so well hadn't changed a bit.

She grinned as he approached her. He glanced at his cigarette with a grimace, crushed it underfoot and pulled her into a quick hug that was over before she could return it. "Sorry about that," he said with a jerk of his head at the crushed butt. "Nasty habit I can't seem to break."

"I haven't seen you around. I thought maybe you weren't living in Serenity anymore."

"I'm not. I just got in this morning. I'd have come earlier, but I was in trial and couldn't get away."

"In trial?"

"Believe it or not, I'm an attorney. And you probably had me pegged as headed for a life of crime."

"No! Of course not. It's just…" She broke off with a laugh. "Well, okay, yes. You weren't exactly the shy, retiring type, and as I recall, you never missed a chance to get into trouble. And now you're an attorney. Defending juvenile delinquents?"

He laughed and reached for another cigarette in his jacket, caught himself and stuffed his hands into the pockets of his pants. "Corporate law. Bankruptcy, mostly." A surge of music from inside the gymnasium filled the space between them, and he studied her. "You look good, Molly. It's great to see you again. I didn't think I ever would."

For once Molly didn't want to talk about the strange set of circumstances that had kept her away. "You know how life is," she said. "You get busy with one thing, and then that leads to another. Pretty soon you've been gone fifteen years."

"But you're here now."

"Yes."

Whit pushed away from the wall and smiled down at her. "I heard you've been asking questions about your mother's accident."

Molly nodded and told herself not to be surprised that he knew. In Serenity news traveled fast. "I'm trying to find out what happened, but I'm running into a little resistance."

"You don't remember it at all?"

"I've lost about a year." She shivered and moved out of the wind. "Six months before the accident and nearly the same after. The last thing I remember clearly is getting ready to start our senior year. The next memory I have is of living in Illinois."

"So you have amnesia?"

"I don't know if it's officially amnesia or whether a doctor would call it something else."

Whit's scowl deepened. "Are you telling me you haven't seen a doctor?"

"Well...no. Dad wasn't terribly worried about it, and by the time I was out on my own, I was used to it."

"O-o-o-kay."

That old, protective urge she felt toward her dad rose to the surface. "He didn't neglect me," she said. "I was perfectly healthy. It's just that we never had health insurance, and you can't just run to the doctor over every little thing under those circumstances."

"Amnesia isn't exactly a little thing."

"It didn't affect me," Molly insisted. She wasn't in the mood to discuss her father's shortcomings or tear apart his decisions. "I went to college. Made good grades. And I've always done well at work. It's just a little chunk of memory that's gone, after all. Besides, it's a beautiful night and I'm having a wonderful time so far, and I don't want to think about anything unpleasant."

Whit nodded slowly. "Fair enough." She could tell he wasn't convinced they should change the subject, but he did, anyway. "I hear you're staying with Beau Julander."

Molly rolled her eyes. "You've only been here a few hours and you already know that?"

"It's a small town, and people have been worried about him since Heather left."

"Well, to set the record straight, I'm not staying *with* Beau, I'm staying in a cabin on his property. We're not an item now, and we're not going to be an item."

Whit held up both hands and backed a step away. "Whoa, put the sword away, I didn't mean to offend you. Frankly, I'm glad to see him looking like himself again. It's about damn time."

"Oh." She flushed, embarrassed by her reaction. "Well, then, I'm sorry. It's just that some people seem to have a problem with it, and I guess I'm a little touchy."

He adjusted his collar and grinned. "Really? I never

would have noticed. So, 'some people' aside, the two of you are getting along well?''

"So far, so good, I guess. He's a great guy and he's been incredibly generous. But I don't have to tell you that. The two of you have been friends forever.''

"Yeah, we have. He's a good friend. Salt of the earth and all that. So what do you think of Serenity now that you're here?''

"It hasn't changed much.''

"It never does. That's one of the best and the worst things about it.''

The music from the gym switched to an old Smokey Robinson song, and a memory flashed through Molly's mind. A dance, just like this one. Her mother swaying to the music in the arms of a man she couldn't remember. It was gone again in a heartbeat, as quickly as it came. Molly tried to call it back, but the image wouldn't form, and after a second or two she realized that Whit was still talking.

"...year after year after year. You always know what you're going to get when you come home again, though. That's one thing. It's predictable.''

Molly pulled herself back into the conversation. "I don't dislike it here. It's just a little small, that's all. And too far off the beaten track.''

Whit slanted a glance at her. "I'd say that's a pretty generous attitude...considering.''

"Considering what?''

"Well, *you* know. Considering what happened and all. Must be hard for you to come back here after all that.''

Something deep inside warned her not to ask. Not tonight. Enjoy the music. Dream through another dance or two with Beau. Indulge her fantasy for a few hours more. She could ask questions tomorrow.

But none of those arguments kept the words from rising to her throat and spilling from her mouth. "After all *what*?"

"Well, *you* know," Whit said again, but his eyes flickered from her to the nearby cars uncomfortably, and he looked as if he might have realized that she really didn't know anything. "Just the divorce and all, and then the accident and your mom dying. And all the talk afterward." He pulled back to look at her. "That must have been hard."

Molly met his gaze. "What divorce? What talk?"

"Your mom and dad. You know how this town is. All the news that's fit to spread in twenty-four hours or less."

She nodded impatiently. "What about my mom and dad? Why did anyone think they were getting divorced? What did people say?"

Giving an uncomfortable laugh, Whit drew back a step. "I don't know the details, Molly. That's just what I heard. I mean, first your dad changed the way he did, and then your mom got killed. There was all kinds of crazy talk right after the accident, especially when your dad decided not to have the funeral here. I figured that was why you and your dad left so soon."

The lights from the parking lot began to swim, and the chill night air suddenly felt too warm. Her senses pulsed with her heartbeat so that the music was alternately loud, then soft, and Whit's face was close one moment and distant the next. "What do you mean, my dad changed?"

"You don't remember that, either?"

"I don't remember *anything*. How did my dad change? Why?"

"I don't know why. I always wondered, though. He was scout leader when I was about eleven, and we all liked him. And then just a few months before your mom died, he changed. I don't know how to describe it. He was *different*. Moody. I mean, one day he's everybody's friend, and the next he's the guy you avoid when you see him pumping gas or eating a burger, y'know? How's he doing now, anyway? Better, I hope."

Molly answered automatically. Apparently there were a few things the grapevine had missed. "He passed away in March."

"Oh. I'm sorry. I didn't know."

She smiled, but her lips felt cold and stiff. "Thanks. I'll get used to having him gone one of these days, I guess." She put a hand on Whit's sleeve. "Is there anything else you remember about what happened? Anything at all?"

Whit shook his head. "I never did know what happened to change him. That's the weird thing about small towns. Just when you start to think there are no secrets at all, you find out that's just a fallacy. If someone wants a secret kept badly enough, it'll be kept."

The magic she'd felt earlier evaporated and she let out a tight laugh. "I'm beginning to find that out. But what secret? That's what I can't figure out. And why doesn't anyone else know about it?" But even as she asked the question, she knew the answer. People did know. But after all this time, someone still had a reason for wanting the truth to stay buried.

But who? And why? And what did it have to do

with her? She couldn't put it off any longer. She had to talk with Clay Julander and find out what he knew. But she had a feeling deep down in her bones that she wasn't going to like what he had to say.

CHAPTER TWELVE

MOLLY MIGHT HAVE been determined to learn the truth, but with Beau back at work, it was Wednesday evening before they could coordinate schedules and work out a meeting with his uncle. It gave her too much time to think, far too much time to fret and wonder and imagine what Clay Julander would tell her.

She was practically jumping out of her skin by the time they left the kids with Beau's mother. A thousand things raced through her mind as Beau drove along the quiet neighborhood streets, but she couldn't seem to get any of them into words.

Beau must have sensed her need for quiet because he didn't say much until he pulled into the driveway of a small, well-kept split-entry house with an extended driveway that held an RV and a sailboat that looked as if it had cost more than the house.

He turned off the engine and shifted in the seat to look at her. "This is it. You sure you're ready?"

Nervousness made Molly's stomach churn, but she nodded and opened the car door. "Ready as I'll ever be."

She started to get out, but Beau put a hand on her arm to stop her. "You don't have to do this. Knowing what happened back then isn't going to change who you are."

His touch threatened to weaken her resolve, so she

pulled away. "You're wrong. It's already taken away what I thought I knew. My parents' relationship was the one constant in my life, but now even that's gone. If I don't find out what happened to them, I'll always have a hole I can't fill."

"You aren't your parents, Molly. You aren't their decisions."

"Of course I am. And so are you and everyone else." She smiled, but she could feel her lips quivering and she knew she looked more frightened than brave. "If I don't find out the whole story, I think I'll go crazy."

Beau climbed out of the Cherokee and came around to stand beside her. "At least let me talk to Clay first."

"Why? So you can decide what to tell me and what to leave out?" She rubbed her arms for warmth and smiled up at him. "I know you're just trying to be nice, but if my dad hadn't censored everything he told me after the accident, I wouldn't be here. I need to hear the truth for myself—all of it."

Beau put an arm around her shoulders and squeezed gently. "I just don't want you to be hurt by what you find out."

It would have been so easy to let herself believe that he felt something for her, but nothing could have been more dangerous to her heart. Still, she allowed herself to lean on him for a minute and draw on his strength. "Maybe I won't be hurt," she said. "Maybe everyone else is wrong."

The look in Beau's eyes told her he didn't believe that any more than she did. He kept his arm around her as they walked to the front door. Too soon, she heard the sound of approaching footsteps and she stiffened in anticipation.

"Don't worry," Beau said softly. "Everything will be okay. I'll make sure of that."

Molly would have given almost anything right then to believe him, but this was just another illusion, and she knew how quickly it could disappear. The only thing she could count on—the only thing she'd *ever* been able to count on—was herself.

The door to Clay Julander's house swung open and he stood before them, every bit as imposing a figure as Beau himself. Molly tensed at the sight of him, but she wasn't sure if she remembered him or if she was just nervous.

At well over six feet, with broad shoulders and a thick head of dark hair streaked with gray, Clay looked years younger than the fifty-plus he must have been. He grinned and pushed open the screen door so they could enter, but once he'd closed the door behind them, he got right down to business. "So you're Molly Lane. It's been a while since I saw you."

"It's been a while since I was in town." She shook the hand he extended and followed him through the living room into a large kitchen at the back of the house. Beau trailed behind her, solid, steady and sober, and her heart filled with gratitude.

Clay motioned them toward the table and opened the refrigerator door. "Can I get you two anything? A beer or a soft drink? I've got some chips, but nothing to go with them. Your aunt Shannon's at work or I'd have her whip up some of that crab dip she makes."

Molly had trouble treating this like a social visit, but she wasn't about to say so. She shook her head, but Beau asked for two sodas and she didn't argue. Holding one would give her something to do with her hands.

Clay carried three cans to the table, set one in front

of Molly and lowered his long frame into a chair. He slid another can toward Beau and popped the top on the third for himself. "So you're here to find out about your mom, are you?"

Molly clutched her cold drink nervously in both hands. "April Dilello suggested that I talk to you. She said you might be able to help me."

"I might. What do you want to know?"

"I was just seventeen when my mother died, and I don't remember much about the accident." She flicked a glance at Beau and went on quickly, "Actually, I don't remember the six months before or nearly that long afterward. That whole year is a big, empty blank in my mind. I came back to Serenity to find answers. Unfortunately it seems that nobody wants to talk about the night Mom died, and I'm hoping you can tell me why."

There was silence for a long moment while Clay took a drink. When at last he set the soda aside, he nodded. "I remember your mother well. Nice lady. Pretty." He tilted his head and regarded Molly for a long moment. "You look like her."

"So people keep telling me," Molly said with a weak smile. "But that's about all they'll tell me—except that she made jewelry."

"That's right. She did. Made some awfully pretty things in that studio of hers. You remember, don't you, Beau?"

Beau shook his head. "I was just a kid obsessed with football and girls. I didn't pay attention to things like that."

His uncle laughed. "Man, those days seem like just yesterday in some ways. I gave a couple of rings to Shannon one Christmas, and a set of earrings for

Mother's Day. Must have been fourteen, fifteen years ago.''

"Fifteen," Molly said automatically. "Why does April Dilello think you can help me? What do you know that she didn't want to tell me?"

With a shrug, Clay took another swallow of his drink and set the can down. "I guess it's no secret that I spent a few evenings over at your place before your mother died—in a professional capacity of course. I didn't really know them to socialize with."

Molly's breath caught and she thought for a moment that she might be sick. She hadn't realized until that moment how much she'd hoped that April had been mistaken. But if what she and Clay said was true, why couldn't she remember? She rubbed one temple with the tips of her fingers. "Why were you there?"

"We were called there. Several times. Neighbors worried about the fighting—wanted us to do something." Clay studied her face for a long moment, assessing her reaction. He must have decided she was strong enough to hear more, because he settled more comfortably in his chair and went on, "Your parents were having trouble, Molly. Lots of arguments. Loud ones. Had to haul your dad down to the jail a couple of times just to separate 'em for the night."

The words cut like cold steel through Molly. "Are you saying that my father… That he…" She couldn't get the words out, but she felt Beau's hand close over hers, and that gave her courage to keep going. "Was there abuse?"

Clay shook his head quickly. "Not physical, no. Never saw any evidence of it, anyway. But verbal, a whole lot. On both sides." His gaze met hers again, and she saw the same kindness she'd always seen in

Beau's. "They were angry as hell with each other, and they didn't mince words."

Her head swam and she felt the last remaining bit of solid ground beneath her feet begin to crumble. Her father's love for her mother was the one thing she'd always counted on. Now it appeared that it had been just a figment of her imagination.

She could feel her mind recoiling, shutting down the way it always did when she got too close to the truth. But this time she wasn't going to let it happen. "Do you have any idea what she was doing on the road to Beaver Creek the night she died?"

"She had several suitcases in the car with her. We figured she was leaving him."

Molly let out a shaky breath and held on to Beau's hand for dear life. It was nothing more than she'd imagined since her conversation with April, but hearing it aloud made it so much worse—and real. Her mother had run away and left her. The same way Heather had left her children. The realization tore through her, burning itself in her mind and her heart. Was that why she'd blocked out the memories? Because her mother had walked out on her? Because she couldn't bear to remember that her mother hadn't loved her enough to stay?

Freeing her hand from Beau's, she thrust her fingers into her hair and cradled her head in her hands. She'd been so sure Whit was mistaken. "I don't understand. My dad hated divorce. You should have seen the way he reacted when I told him that my marriage to Ethan was over. He didn't care what was wrong between us and insisted I should stay and make it work. And now you're telling me that he and my mother were on the verge of divorce when she died?"

"I don't know what happened to your dad after he left here, Molly. I don't know what he came to believe, or why he felt the way he did. But I do know what happened here. There was a petition for divorce filed with the court just two days before your mother died."

She sank back in her chair and tried desperately to process what she'd just learned. But the biggest question of all was still unanswered, and she knew she couldn't put it all together until she heard the words for herself. "When my mother died," she said, lifting her gaze to meet Clay's again, "was she leaving *him?* Or both of us?"

"She was leaving him."

That was so different from what she'd been expecting, Molly narrowed her eyes and looked at him hard. "Are you sure? Or are you just saying that to make me feel better?"

Clay glanced quickly at Beau, then back at her. "I'm sure."

She dropped her hands and sat up a little straighter. "How can you be sure? How do you know?"

"Because you were in the car with your mother when she died, Molly. I thought you knew that."

BEAU WATCHED the blood drain from Molly's face as the bombshell his uncle had just dropped hit her. Damn, but he wished he'd asked Clay what he knew when he'd talked to him earlier that morning. Maybe he could have helped prepare her.

He met Clay's worried gaze over the top of Molly's head. "Why didn't I know that?" Beau demanded.

"I don't know, but I was one of the first officers on the scene, and I pulled Molly from the car myself."

Molly's hand trembled in his. Fear, shock and disbelief were mirrored in her eyes. "But how…" She broke off uncertainly, then tried again. "Why didn't my dad ever tell me that?"

Feeling utterly useless, Beau took her hand in his. "We may never understand his reasons, Molly, but I'm sure he did what he thought was best for you."

"No matter what problems he had with your mom at the end, your dad was a good man," Clay assured her. "We all knew he adored you."

She jerked her hand from Beau's and stood. "He adored me so much he spent the rest of his life lying to me?"

"He probably didn't want to hurt you," Beau said. "You'd lost your mother. Life at home hadn't been happy for quite a while. Maybe he thought you'd been through enough."

Molly's eyes grew cold and hard. "Are you defending him?"

"No." Beau stood to face her. He longed to take her in his arms and offer some comfort, but he could tell she wouldn't welcome anything from him right now. "I'm not defending him. I'm guessing. I'm trying to put myself in his place."

"So that's what *you'd* do?"

"No! Of course not. Dammit, Molly, I'm trying to help."

She turned away. "Well, don't. He lied to me for fifteen years! He let me think that he couldn't talk about Mom's accident because he was so destroyed by losing her. Now I find out that he wouldn't talk about it because he just didn't want me to know the truth."

"You don't know that, Molly."

"I don't?" She glared at him over her shoulder. "He let me grow up thinking that we were the happiest family in the world. He let me believe that he was grieving horribly for my mother. So much that I learned to keep my questions to myself so I wouldn't hurt him. Tell me, Beau, which part of that was the truth?''

He flinched under the fury in her eyes and shook his head. ''I can't. But I know what it's like to be a father, and I know that he must have had some reason for what he did—a reason he thought was a good one.''

Holding up both hands as if to ward off the words, she looked around the room and focused on the bag she'd left lying on the floor beside her chair. ''Don't say any more. I can't hear it right now.'' She snagged her bag and headed for the door, but halfway across the room, she turned back to Clay. ''Thank you,'' she said in a hoarse whisper. ''I...I'm sorry.'' And with that, she was gone.

Beau stood, frozen, until he heard the front door close. But when he would have gone after her, Clay caught his arm and stopped him.

''Leave her be, Beau.''

''I can't. She's too upset.''

''Yeah, she's upset, but she needs some space. Let her walk a bit. It'll give her a chance to burn off some of that energy.'' He turned toward the fridge again. ''Want another soda?''

Beau gaped at him in disbelief, but he realized that Molly would probably turn to Elaine or Jennifer for comfort, and maybe that was who she needed right now. But that didn't make him feel better. ''What I *want*,'' he snarled, ''is a few answers. Why didn't we ever know that Molly was in that accident?''

''I couldn't say.''

''You'd better say,'' Beau warned. ''If you know

anything else, you'd better come clean. About all of it. Right now.''

"I don't know anything else," Clay said evenly. "We transported her to the hospital in Jackson. When they released her, Frank took Molly away. We figured it was so she could be near family, but we never knew for sure.''

"You should have found out.''

"Why? There was no evidence of foul play. We had no reason to question him, and he didn't want anything to do with any of us after that night.'' Clay pulled out two fresh cans and handed one to Beau. "We're never going to know what happened between those two, Beau. The truth died with Frank, and Molly's going to have to accept that. He was so protective of her the chief didn't even tell Hannah down at the paper about Molly being in the car. He thought it was best.''

Beau shoved away from the table and paced in front of the window for a long time, trying to accept the story himself. But he couldn't swallow it, and he knew Molly never would. He wheeled back to face Clay once more. "What did they argue about?''

"I don't know.''

"Bullshit! You were there. You heard them. Don't lie to me, Clay. This is too important.''

His uncle took his sweet time popping the top on his can and taking a seat at the kitchen table. Only habit and respect kept Beau from grabbing him by the collar and demanding the truth from him. When he couldn't stand it any longer, he planted his fists on the table and glared at Clay. "*Tell* me.''

Clay looked him square in the eye. "Frank and Ruby are both dead, Beau. Let 'em rest in peace.''

"And what about Molly?''

"You really think finding out what tore her parents apart is going to help her?"

"What right do you have to hide the truth from her?"

"Asking questions isn't going to help her, Beau. Trust me. You think she's torn up right now, just wait."

"So you *do* know." Beau raked his fingers through his hair, agitated and confused. "Tell me what it is so I can help her."

"I don't know anything for sure," Clay said. "I have bits and pieces of conversations and arguments, and I have a few suspicions I've never voiced aloud to another living soul. But if you think I'm going to tell you what they are, you're crazy." He gestured toward the door with his can. "You saw how she acted when she thought her mother had walked out on her. I'm not feeding any more maybes into that head of hers."

"Well, you can't just leave her like this. It's not fair." Beau paced to the far end of the kitchen, but his nerves felt as if they were on fire, and he'd just about reached the end of his patience. "You've always been fair, Clay. As fair as a man can be, anyway. So why are you doing this now?"

Clay let out a sigh and pushed his can away. "Why do you care so much, Beau? Why can't you just let it be?"

"Because this is eating her up alive. Can't you see that?"

"Sure I can, but speculating and making up stories, digging up things that are better left alone could be even worse. What I want to know is, what's she to you?"

"She's a friend. I told you that on the phone."

''I know you did.'' Clay hooked one arm over the back of his chair. ''Can't say as I believe you, though. Seems to me you're smitten, and if you won't admit it, you're either lying to me or you're lying to yourself.''

''What I feel or don't feel isn't the issue!'' Beau shouted. ''Dammit, Uncle Clay, quit trying to change the subject, and just tell me what you know about Frank and Ruby's divorce.''

For a minute that felt like an hour, Clay sat perfectly still, considering Beau's demands. Beau had always admired the way his uncle never spoke without thinking, but today it made him want to hit something. ''All I know,'' he said at last, ''is that Frank found out something Ruby didn't want him to know. Whatever it was, he changed into a whole different person because of it. Like I said before, I didn't know him to socialize with, but he was one of those guys everybody likes. Lots of friends. Always smiling. I don't know what Ruby was hiding, but that friendly guy disappeared the day Frank found out about it.''

''And they never said anything in front of you that would give you a clue?''

Clay ran a finger along the table's edge. ''They said a few things in front of me, but nothing I could get a firm handle on. They might have been at each other's throats, but they were mighty careful about what they said once we got there. It's been a long time since then, Beau. Too much water under the bridge. Too many other things I've heard and forgotten. I wouldn't know how to separate what I heard from what I made up.''

Everything inside Beau rebelled at his helplessness. ''So nobody knows what really happened?''

''I didn't say that.'' Clay stood again and fixed him

with a look. "There's one person who does, and I reckon she'll remember when she's ready. If she doesn't, then maybe that's for the best, too."

A WEEK LATER, Beau drained the last of his soda from lunch at the Burger Shack, tossed a handful of uneaten fries onto the orange plastic tray on the table in front of him and checked his watch for the twentieth time in as many minutes.

"It's only two," Aaron said from across the table. "Would you relax? Harvey said he might be a few minutes late."

Relax? Beau had been on pins and needles since that day in Clay's kitchen, waiting for the other shoe to drop. One of these days, Molly was going to remember what happened between her parents, and he didn't know how she would react.

At least the two of them had reached a truce of sorts, but they still hadn't gone back to the easy way things had been between them in the beginning. He'd tried half a dozen times to talk to her alone, but she inevitably found some excuse to avoid him. Oh, she said things were fine between them, and she'd accepted his offer to stay in the cabin even though there was space at the motel now. She claimed to have forgotten why she was angry with him in the first place. But things weren't fine, and Beau cared a whole lot more than he should have.

To make matters worse, Mayor Biggs was still dragging his feet on finding a replacement for Beau on the WinterFest committee, and everyone—even his own mother—had an opinion about his efforts to resign.

When he realized Aaron was looking at him strangely, he tugged his sleeve down over his watch and leaned back in the booth. "I'm just wondering if we've missed Harvey, that's all. I could belt him for making us negotiate the use of that field for WinterFest parking. We've used it for ten years without trouble. What the hell is wrong with him?"

Aaron snorted a laugh and dumped sugar into his second cup of coffee. "Forget Harvey. What's wrong with *you?*"

"With me? Nothing." He could hear the harsh edge to his voice, so he tossed off a smile. "Really. I'm fine."

"Really." Aaron dabbed a finger into his coffee, checked the sugar content thoughtfully and tore open a package of creamer. "What is it? The kids? Work? Doris?" He stirred his coffee for a minute, then looked up at Beau with one raised eyebrow. "Molly?"

Beau tried to laugh off the question, but it was a useless effort. That annoying eyebrow of Aaron's winged a little higher, and he knew he'd never be able to pull off a convincing lie. "Okay, you're right. It's Molly. I'm worried about her."

Aaron's eyebrow dropped back into place and he took a noisy sip from his cup. "I saw her yesterday with Elaine at the Chicken Inn. She seemed all right to me."

Of course she did—to the casual observer. At least she wasn't pushing Elaine and Jennifer away. He was glad of that. He toyed with a paper jack-o'-lantern advertising pumpkin milk shakes and tried to decide how much to say. He didn't want to broadcast Molly's troubles all over town, but Aaron was his best friend. He'd been a sounding board for every tough issue Beau'd had to work through in his life, and he knew how to keep his mouth shut when the occasion demanded.

Pushing aside the pumpkin, Beau raked his fingers through his hair and glanced around to make sure nobody was listening. The Burger Shack was crowded, but nobody seemed to be paying attention to their conversation, so he decided to take a chance. "I guess you've heard that she's trying to find out about her mom's accident?"

"I have. What about it?"

"Somebody suggested that she talk to my uncle Clay. Apparently, Frank and Ruby Lane had some domestic trouble in the last few months before Ruby's accident. Clay responded to calls from the neighbors complaining about their loud fights."

"Molly didn't know that?"

"She can't remember anything about the last six months her mother was alive, and her dad would never talk about it. He died a few months ago, so when she got the invitation to Homecoming, she decided to come back to Serenity and find out for herself what happened. According to Clay, she was in the car with her mother when it went off the road."

Aaron whistled softly. "She doesn't remember that, either?"

Beau shook his head. "What I don't get is why her dad never told her that. Why would you keep that from your kid?"

Aaron shrugged. "Hell, I don't know. Maybe he didn't want to upset her."

"Well, if that's what he wanted, it didn't work. The man never spoke about the accident in fifteen years. Not one word, even though his daughter had lost her mother." He could feel Aaron getting ready to argue Frank's defense, but he cut him off. "I know, I know. She couldn't remember. No sense upsetting her and all that. But how did he know she wouldn't remember eventually? Why would you take a chance like that? Why just waltz through life and pretend it never happened?'' He looked his friend directly in the eye. ''Clay says that Ruby was keeping some secret and that Frank found out about it. But I'll tell you what *I* think. I think he was willing to take the chance he did with Molly because he was hiding something. Something big.''

Aaron stuck the stir stick between his teeth and leaned back in his seat. ''Like what?''

''I wish I knew.'' Beau crumpled a napkin and added it to the pile on his tray. ''It's driving me crazy. I can't even imagine how frustrated Molly must be.''

''How's she handling it?''

''I don't know. She's still here. Says she's staying until she knows the whole truth.'' Beau added a straw wrapper to the heap. ''I see her every day, and she seems fine on the surface, but she's pulled way back in on herself. The most serious conversation we've had in a week was when she asked to use my computer so she could look up something on the Internet.''

''And that bothers you?''

''It bothers me a lot.''

''Because…?''

''Because she's a friend. Because I hate to see anybody going through a rough time.''

Aaron laughed and slid down in his seat. ''Wow. What a saint. Now what's the real reason?''

Beau was beginning to wish he'd never started the conversation. He never expected to hide anything from Aaron, but he should have remembered that Aaron would never let Beau hide anything from himself, either. He drummed his fingers on the tabletop for a moment while he tried to argue himself out of the realization he'd been fighting all week.

"You care about her, don't you," Aaron said before Beau was ready. "You're falling for her."

"I care about her," Beau agreed. But that was where he drew the line. He had to. He'd been through hell in the past few years because he'd made decisions with his heart. It was time to let his head do what it had been created for. "She's a good friend," he said. "I hate to see her struggling through this alone."

"Doesn't sound like she's alone to me. But let's skip to the important question. What are you going to do?"

"Keep my ears open. Try to find the answers she's looking for."

"In your spare time?"

"Something like that."

Aaron arched that damn eyebrow again. "And the rest? You and Molly? What are you going to do about that?"

"Not a thing. There is no Molly and me. She's leaving as soon as she finds what she came for, and I'll still be here. End of story."

"Is that what you want?" The stir stick between Aaron's teeth bobbed up and down as he talked, and Beau fought the urge to snatch it out of his mouth.

"It's what *is*," he said with a casual shrug.

"Now. But things can change."

Beau let out a needle-sharp laugh, decided Harvey wasn't going to show and slid out of the booth. "That's where you're wrong, Aaron. What is, is. Things don't change. People don't change. And only a kid walks around with his head in the clouds, thinking he can make things work out the way he wants them to."

As far as Beau was concerned, he'd already been acting like a kid for too long. It was time to grow up.

CHAPTER THIRTEEN

"MOLLY! MOLLY! Come quick! Somebody's sent you something."

Startled out of the book she'd been reading, Molly sat up quickly and looked around to get her bearings. Clouds hung heavily in the sky, and the trees, which had still had their leaves when she arrived in Serenity just three weeks earlier, stood stark and bare.

The holidays were growing relentlessly closer, and even the thought of spending them with Cassandra didn't wipe the ache from her heart. She couldn't stay in Serenity forever. She knew that, but she couldn't make herself leave, either.

The first flakes of snow from a winterlike storm drifted past her window, and she could see Nicky, wearing just a sweatshirt and jeans, barreling across the lawn toward the cabin.

She hurried to the door, throwing it open just as the boy jumped onto the porch. His little chest heaved with excitement and his breath formed a cloud in front of him as he tried to stop panting. "You've...gotta...come." He bent at the waist and gripped his knees. "Right...now."

"I will, but what are you doing running around without your coat? It's freezing out there." Molly tried to draw him into the cabin, but he pulled back and shook his head.

"No! You have to come quick. Somebody sent you something. Boxes and boxes of stuff. It's all up at the house." He danced a little in his excitement and pointed across the lawn as if she might have forgotten where the house was.

Molly gave up and reached for her sweater. She'd spent far too much money ordering supplies over the Internet during the past week, and she'd been having second thoughts. She justified her decisions because she needed to stay busy while she was here, but she was really just creating false reasons to stay.

She had no business taking advantage of Beau's hospitality and no idea what made her think she could come close to recreating her mother's designs. She'd probably just thrown away a chunk of money from her dad's life insurance that could have gone for something more practical.

But now that the supplies were here, exhilaration bubbled up inside her again. It had been a long time since she'd felt excited about anything. It felt so good she almost didn't care whether she succeeded or failed.

She closed the cabin door and hurried down the steps. Nicky jumped to the ground, fell to his knees and got up running. Laughing, Molly put a little zip into her step and started across the lawn behind the boy, who could hardly contain himself.

Apparently he decided she still wasn't moving fast enough, because partway there he turned back and grabbed her hand. It was a completely spontaneous gesture, and Molly knew it meant nothing to Nicky, but her emotions had been raw since that day in Clay's sunny kitchen, and her eyes blurred with unshed tears.

She wasn't angry with Beau. She'd realized how over the top her reaction had been before she'd walked even just a couple of blocks that afternoon. But everything new she learned about her parents left her that much less certain of herself, and though she longed to find comfort in her friendship with Beau, she refused to let herself take refuge from the world. Not there. Not anywhere.

It was a completely logical decision, but it didn't do a thing to lessen the confusion in his eyes or still the whispers of her heart.

"Come on, Molly." Nicky dragged at her, making her move faster than she would have on her own.

She tried to laugh at the picture she knew they must make, but the sound caught in her throat. The cold air burned her cheeks and nose, and the scent of burning leaves reached her from somewhere nearby.

Her toe hit a bump in the lawn, and she nearly lost her balance. Tightening her grip on Nicky's hand, she managed to slow the determined little boy. "Hold on," she said, gasping for breath and laughing at the same time. "Let's get there without breaking my neck."

"But you gotta *see!* There's probably a hundred boxes."

"If there are a hundred, then someone's made a mistake." She regulated their pace a little more, and Nicky finally stopped fighting and fell into step beside her. "It's not really that exciting," she warned. "It's just some supplies I ordered for my new business." But just saying the words aloud made her fingers tingle and she felt as if a flurry of butterflies had been turned loose inside her.

"What kind of business?"

"I'm going to make jewelry like my mother did."

Some of the excitement in Nicky's blue eyes died away. "Jewelry? For *girls?*"

"I think so—at least most of it."

They reached the back of the house and Nicky released her hand to charge up the steps. "Well, that's dumb. Why don't you make something for boys?"

"Maybe I will someday." Molly followed him into the kitchen and closed the door to keep the cold out.

Brianne stood in front of a stack of brown cardboard boxes piled near the window. She turned one small box over in her hands and studied it carefully, but she jumped when the door opened, and set the box down with a guilty flush.

It was the first thing Molly had seen the girl show any real interest in, and she didn't want to scare her off, so she pretended not to notice. "Oh, this is great. They must have delivered everything at once. Who's that one from, Brianne?" She bobbed her head toward the box Brianne had been holding and picked up another to study the label.

The girl seemed to relax a little. "It's from someplace called JewelArt in California."

"Perfect. And this one's from Lisa's Jewelry Cottage. I can't wait to see whether the gemstones are as good as they looked on the computer." Molly glanced around and pretended to consider her options. "I'd like to get these boxes open and make sure everything's here. I don't suppose the two of you would be willing to help me get all this to the cabin, would you?"

Nicky jumped at the chance, but Brianne showed a little more restraint. "You want us to help you now?" she asked.

"If you don't mind. I don't want your dad to come home and find a mess."

Brianne actually laughed. "Yeah, that'd be *real* different."

"Things are getting better around here," Molly protested. "A little. And anyway, there's no reason I should add to the problem."

Nicky picked up two boxes at once and tucked one beneath his arm. "I'll help. I can carry lots. Brianne doesn't even have to help if she doesn't want."

To Molly's surprise, Brianne shushed him and planted her hands on her hips. "We don't have to carry all this stuff. Nicky has an old wagon somewhere. We can use that and take everything at the same time."

We. Molly liked the sound of that—maybe a little too much. "That's a great idea. Do you know where it is?"

"Probably in the shed—with all my mom's stuff."

No telling how the kids would react to seeing their mother's belongings, and Molly didn't want to ruin the moment by opening the door on painful memories. "Well, then, we probably should wait to ask your dad before we go rooting around and making a mess. How about a wheelbarrow? Does he have one of those?"

Nicky nodded solemnly. "In the shed."

"I see." Molly laughed and glanced out the window at the gathering darkness, then back at the stack of boxes. "Well... I guess there's not so much. We might have to make a couple of trips, but the boxes aren't heavy. What do you say? Should we waste time looking for the wagon or should we just load up and carry them?"

Nicky seemed oblivious to the hidden meaning behind the question, but Molly was sure that Brianne knew exactly what she was trying to do. The girl looked her up and down for an uncomfortably long time before she shrugged and picked up a box. "Let's carry them. There aren't *that* many."

Relieved, Molly helped the kids load up, grabbed as many boxes as she could and followed them out the door. She couldn't help thinking that she'd just scored a major victory, but victory in a war she wasn't going to be around to win seemed hollow.

These weren't her children. She barely knew them. But the thought of leaving when she'd finally started making progress with them made her sad.

Even more important, now that they'd started to respond to her, how would they react when she left?

She watched Brianne take a box that teetered dangerously on the stack Nicky was holding and told herself not to get carried away. Nicky liked her, but he was hardly attached, and one civil conversation with Brianne didn't exactly take their relationship to a whole new level. She was just longing for a family of her own, that's all. Wishing for things that could never be.

She shook off the slight melancholy and concentrated on recapturing her excitement, but it wasn't easy. She was tired of being alone, tired of hiding her true feelings, tired of living in the past. What she wanted more than anything, she realized suddenly, was to have a future.

IT TOOK ANOTHER two days after his conversation with Aaron for Beau to convince himself he needed to talk to Molly—and find the time to do it. The first night he'd arrived home late after a frustrating meeting with the mayor, and Molly had already been in bed—at least, her lights were out. The second day had passed in a blur of work, soccer practices, dance lessons and arguments with bullheaded people over the best way to conduct an ice-block carving competition during WinterFest.

Now it was Friday night, and he finally had a minute to call his own. He'd sent Nicky to invite Molly to dinner, and she'd come of course, but she'd kept him at arm's length with superficial conversation, just as she had for the past ten days.

Beau wondered if the kids could feel the difference in her. If anything, their relationship with her seemed stronger, while his seemed worse. There was something wrong with this picture.

He wasn't even sure what he wanted. He only knew that he didn't like this wall that had gone up between them, and he missed the time they'd once spent together laughing and talking. So he waited until the kids were in bed and asleep, then set off across the lawn to…do something. He'd figure it out when he got there.

He walked quickly, and as he drew near the cabin, he could see her through the window, sitting at the table, completely focused on something she held in her hands.

His heart turned over in his chest and he nearly lost his nerve, but he'd never been afraid of anything in his life before the divorce, and he wouldn't be able to look himself in the mirror if he ran scared now. Still, crossing the lawn and climbing those stairs with the memory of Heather's ugly words ringing in his ears was one of the hardest things he'd ever done.

Molly apparently heard him coming. Her head shot up with his first footstep on the porch, and she was at the door and holding it open before he could reach it. She'd removed her makeup and pulled her hair up with a clip, but soft curls fell around her face and made him long to touch them. She wore a pale-blue robe that looked about a million years old over a pair of pajamas covered with cartoon ducks, but Beau was quite sure he'd never seen a woman more alluring. Only uncertainty kept his imagination from racing off to places he shouldn't let it go.

The light inside the cabin formed a sort of halo around her, and that slow burn he'd almost given up hope of feeling again ignited deep inside him. He made himself smile. This was as easy as passing a football, he told himself. It took just a little determination, a little focus...

Smiling wasn't so hard. But making his mouth work to form words was a little harder. "Am I interrupting something?"

She shook her head and motioned toward the table. "I'm just sorting supplies. I thought I'd take your suggestion and try recreating some of my mom's designs."

She sounded normal, but he caught a glimpse of the pulse point just above her collarbone, and when he saw it jump, as if she was aware of him, too, he felt himself relaxing enough to carry on a conversation. "Well, you'll be great at it, I'm sure." He propped one hand against the door frame and leaned in just a little, needing to be where she was and wanting her to ask him to be. "Listen, Molly, we need to talk."

Her worried gaze shot to his face and he hurried to set her mind at ease. "There's nothing wrong. Not anything you've done, that is. But I don't like the way things have been between us since that day at Uncle Clay's, and I want to fix it."

She hesitated for a moment, then stepped away from the door and motioned him inside. "I've already told you that I'm not angry," she said when she'd closed the door behind him. "I know what you were trying to say. I just overreacted."

"Yeah, well, I said the last thing you wanted to hear right then. Have you found out anything more?"

"No, but I haven't really tried." She turned away, kneading her forehead with her fingertips. "I just can't figure it out, Beau. I've thought and thought, but none of it makes any sense. My dad was one of the gentlest people I've ever known. I can't imagine him fighting with my mother so fiercely that the police would need to interfere. But I also can't imagine him doing something so wrong that my mother would get that angry." She turned back to face him and her eyes swam with unshed tears. "The idea that they were heading into divorce court is so preposterous it just makes me crazy. There's more to the story. I just know it."

He needed to do something, so he closed the distance between them and pulled her into his arms. "Then we'll find it, Molly. I promise you we will."

She held herself stiffly for a moment, then relaxed against him, wrapping her arms around his waist and hanging on as if he held the key to her very survival. "I've been going through the days, ordering jewelry supplies and pretending that I can make it all better by stringing some beads on wire. I'm an expert at putting things out of my mind and forgetting what's too unpleasant to remember. But it's not going to go away this time. Some days that's what I want. Other days, I think I'll die if I don't remember."

He cradled her gently, brushing his lips across the top of her head and smoothing his hands along the soft fabric of her robe. "What are you saying? That you're choosing not to remember?"

She lifted her gaze to meet his. "I don't know. Maybe I am. Maybe I walked away from that accident and decided it was all too ugly to think about. Maybe

I was tired of hearing my parents argue. And maybe I decided to pretend it never happened.''

"Give yourself time, Molly. You can't undo fifteen years in a week or two.''

She put a hand on his chest. She didn't push him away, but he could feel the agitation starting to take control of her again. "Meanwhile, I'm taking horrible advantage of you. I should at least go back to the motel.''

"Absolutely not. The cabin would just sit empty if you weren't here. And besides, the kids like having you around, and I feel better knowing they're not alone, even for only a couple of hours after school. So just relax and let yourself deal with this.''

"I can't bear to think I'll have to go through years of this. I'd rather forget about it completely.'' She laughed harshly and stepped away. "And why don't I? Obviously my dad was good at forgetting about things *he* didn't want to remember. Maybe I should just go with the family tradition and avoid reality completely.''

Beau hated what this was doing to her. "You're being too hard on yourself,'' he told her. "Strange things happen to people when they go through something traumatic, and they don't always get to choose their reactions.''

"You don't get it, do you?'' Her voice sounded frantic. "We talked to Clay ten days ago. I've known for over a week that I was in the car with my mom when she died. I've had all this time to dig into records, ask questions and find out the rest, but every day I find some excuse not to do it. I say I want to know the truth, but I sure don't act like it.''

Beau sat on the arm of the couch. "I think you can cut yourself a little slack, Molly. You've been dealt a few surprises since you've been here. I'm sure it's not easy to take it all in."

"It shouldn't take this long." She turned back to the table.

"I didn't realize there was a time limit," he said, trying to lighten the moment. When she didn't smile, he stood again and followed her. "I don't know how you can put a time limit on something like that. Look how long it's taken me to come to terms with the surprise Heather dropped on me. Are you saying I should have just dealt with it eight or nine months ago? Because if that's what you think happened, I've got news for you."

Dropping into a chair, she began sorting tiny pieces of something shiny with quick, angry movements. "That's different," she said without looking up. "You haven't made avoiding reality the work of a lifetime. But you know what? This isn't getting us anywhere, so why don't we just drop it?"

She stopped working and met his gaze, and he could see that she'd already withdrawn. But he wasn't about to let her run him off.

He drew up a chair and straddled it, watching her intently as she kept sorting.

After a few seconds, her gaze returned to his face. "What?"

"Nothing. Just watching."

"It's that interesting?"

"Riveting."

She rolled her eyes and went back to work. "You're easily amused, aren't you."

"So I've been told." He rocked the chair up on two legs and picked up a shiny pink stone. "This is pretty. What is it?"

"Rose quartz."

"What are you going to do with it?"

"I'll probably make a necklace." She reached out with an impatient hand and took the stone from him. "Maybe for Brianne, if you think she'd like it."

Beau nodded and pretended to give that some thought. "She probably would. It would look better on her than it would on Nicky or me."

Molly ignored his feeble attempt at humor, but when he didn't move for several minutes, she leaned back in her seat and met his gaze. *"What?"* she asked.

"You look good in this cabin," he said impulsively. "Like it was made just for you."

The sigh she released sounded exasperated, but her lips quirked and Beau could have sworn he saw a hint of a smile there. "I thought you said your grandparents built this place."

"I did."

"So you're saying I look old?"

Chuckling, he leaned over and captured her lips with his for the briefest kiss in history. Then he stood and turned the chair back around. "Yes, Molly, that's exactly what I'm saying." He bent and kissed her again, this time taking just a little more time and putting all the things he couldn't let himself say into the effort. She responded well enough to satisfy him, so he straightened, cupped her chin in his hand and lifted her face so he could see into her eyes. "Good night, Molly."

He heard her whispered "good night" as he stepped outside, a split second before he shut the door, but he carried the pleasure of it, and the look on her face, across the frozen lawn with him. He liked the fact Molly wasn't afraid to look at herself, even if she sometimes didn't like what she found. And though he still wasn't sure what he wanted from the future, he felt better about his ability to figure it out.

All he needed was time.

BEAU CAME AWAKE suddenly the next morning and bolted upright in bed. He blinked a few times to clear his eyes and realized that the sun was already streaming into the room. He rolled over and dragged the alarm clock around so he could see it. Eight o'clock! How in the hell had that happened?

Obviously he'd stayed awake too long thinking about Molly and wondering about the future. He wasn't thinking commitment, but the prospect of exploring possibilities made the days ahead look brighter.

He scrambled out of bed, tugged on a pair of sweat-pants and raced down the stairs to put coffee on. Thankfully, Gwen had canceled the kids' piano lessons this week so she could carve pumpkins with Riley's family, but he still had a million things to do, starting with an early meeting to discuss the city's Christmas decorations. At least this was one meeting he could get the kids involved in.

He felt a sharp pang of regret that Molly wouldn't be here for the holidays. He'd love to share WinterFest with her—the snowball toss, the sleigh rides, the snow-shoe races and even the snowman-building competi-tion. But he couldn't think about that now. He was already running so late he'd be lucky to finish every-thing before midnight.

Even with so much on his mind, he had a hard time not grinning as he put on the coffee. He pulled a load of clean towels from the dryer and left them sitting on the table while he dug through the fridge for breakfast makings. But his mind wasn't on laundry and bacon.

Whistling softly, he stuffed a load of sheets into the washer, then carried his mug of coffee back to the table and set to work. He even managed to keep himself from checking out the window for Molly between folding each towel.

He finished the task in record time and carried the towels upstairs to the linen closet, which he suddenly noticed was in desperate need of reorganization. Vowing to put them away neatly *next* week, he stuffed everything into the empty spots and hurried downstairs again to start breakfast.

He pulled bowls and pancake mix from the cupboards, eggs from the fridge and juice from the freezer. With a quick look out the window at the cabin, he tried sending a subliminal message to Molly that it was time to wake up. He couldn't wait to see her again.

Laughing at himself, he put the frozen juice and water in a pitcher, started to pour pancake mix into the bowl, then left the box on top of the washer while he dug through the cupboard for a measuring cup he could have sworn was there a few days earlier. When he couldn't find it at the front of the cupboard, he stretched high to check the back, craning to see over the jumble of bowls, plastic containers, ice-cube trays and other things he couldn't identify—but if the measuring cup was there, it was cleverly hidden.

He let out a growl of frustration and turned toward the next cupboard. His hand knocked over the pitcher, sending a shower of pale-pink water and half-melted juice concentrate to the floor before he could right it. At the same moment the washer clicked onto the spin cycle.

Cursing under his breath, Beau grabbed a dish towel and tossed it onto the floor. As he dropped to his knees and took one swipe at the mess, the washer let out an ungodly noise and began to shake as if something or someone was trapped inside. He shot to his feet again and lurched toward the machine, watching in horror as the five-pound package of pancake mix gyrated to the edge of the washer and plunged to the floor.

"No-o-o-o!" He dived after it, but the package split on contact and a cloud of pancake mix flew into the air, up his nostrils and into his eyes. He sneezed twice and swiped at his face with his shirttail. In frustration, he aimed a kick at the closest cupboard, forgetting that he wasn't wearing shoes until the pain shot through his foot and up his leg.

"Need some help?"

He glanced over to see Molly standing near the island, watching his disaster-in-the-making. Her eyes were clear and bright, her smile warm and friendly, and relief quickly overshadowed the humiliation of being caught covered in pancake flour and juice.

"Help? No." He scrambled to his feet and studied the mess on the floor with a wry expression. "Why do you ask?"

"No reason."

"That's what I thought. Obviously, I have everything under control." Molly's lips twitched, and Beau's heart soared with hope that they'd put the uneasiness behind them.

As she stepped around the counter, Beau drank in the sight of her. She wore jeans and a plain, long-sleeve white T-shirt tucked in at the waist. Her thumbs were hooked in her back pockets, causing her breasts to press against the thin white fabric, accentuating the lacy bra covering their soft swell. "I realize you don't need help from me, but out of curiosity, where's your broom?"

Beau jerked his gaze back up to her face. "Broom?"

"That thing with the handle on one end and bristles on the other? I'm sure you've seen one."

Her hair fell in lazy curls to her shoulders, and Beau had a sudden urge to forget about breakfast and remind himself why men and women had been created differently. He was having one helluva time concentrating on what she was saying. *Broom,* he reminded himself. "I've seen one. I just haven't decided whether or not to use it yet. I'm still pondering my options."

Her eyes sparkled with suppressed laughter and Beau added another entry to the list of things he was learning to love about her. "I'd suggest the broom first, then maybe a mop."

"A mop."

"Spongy thing. Long handle. Needs water." She glanced at the puddle on the floor. "I wish I'd gotten here sooner. I could have told you that juice doesn't work, as well."

He gave himself over to the game and narrowed his eyes in mock disbelief as he pulled the broom from the closet. "Are you sure? It's prettier than water. Pink."

"That's true," she said, somehow still managing not to smile, "but your floor isn't pink."

"Not yet."

She nodded, conceding the point, and turned away to pull the mop and bucket from the closet. "Did you *want* a pink floor?"

Beau swept a mound of pancake mix onto the dustpan and carried it to the garbage can. "I'm thinking about it. Brianne likes pink. It's a perfectly good color.

And it might even help me get in touch with my feminine side.''

Molly laughed, just once, before she sobered again. ''It might, but that's not really the thing to do anymore.''

''No?''

''I don't want to sound rude, but it's sort of… nineties.''

''Shows you what I know. And after I went to all this trouble, too.'' He stepped across a particularly noxious blob of pink dough and tackled another heap of dry mix. ''So what are men into these days?''

''I think it's all about 'being real.' Facing things squarely.'' She wagged a dismissive hand through the air. ''You know the drill. Dealing with life head-on. Taking it on the jaw. That sort of macho, manly, testosterone-y thing.''

''Head-on? Are you sure?''

''Well, not a hundred percent, but fairly sure. Honesty seems to be the thing these days for both sexes.'' She carried the bucket to the sink, found floor cleaner and mixed it with hot water. ''It's not a bad idea, actually. It comes highly recommended.''

''Honesty, huh?'' He scratched his chin thoughtfully. ''That sounds almost dangerous. Are you sure it works?''

''Well, I can't be positive, of course. It's a new idea and I've never been involved with anyone who actually did it…'' She shut off the water and turned back to him. ''But it sounds nice, and I think I'd like to try. If you're interested, we could work on it together. Maybe go back over the past few weeks and try again?''

Beau's throat closed and he could have sworn that his heart took up residence behind his ears. He couldn't hear anything but its incessant drumming for several seconds, and the blood in his veins felt as if someone had set it on fire. "What would you do differently?"

The humor fled her eyes and stark emotion replaced it. "Well, for one thing, I'd be more honest about my feelings for you."

He tried to smile. "Would those be *good* feelings?"

"That depends on your point of view, but I think so."

"That sounds promising." He left the broom and dustpan leaning against the fridge and moved closer to her. "I'd probably be forced to admit that I've missed this a whole lot more than I should."

She smiled and her eyes softened even further. "So have I."

Beau felt himself being drawn into their depths, and he suddenly wanted more than anything to spend however long it took to uncover all the mysteries there. "So we're friends again?"

She nodded without looking away. "I'd like that."

"*Only* friends?"

Her eyes widened slightly, but she shook her head and her lips curved into a slow, seductive smile. "I don't think so."

He slid his arms around her and pulled her close, sparing one brief thought for the kids and willing them to sleep just five minutes longer.

She snuggled into his arms and frowned up at him thoughtfully. "I guess if we're really going to get into this honesty thing, there's one more little tidbit I should share. I was madly in love with you back in high school. I would have given almost anything to take Heather's place."

The confession both stunned and delighted him, but

he wasn't about to waste time analyzing which feeling was stronger. The kids might wake up at any minute. He drew her closer and lowered his head until their lips were almost touching. "Maybe you should have told me back then."

"I was too shy."

"Yeah? But think of all the time we've wasted." And with that, he covered her mouth with his and put an end to the conversation. There'd be plenty of opportunity to talk later. Right now it was time to feed a starving man—and he didn't mean eggs and pancakes, either.

CHAPTER FOURTEEN

BEAU SQUINTED into the deceptive October sunshine and tugged the collar of his jacket up to protect his ears from the biting cold as he worked. A small pile of luggage sat on the tarmac a few feet from the Cessna, waiting for him to load up. His passengers, two guys who needed transportation back to Jackson after a successful elk hunt, had conceded to the cold and gone inside for stale coffee and doughnuts.

Perfect weather for Halloween. Perfect weather for a flight. In fact, everything had been pretty damn perfect for nearly a week. If he wasn't careful, he could get used to this.

Molly had been in Serenity for a month already, and there were times when Beau let himself forget that she wasn't going to be around forever. He liked coming home from work and finding her there with the kids. He got a kick out of cutting firewood for the cabin while she worked on her jewelry. No matter how many times he'd told her she didn't need to cook for them, it was a rare workday when he didn't walk through the door to the aroma of something in the oven or on the stove. But on his days off, he tried to pull his weight by fixing chili and biscuits or Brianne's favorite baked potato bar.

Yep, he could get used to this. And maybe Aaron was right. Maybe this *was* his chance.

He heard footsteps behind him and turned, expecting to find his passengers returning. But instead, he found Doris striding toward him, looking as if someone had just run off with her prize pickle recipe. He groaned silently and prayed for patience.

"Doris."

"We need to talk, Beau."

He decided not to assume the worst. "About what?"

"I think you know what."

"This isn't really a good time," he said, nodding toward the luggage in case she hadn't noticed it. "I have passengers inside, and I'm due for takeoff in just a couple of minutes."

"This can't wait. I'm worried about the kids."

"Did something happen?"

"*Yes,* something happened. It's been happening for a month, and I'm tired of hoping you'll wake up and be reasonable about this."

Would the woman never give up? Beau shook his head and hefted a duffel bag. He stuffed it into the Cessna's nose compartment and turned back for another. "I thought we'd agreed not to have this conversation again."

Doris tugged her cardigan sweater closer and folded her arms. The wind tousled her hair and the cold had already turned her nose and ears pink, but she looked ready to settle in for a long battle. "I don't approve of what you're doing over there with that woman. What will it take to get you to stop?"

Beau had to reach around her to get the rest of the bags. "I can't discuss this now, Doris. I'm scheduled to take off and my passengers are waiting."

"This doesn't have to take long. I just want you to promise me you'll be reasonable. That you'll start to care about Brianne and Nicky and the impression you're making on them, and that you'll send—'' she waved a hand as if she couldn't remember ''—Molly to stay somewhere else.''

Beau wedged the two small bags into the Cessna's nose and stepped back to latch it. ''In the first place, Doris, what I do isn't your concern. In the second, Molly and I aren't doing anything wrong.'' He stepped around her and stowed two leather briefcases behind the passenger seats. ''And third, I really don't want Molly to go anywhere.'' He turned back to face her. ''As a matter of fact, I'm hoping she'll decide to stay for a long, long time.''

''Oh, please, Beau. You don't know what you're talking about. You haven't been divorced that long, and you were in love with Heather since you were teenagers. Now someone comes back who knew you then and still sees you as the quarterback on the high-school football team, and you're going take a little flirtation with her seriously?''

Struggling to keep his temper, Beau moved past her again. Doris had been a constant presence in his marriage, a thorn in his side for fifteen long years. She'd controlled everything Heather had ever done, and through Heather, him. But he still wasn't willing to let down his guard and tell her everything in his mind. Call it respect, call it weakness, he wasn't sure which. But he bit his tongue as he always did.

And she came after him, as *she* always did. ''Don't you dare walk away from me. Everyone knew Molly had a thing for you in school, but Heather always stood in her way. Now Heather's gone, and who shows up? It's quite a coincidence, isn't it?''

''Don't be ridiculous. She's not here for me.''

"*Is* it ridiculous?" Doris's footsteps echoed on the tarmac behind him. "Why don't you go ask a few people, Beau? Eve knows. Heather always knew."

"I wouldn't trust Heather to tell me what time it is," Beau snapped. "And Eve's almost as bad."

"And Molly's just like her mother, sniffing around for any man who'd have her."

Suddenly furious, Beau whipped around and put himself at eye level with her. "You're a mean-spirited woman, Doris. You always have been. You drove Heather crazy with your constant nagging, and you're about to do the same thing to me."

Her mouth dropped open, but she snapped it shut again, and fire flashed in her eyes.

Beau didn't care. "For the kids' sake, I've put up with everything you've dished out, but you've gone too far this time. I'm going to tell you this just once. Leave Molly alone. And if I ever hear you say anything that vile about her mother again, it'll be the last time the kids go anywhere with you alone."

It was a rash threat, but he didn't let himself apologize. Doris had to realize how irrational she'd become, or the situation really would get out of hand, and the kids would be the ones who suffered.

Doris's pale eyes grew icy. "You don't mean that."

"Try me and find out."

"I'll take you to court. I'll petition for custody of those kids myself."

Perhaps he'd gone too far, Beau thought, especially with customers likely to come back at any moment. He also knew that if he kept arguing with her, things would go downhill—as if they could go any farther downhill than they already had. Clenching his fists as tightly as his teeth, he wheeled away from her and started across the tarmac toward his office.

"Don't you *dare* walk away from me," she shouted after him. "I mean it, Beau."

He kept walking, but only because he didn't completely trust himself not to do something he'd regret. Maybe he'd pushed her too far this time, but she had to understand that there were some lines folks didn't cross. Getting dealt a raw hand in life didn't justify becoming mean-spirited. And if she followed through on her threat and fought him for custody of the kids in court? Well, then he supposed Doris Preston would finally find out what he was made of.

"COME OUT WITH ME," he whispered to Molly that evening during a rare moment alone.

Scowling in concentration, she looked up from the lasagna she'd been layering into a pan. "Out?"

"For dinner. Let the kids have the lasagna. We'll go somewhere, just the two of us."

Molly's eyes grew wide. "On a date?"

"That's what I had in mind."

She tilted her head to one side and considered him for a moment. "Well, I do truly love my lasagna, but I guess leftovers would be just as good. Are you sure that's what you want?"

"Why wouldn't I?"

She lifted a shoulder casually, but a shadow crossed her eyes. "You know how people are. If we go out in public together—alone—people will talk. I'll be leaving sooner or later. You and the kids are the ones who'll have to live with it."

Leaving. He ignored the pang he felt and leaned into the corner, crossing his arms over his chest. "Don't worry about talk. We've gotten used to talk this year. Besides, I'm a big boy. I can handle it.''

Her gaze traveled the length of him and a slow smile curved her lips. She cleared her throat and looked at the lasagna noodle she held in her hands as if she didn't know what it was. "It's not you I'm worried about," she said after she gathered her wits. "Brianne seems to be doing a lot better lately. I don't want to do anything that might send her into a tailspin."

"And you think that going on a date with me will do that?"

"I don't know." She met his gaze squarely. "I think that her grandmother will cause trouble if you and I go out in public."

"Doris is one of the reasons I want to talk to you—alone. She stopped by to see me today at the airstrip. I think you should know what she's saying."

"About me?"

Beau nodded. The rest could keep until they were alone.

Molly's gaze faltered. "You know she's not happy about me being here."

"She made that pretty clear," he admitted, "but how do you know?"

"She told me."

Beau's good mood evaporated. "She what?"

"She told me."

"I got that part." He struggled not to let his anger with Doris spill over to Molly. "When did she tell you?"

"The other day at the FoodWay. I was there picking up a few groceries and she made a point of... introducing herself."

The anger he'd somehow managed to keep suppressed all day burst to life as if someone had tossed a lit match onto gas-soaked kindling. He'd had enough. More than enough. He turned away as he struggled to get it under control. "She's gone too far," he ground out when he could speak again. "I don't know what it's going to take to wake her up, but she can't keep doing this. I'm sorry, Molly."

"It's not your fault."

"Oh, but it is. She's been this way since Heather and I got married. Even earlier, if you want the truth. From the minute we told her Heather was pregnant, she started nosing her way into our lives, and I let her in because I was a kid and I felt so damn guilty about what we'd done. My parents were disappointed, but they took it in stride. Doris…" He paused and shook his head. "She's held every mistake I've ever made over my head, and she did the same with Heather. Miserable as she's been making me, I'll tell you who I'd hate to be right now, and that's Heather. She'll pay for leaving here for the rest of her life. Doris will make sure of it."

Molly touched his arm tentatively. "At least she's not alone. She has Dawn…and you."

He whirled back to face her. "Me?"

Molly went back to work, spooning great daubs of filling into the pan. "I know she hurt you, Beau. I understand you don't want to put your marriage back together, and I'm not suggesting you should." She set the bowl aside and looked into his eyes. "But regardless of what happened in the end, the two of you really have been friends forever. You've been through hell and back again. And you have children together. Wouldn't it be better for everyone if you could stop being angry with her and just be her friend? I know the kids would like it.''

''You're forgetting one thing. She isn't interested in seeing the kids.''

''I don't think you can be sure of that. If she *was* living a lie during her marriage to you, she must have been unhappy. Now you're hurt and angry, and her mother's...well, Doris. And let's face facts—Heather's obviously not strong enough to come back here and see the children she disappointed when there's not a soul in the world who'll back her. Dawn wouldn't be much help in that situation.''

Molly was wrong, and Beau wanted to tell her so, but deep down he knew that her argument made a certain kind of sense. He let out a brittle laugh and turned away, testing Molly's analysis in a dozen different ways and trying to find the flaws.

''If you shut her out,'' Molly said after a long moment, ''then you're really doing the same thing my dad did with me.''

He whipped back toward her. ''It's not the same thing at all. She left me.''

''And apparently my mom left Dad. She just didn't live long enough for anyone else to know about it.''

He dropped heavily into a chair and held his head with his hands, still trying to find faults in her logic and losing at every turn. ''You're asking me to forgive her for lying to me? For hurting the kids? For ignoring them and putting herself first?''

''Yes. Because if you don't, you're putting your own hurt before the kids. You can't really believe that staying this angry with her is good for Brianne and Nicky. Whether or not she accepts your offer isn't the issue. For the kids' sake, you have to find a way to make it.''

A rush of affection swept through him for this woman who showed such concern for his children. He stood uncertainly and rounded the island. Some logical part of his brain warned him to think, but he was tired of thinking, and so very tired of fighting life's battles alone.

He cupped her face in his hands and leaned in close, half expecting her to pull away but praying she wouldn't. He brushed her lips once. Twice. Then covered them with his and poured everything he was feeling into the moment between them.

He could feel her heart beating against his chest, the rapid rise and fall and the unsteady breaths that spoke of her own emotions. He'd never been good at speaking his heart. He was much better at showing what he felt. But he could put everything he was feeling into one word, and he whispered it softly as he ended the kiss and pulled away slightly so he could look into her eyes.

"Stay."

Her eyes were closed, but they flew open at the sound of his voice and searched his for an explanation.

"Stay here for a while," he said hoarsely. And then, because she still looked confused, he added, "Stay, even if you find out what happened with your mom and dad tomorrow. Stay for Thanksgiving. Share Christmas with us. Spend New Year's Eve with me. Maybe with enough time, you and I can figure this thing out."

When she didn't immediately respond, he made himself be even more honest. "I never expected to feel something like this so soon after Heather. I don't want you to leave. Stay, and give us a chance to see where things go."

She put her hands on his chest, but instead of pushing him away, she splayed her fingers and studied them
as if she wanted to memorize the way they looked
there. Warmth spiraled through him from those places
where her skin made contact with his, and he wished
they were at the cabin, alone, instead of standing in his
kitchen, about to be descended upon by the kids he
could hear stirring overhead.

"It would also give us a chance to confuse your kids
more than they already are," she argued reasonably.
"And to hurt them all over again when I leave."

"There's no law that says you have to leave at all,"
Beau reminded her. "Serenity's a good place to live.
Good people. Beautiful scenery.

"And zero opportunity," she said with a little shake
of her head. "I haven't worked in nearly six weeks,
and I can't count on Mom's jewelry to get me by."

"So get a job here."

She smiled softly, but there was a deep sadness in
her eyes. She pulled her hands away and put some
distance between them as the kids began to come down
the stairs. "I don't want a job, Beau. I want a career."

"And you can't have one here?"

"Where? At the FoodWay? It's a nice town, and
most of the people are wonderful, but it's not exactly
a hub of industry. There's no call for a graphic-design
artist here, and the market's so glutted I can't hope to
get anywhere on my own. I need to be out there where
the action is."

"Serenity's not the end of the world."

"I know that, but I'm just not interested in waiting
tables or checking groceries."

He swallowed his disappointment and shoved aside
the flicker of irritation at her attitude toward the town

he loved. Much as he wanted to argue with her, she was right. Serenity was small and out of the way. Too far from anywhere to have any allure for someone like Molly.

"What about the jewelry?"

"It's a nice hobby. It might even add to my income a little. But it's never going to support me."

He turned away and tried to get his disappointment under control. Her argument was logical. It made perfect sense. But it didn't change the way he felt. He just had no idea how he'd ever convince her to stay when he had nothing to offer but himself.

A LITTLE AFTER noon the next day, Molly paced the foyer of the Chicken Inn as she waited for Elaine to arrive. She had a million things to share with her friend, beginning with the simple pair of earrings she'd made before she left the cabin and ending with Beau's unexpected request last night.

In spite of what she'd told him, she'd spent hours toying with the idea of staying. Beau's sense of humor delighted her. His obvious love for his children, his never-ending service to the city and that streak of self-doubt that she glimpsed occasionally all worked together to create an incredible man who captivated her at every turn.

Could she? Should she? The temptation was almost too strong to resist.

Elaine arrived just a few minutes later, and almost immediately the hostess led them to a table. There were a few other customers at tables scattered around the dining area, but no one sat at the neighboring tables, and Molly was glad for the chance to talk freely.

Elaine draped her napkin across her lap and

smoothed it thoughtfully, then, tilting her head, she studied Molly and said, "You look happy. Things are going well?"

"Very well." Molly pulled the small box holding the earrings from her purse and handed it over for Elaine's inspection. "What do you think? Not bad for a first effort, huh?"

After studying the earrings carefully for a moment, Elaine agreed. "Not bad at all. You made these?"

"I did." The waitress arrived with salads, and Molly unrolled the napkin holding her silverware. "Beau thinks I can make a living at this, but I'm still not sure. Still, it's a nice hobby, and I actually felt kind of connected to my mom when I was making those."

"Well, I'm glad," Elaine said, closing the box and passing it back to Molly. "It would be really nice if this worked into a little business for you. My mom always said that Ruby Lane made the best jewelry around." Elaine speared her salad with her fork, but didn't eat. "Have you found out anything more about her accident?"

"Just what I told you the other day on the phone. I know I need to keep digging, but Clay's news really rocked me. It's going to take a while to come to terms with it, I guess."

"So how long will you be staying?"

"I don't know. A while."

Elaine turned her attention to her salad. "And how are things with Beau?"

Molly grinned like a teenager. "Things with Beau are just fine. He's really great, isn't he?"

"He always has been." Elaine worked the salt and pepper grinders over her salad, then settled them back in place slowly and deliberately. "He was pretty torn up when Heather left, you know."

"I'm sure he was." Molly realized that sounded almost patronizing and checked herself. "I know he was. There are times even now when you can tell how much it hurt him." She wondered if Elaine knew the truth about why Heather left, but she wasn't going to betray Beau's confidence. "The kids have had a rough time, too, but I think Brianne is actually starting to like me, and Nicky's just a great kid."

"Yeah, he is." Elaine looked up at Molly. "He and Jacob play together sometimes." Her expression seemed almost cool, and Molly shifted with a sudden uneasiness.

"Is something wrong?"

Although Elaine smiled, there was no warmth in it. "Wrong? I don't know what you mean."

"You're angry with me, I can tell. Why? What did I do?"

"I wouldn't say I'm angry. Just cautious. Concerned." Elaine stabbed her fork aimlessly into her salad bowl several more times. "I don't know, Molly. This whole thing with Beau just seems wrong to me. I mean, it's kind of like you're over there playing house, isn't it?"

Molly froze. "No! It's not like that at all!"

"Isn't it? You're over there in Beau's cabin, making stuffed French toast for his kids, and lasagna for the family, but you don't have any intention of staying and making this thing between you real." She put her fork down. "What would *you* call it?"

Feeling a bit ill suddenly, Molly put her own fork on her plate and locked her hands in her lap. "That's not what I'm doing. Beau and I have become close,

but he knows I'm not planning to stay. I told him so
again last night.''

"And the kids? Have you told them?''

"Of course I have.'' But a pang of guilt zapped her
when she realized how long it had been since she'd
brought it up.

"Look,'' Elaine said. "You're my friend and I want
you to be happy. But Beau's a friend, too. A *good*
friend. I know you want a family, Molly. I know you
want children of your own. It's obvious every time
somebody else talks about their kids. But if all you're
doing is using Beau's kids to ease your longing, that's
not right—for any of you.''

Molly recoiled as if Elaine had struck her. "That's
not what I'm doing.''

Elaine looked her straight in the eye. "You know I
love you. And if you were doing this with anybody
else, I probably wouldn't say a word. But that family's
been through enough. If you're not planning to stay,
then all you're doing is playing with their feelings. If
you're serious about Beau and the kids, then I won't
say another word. But if you're not in this relationship
for the long haul, I'm asking you—as your friend and
Beau's—to walk away and let them heal.''

Molly's first response was to argue, but she knew in
her heart that Elaine was right. She wasn't in this for
the long haul. Even if she wanted to, she couldn't stay.
There was nothing for her here, and much as she'd
enjoyed pretending she could live this kind of life forever, she knew she'd never be happy if her days con-
sisted only of laundry, dishes and dinners.

Elaine had circled the wagons to protect Serenity's
Golden Boy, and there would be others. No one would
want to see him hurt again—especially Molly. Much

as she hated to admit it, Elaine had a point. She couldn't continue to pretend that Beau and his kids had any place in her life. Even more important, she couldn't continue to pretend that she had a place in theirs.

IT WAS A WHOLE LOT easier to make the decision than to act on it. When Molly woke up the next morning, Brianne was waiting in one of the porch chairs, ready to help sort supplies and interested—though she didn't want to admit it—in learning how to make jewelry. Even with her own arguments ringing in her ears, Molly hadn't been able to turn the girl away. Not that day. Nor the next day after school or any day of the following two weeks.

With Brianne at the cabin every afternoon, Nicky was never far away. When the weather was good, he'd ride his bike, play football with imaginary playmates or bring neighborhood friends by to show off in front of the windows. After dark or when the weather was too cold, he'd construct towers out of building blocks on the rug in front of the fireplace or sit beside Molly and chatter about things that happened in school. At the end of every day, Molly promised herself that she'd make the break first thing the next morning.

Beau spent long hours away from home, flying charters or working with the committees on Christmas and WinterFest plans. He took the kids with him when he could, and she could tell he felt worse than they did when he had to leave them.

By mid-November she and the kids had established a daily routine. While the kids were at school, Molly created sketches of the jewelry women around town had lent her, did research on the Internet and read everything she could get her hands on that dealt with starting a small business. In the afternoons she'd throw dinner together, do a load of laundry, dust, vacuum or tidy a corner while the kids did homework, then they'd all scurry across to the cabin, where they'd stay until Beau came home.

Whatever housework she did was a small price to pay for continued use of the cabin.

One weekend, she and Beau had had breakfast at the diner while the kids had their piano lessons with Gwen. Beau's mother, Vickie, had invited her for dinner on Sunday, and both she and Gwen had treated Molly like one of the family. Beau's dad, and even Beau's younger brother, Lucas, who was too busy dating to spend much time at home, had welcomed her without batting an eye.

Molly hadn't forgotten that she still had questions about her mother's accident, but every day she found a reason not to ask them. As long as she still had questions, she also had an excuse to stay.

The kids were only part of her reason for hanging around. Beau might not have many free moments, but she certainly got her fair share of the ones he did have. Long walks along the creekbed, dinners at the Chicken Inn, stolen kisses in the moonlight, evenings spent with the kids, rented movies and popcorn… Add the friendships she'd renewed in town, and it was heaven on earth. Molly went back and forth, one day convinced that she really could stay, the next irritated with herself for letting the situation continue.

On a cold Wednesday afternoon, she bundled herself into the coat she'd borrowed from Beau a few days earlier, stuffed her feet into the hiking boots she'd ordered online and trudged across the frozen lawn toward the house. Beau had flown a charter to Idaho Falls, but the kids would be home any minute, and she wanted to have cocoa ready when they arrived.

It was only a short walk from the cabin, but arctic air was blowing into the valley from the north, and the temperatures had dropped to nearly freezing overnight. Today, for the first time, she was having to face grim reality. The cabin was comfortable as long as she kept the fire burning, but it became uncomfortable quickly if she got distracted and didn't replenish the firewood soon enough. Much as she might like to, she wouldn't be able to stay in the cabin all winter unless Beau followed through on his plans to winterize it.

Inside the kitchen, she draped her coat over a chair and set to work. She filled the kettle with water and turned on the burner, then settled in with a paperback novel to wait for the kids. After only a page or two, the phone rang. Someone had left the cordless phone on the table, so she glanced idly at the caller ID screen. When she recognized Beau's cell-phone number, she lunged for the phone and punched the talk button, hoping she'd gotten to it before the call transferred to voice mail.

"I'm here," she said. "Don't hang up."

Beau laughed softly. "I was hoping you might be. What is it, laundry day?"

She'd been using his washer and dryer for weeks, and they'd fallen into a rhythm with laundry, as well. "Not today. Probably tomorrow." She glanced at her watch and frowned. "I thought you'd be in the air by now. Is everything all right?"

"Change of plans," he said. "There's a bad storm rolling in and there's no way I'll get out of here tonight."

She felt a pang of disappointment followed by shock at how much she'd grown used to being around him.

"I have another charter in the morning," he said, "so I probably won't be home until late tomorrow."

Molly got up to turn off the kettle. "Do you have someplace to stay?"

"I have a room at a motel near the airport. I'll make sure you have the number before I hang up. I hate to do this, Molly, but do you think you could stay with the kids for the night? They'd probably be okay there on their own, but I'd feel a whole lot better knowing they had an adult with them."

"Of course I'll stay. You don't even need to ask."

"Great. Use my room. There are clean sheets in the linen closet. Tell Brie I said for her to help you change them."

The thought of sleeping in Beau's bed lit a flicker of anticipation in her belly. "I'm capable of changing a set of sheets on my own," she said with a laugh. "If it's too difficult, I'll just make up a bed on the sofa." Which might be smart, but not nearly as much fun. "Is there anyone you need me to call? Don't you have a meeting with the planning committee tonight?"

"Canceled, but Rosetta Carlisle might drop off some information she's found about the snowball toss. If she does, just put it on my desk and I'll see it when I come home. And if you have a minute while you're online, could you check my e-mails?" He rattled off his screen name and password, and Molly scribbled them in the notebook he now kept near the phone. "The supplier we've always used for Wiffle balls went out of business during the summer, and I'm hoping bids from a couple of new companies will be there."

Molly folded the note and tucked it between the

pages of her novel. "You mean that people still walk off with the 'snowballs'?"

"It's worse than ever. We lose so many every year you'd think people needed them for food."

"What if the bids are there? What would you like me to do?"

"Accept the best one. We need three hundred balls by this time next month. I'll fill out the purchase order when I get back."

"You trust me with your Wiffle balls? I'm flattered."

"I trust you with a helluva lot more than that." His voice was low and intimate, and it sent the most delicious curls of anticipation through her. "I'm also trusting you not to drool on my pillow."

Molly laughed, and the rush of affection she felt for him nearly overwhelmed her. "I'll use my own. Then you don't have to worry."

"Oh, I'm not worried. Just a little annoyed by my rotten luck. I finally get you into my bed, and I can't even be there to enjoy it." A beep interrupted and he muttered something she didn't understand. "My battery's shot," he said. "I'll call later to talk to the kids."

The connection died suddenly and Molly hung up. Thanksgiving was in just two weeks, she realized as she returned the phone to the table. In a month, WinterFest would be in full swing. Two weeks after that it would be Christmas, then New Year's, and a whole new year would be under way.

She'd intended to leave Serenity eventually, but she'd been dragging out her visit with one excuse or another for weeks. Crossing to the window, she stared out at the yard, the frozen fields stretching away on one side, the roofs of neighbors' homes on the other.

Low clouds hugged the mountains rimming the valley, and she realized suddenly what she must always have known—she didn't want to leave.

Not now. Not in a few weeks. Not ever.

CHAPTER FIFTEEN

THE BIDS CAME through just before noon the next day. Molly had moved Beau's laptop to the kitchen table after the kids left for school so she could work without disturbing the notes and files spread all over his study. She considered both bids carefully, settled on the one that looked best to her, then sent the e-mail placing an order for three hundred Wiffle balls.

Hoping she'd made the right choice, she got up from her chair to make tea. As she reached for the kettle, she caught movement out the kitchen window. When she looked closer, she realized that Doris Preston was marching up the walk toward the door, wearing a look that meant business.

What was she doing here, and why now?

Determined not to let the woman intimidate her, Molly took a couple of deep breaths for courage and crossed to the door. She opened it just as Doris reached for the knob, and felt a flash of irritation that the woman didn't even have the courtesy to knock.

"Mrs. Preston. What a surprise." Molly didn't trust Doris not to look for something she could use against her later, so she kept a friendly smile in place. "Beau's away on a flight and the kids are at school. What can I do for you?"

"Not a thing, Molly. I'm just here to pick up a few things for the children." She brushed past Molly and into the kitchen, where she tugged off her gloves, one finger at a time.

Confused, Molly shut the door behind her and leaned against it. "For the children?"

"Brianne and Nicky. They'll be coming to stay with me after school."

"Oh. I didn't realize…" Molly pushed away from the door and glanced at the cordless phone sitting beside the laptop computer. "I must have been online when Beau called. I didn't know you were coming."

Doris spied one of Brianne's sweaters on a chair and practically swooped down on it. "Beau doesn't know I'm here," she said with a thin smile. "I heard that he was away and I decided to take matters into my own hands. There's no reason for you to be burdened with the kids. They're *my* grandchildren."

"You haven't talked this over with Beau?"

"Beau doesn't discuss the children with me these days." Doris ran a glance the length of Molly and turned away again. "I wonder why."

Her implication couldn't have been clearer, but it was so unfair Molly felt as if she'd been kicked. "You think it's my fault?"

"Well, someone's behind it. Things were fine around here until you came to town."

"That's not true," Molly protested. "Beau had already asked you to stay away before I arrived. I didn't get to town until later."

"That may be true—technically." Doris finished folding Brianne's sweater and held it close. "But if you hadn't come back when you did, I'm sure he and I would have patched up our differences a long time ago."

Was this some kind of joke? A bad dream? It certainly couldn't be real. Molly studied the older woman's face, trying to find some hint of a smile or a flicker of amusement in her eyes, but she saw only anger. "Surely you don't believe that. Why would I want to keep you and Beau from reconciling your differences?"

"That's the question, isn't it? I've asked myself the same thing a hundred times these past few weeks. I suppose some people are like that, always stirring up trouble…"

Molly couldn't believe what she was hearing. "I'm not here to stir up trouble," she said. "I'm just here to find out about my mother."

"*Still?* You mean nobody's told you the truth yet?"

Molly shook her head. She wasn't sure why, but she didn't want to talk about her mother with this angry, venomous woman.

"Well, that figures." Doris picked up one of Nicky's trucks from a corner of the room and moved it to another. "Really, Molly, this is pointless. I'm here to pick up a few things for the kids, not to argue with you. I wouldn't want the children to be a burden on you."

Molly's cheeks flamed with heat, but she managed to sound reasonable when she said, "In the first place, the kids aren't a burden. And in the second place, Beau asked me to stay with them. He's expecting to find them here when he comes home."

"That's easily fixed. I'll leave him a note and tell him where they are. I can have them back here five minutes after he calls."

Although she forced a smile, inside Molly was shaking like a leaf. Doris wasn't particularly frightening, so what was it about this that bothered her so? "It's not really a question of how soon you could bring them back,'' she said. Her voice still sounded almost normal, much to her surprise. ''I told Beau I'd stay with the kids, and I really can't change plans without his consent.''

Doris sighed and propped her hands on the table as if she meant business. ''I don't think you understand, Molly. I'm not asking for permission. I'm *telling* you that I'm not letting my grandchildren back into this house until their father gets home.''

Her voice was filled with such venom Molly had to fight not to recoil from it. ''Is it just because Beau's gone, or are you saying that you have a problem with *me?*''

The expression on Doris's face left little to wonder about. ''I really don't think we need to dig up all that old unpleasantness, do we?''

Molly stopped moving completely. ''What old unpleasantness?''

''Oh, I think we both know the answer to that.'' Doris gave an airy wave of her hand. ''You know what they say—the apple doesn't fall far from the tree.''

''And I'm supposed to be the apple in your analogy?''

Doris looked at Molly over the tops of her glasses. ''I don't blame you for what your mother did, Molly, but where children are concerned, you simply can't take chances. Everybody knew what your mother was up to back then—everybody but poor Frank, that is. But he found out eventually. The truth always comes out, no matter how hard people try to hide it.''

The pounding of Molly's heart should have drowned out Doris's hateful words, but they came through loud and clear. A dozen questions rose to Molly's lips, but she wouldn't let herself ask them. Doris was too angry, too filled with whatever ugly emotion drove her, and Molly didn't want it to throw shadows on her mother's memory and make things worse.

She picked up Brianne's sweater, where Doris had dropped it, and very deliberately carried it to the washing machine. "I'm sorry, Doris, but I can't let you take the kids' things without Beau's permission. You're welcome to call him. If he's not flying, I'm sure he'll have his cell phone on. I just need to know that he's agreeable. I'm sure you understand."

"You don't have the right to tell me no. Those are my grandchildren."

"I understand that, but Beau is their father, and he asked *me* to stay with them." Something flashed in the back of her mind, but it was gone so quickly she couldn't identify it. Again, she tried appealing to Doris's better nature. "I know you're concerned about Brianne and Nicky. The past year has been rough on them—even an outsider can see that. It's also obvious that you love them and you want what's best for them."

"Don't patronize me," Doris snapped. "It's insulting."

Molly held up both hands to avoid the accusation. "I'm not trying to do either. I know how hard divorce can be, and I know that when one person makes a decision, it affects everyone around them. I know you love Heather, and this has been hard on you, too."

Doris didn't respond, which was enough to give Molly hope that maybe she'd listen. She'd never forgive herself if she made Beau's situation worse.

Motioning toward the table, she tried again. "Why don't you sit down? I was just about to make some tea, and I'm sure if we try, we can find a compromise."

"I don't need a compromise with *you*."

"But you do. It's not about me or about you. Brianne and Nicky are the ones who matter, and they'll be hurt if you and I can't at least be civil to one another as long as I'm here."

Doris's frown was grim, but she was obviously considering the suggestion.

Molly grabbed the kettle and headed for the sink, chattering as if Doris had uttered a gracious acceptance. "I've been meaning to talk to Beau about Brianne," she said as she filled the kettle. "She's nearly thirteen, and she seems very interested in hair and makeup and clothes and shoes." She stole a glance at Doris, who moved slowly toward a chair and gripped it with both hands. "I was going to suggest a shopping trip—maybe to Jackson? But I'm sure she'd rather go with you than me."

To Molly's surprise, Doris almost smiled. "I'm not so sure about that, but thank you. It's a nice gesture."

"The kids love you, Doris. You've been through something very upsetting together, and they need you to help them make sense of it. But I know from experience that it will only hurt them, to hide things from them or try to paint a pretty picture over the truth."

She found tea in the cupboard and smiled sadly. "I don't know exactly what happened between my parents before my mom died, but I *do* know it isn't even close to what my dad told me. I found out a couple of weeks ago that my parents were having problems in their marriage. I'm thirty-three, and I never knew that before I came back here. I'm so angry with him now, I can hardly stand to think about him—not because he and my mom were having trouble, but because he lied to me about it." She carried cups and saucers to the table.

"The truth is sometimes hard to take, but even when you're a kid, the truth is better than a lie."

"I don't believe that. I don't believe it would be better for those children to be told their mother isn't coming back."

"It would be better than being told she's coming back to live with their father when you know that's not going to happen."

"I don't *know* that," Doris insisted, but the sadness in her eyes told a different story. She shot to her feet again and turned her back on Molly. "It's a phase, that's all. A ridiculous, hurtful, selfish, indulgent phase."

The pain she was feeling grew more evident with every word, and Molly wondered if the poor woman had ever let herself discuss Heather's decision with anyone. Judging from the way she moved and the look on her face, Molly would bet she'd kept the hurt and anger locked away all this time.

The kettle began to whistle and Molly turned to get it. "I don't know Heather well enough to understand why she made the choices she made, but I don't think you should keep blaming yourself for what she did."

Doris whipped back around, and the grief on her face was so powerful Molly felt as if it might tear her in two. "I'm her *mother*. She is what she is because of me. I don't know what I did wrong. I don't know where I made my mistakes. I've gone over everything a million times since she came and told me what she was going to do. Maybe if I'd intervened more when she argued with her father. Maybe if I'd been stricter. If I'd taken her to church more often. Or less. Maybe I was *too* strict."

The older woman covered her face with her hands,

and her shoulders began to shake. "I've tried to make it up to those poor kids, but I can't. No matter how much I do, it's just never enough."

Molly abandoned the tea and moved closer to the woman, whose pain seemed to fill the entire room. "Oh, but, Mrs. Preston, don't you see? You don't have to make anything up to them. They don't blame you for what their mother did, and nobody expects you to 'fix' what their mother has done. You can't make Heather's choices for her. You're not personally responsible for the ones she makes. And if this isn't a choice, if she really can't change who she is, then doesn't she need you to just love her?"

"Do you have any idea what people will think if they find out?" The question came out in a rush of agony.

Molly's heart softened even more. "Some people might think the worst, but some won't. And surely Heather matters more to you than a bunch of neighbors. She's your own flesh and blood."

When Doris didn't say anything, Molly decided to leave that subject alone.

"What the kids need is for you to fill part of the gap Heather's left by going away. But that should be easy when you love somebody as much as you love them."

Doris dropped her hands and regarded Molly intently. "I guess I owe you an apology," she said after what felt like forever. "I misjudged you." She smiled ruefully and dug into her handbag, finally producing a tissue, which she put to work wiping away the remnants of her tears. "You really aren't anything like Ruby, are you?"

Molly's smile evaporated. "I don't understand." She wasn't sure she wanted to.

"It's a compliment, dear," Doris said, wagging the tissue in the space between them. "Your mother was a wonderful woman in a lot of ways, but she wasn't perfect, was she? And when you think about what she put your poor father through…"

Molly could hardly bear the thought of hearing the truth from Doris, but she forced herself to ask, "What did she put him through?"

"Well, I don't know all the details of course. But I do know that Ruby could be quite the flirt when we were younger. The men our age were just wild for her." Judging from the expression on Doris's face, a young man *she'd* cared about had probably been one of them. "All I know is that she lied to Frank about something. Whatever it was, it nearly destroyed him. I never could feel the same about her afterward."

"But you don't know what?"

"No, but I can guess."

Molly wasn't interested in Doris's speculations. She'd already endured enough of those.

"It's not good to speak ill of the dead," Doris said, "but I'm glad to see you're not like her, after all." She tucked the tissue away and glanced at the clock on the wall behind her. "I know you're making tea, but I really can't stay. I'll phone Beau in a day or two about taking Brianne shopping. You'll let him know?"

Molly nodded. She couldn't do anything else.

But as she watched Doris walk back to her car, she knew she'd just been pushed into making a decision she'd been putting off too long. Sooner or later, she was going to learn the truth about her parents' marriage. It was inevitable. The only real questions were how and when.

IT WAS WELL after dark before Beau finally finished up at the airstrip and headed home. His eyes burned and every muscle in his body felt as if someone had tied it in a knot, but he'd made a substantial amount of money for two days' work and wasn't about to complain. He just hoped that the kids hadn't been too much for Molly. She'd sounded fine when he talked to her that morning, but he hadn't had a spare minute since to check in with her.

The Halloween decorations along Front Street had given way to Thanksgiving, and Beau realized with a start that the holiday was just a couple of weeks away. His mom had invited them all for dinner, including Molly, but he hadn't discussed the invitation with her. Nor had he checked with Doris to make sure the kids would be included in Preston family celebrations.

Life was slowly becoming more organized. He still had a way to go, but the house wasn't a complete disaster anymore, and he had a lot to celebrate this year.

The idea of contacting Heather skittered across his mind, but he shoved it away again. Molly was probably right about him taking the initiative to invite her back into the kids' lives, and he might take her advice one of these days. He just wasn't ready to do so yet.

He pulled into the driveway and turned off the engine, yawning hard enough to make his eyes water. Lights burned in the windows, and the house looked more inviting than it had in months.

On the porch he stopped to watch his family through the window for a few minutes. He was captivated by the sight of Brianne's smile, the sound of Nicky's laughter and the joy on Molly's face. As if someone had opened a door, he felt warmth and something he couldn't identify rushing through him.

Long before Heather had told him the truth, he'd suspected that something was wrong, and his doubts and fears had been eating at him for a long, long time. It had been years since he'd felt anything but tightness and anger and suspicion in the deepest part of him, but those emotions were gone, and he had Molly to thank. And if he and Heather eventually made peace, he'd have Molly to thank for that, too.

He watched as she turned, laughing, and took a sparkly item out of a bag at her feet. Pulling Brianne's hair up on one side, she secured it with the jeweled clip. The delight on his daughter's face shocked him, and his reaction told him that it had been far longer than he'd realized since she'd been truly happy, as well.

Without even trying, Molly had worked miracles in all their lives, and in that moment Beau knew he couldn't let her leave Serenity.

Eager to join them, he reached for the doorknob, but the vibration of his cell phone in his pocket made him draw back his hand. He pulled the phone out, saw Doris's name on the screen and groaned softly. She was the last person he wanted to talk to right now, but maybe it was a good thing she'd called before he got inside where the kids could hear.

He stepped into the shadows and steeled himself for the usual argument, the same old discussion.

"I know you've been away for a couple of days," Doris said when he answered, "but I'd like to talk to you. Is this a good time?"

"Not really. I'm just getting home. I haven't even walked in the door yet."

"It'll only take a minute." She took a deep breath and let it out again slowly. "I'll get the hard part over with first. I owe you an apology. Heather leaving the way she did, announcing after thirty years that she's...not herself...'' She laughed nervously. ''Let's just say that I haven't dealt well with what's happened, and I've tried to place the burden for fixing everything on your shoulders. I shouldn't have done that, and I'm sorry.''

Beau leaned against the porch railing and tried to take in what she'd just told him. ''Okay, but... how...?''

Doris went on as if he hadn't spoken. ''I'd like to stop being angry, the two of us. I thought maybe I could take each of the kids for a day—if that's okay with you. Molly suggested that Brianne might like a shopping trip, and I'm sure Nicky could use some new things, too. I promise there'll be no talk about reconciliations. I won't mention Heather unless the kids bring her up.''

Letting out his own deep breath, Beau glanced toward the bay window. ''That sounds fine, but...''

Doris laughed. ''You're surprised.''

''To put it mildly.'' He pulled out the gloves he'd stuffed into his pockets and put them on again. ''Don't get me wrong—I don't have a problem with what you're suggesting, but I don't get it. What happened?''

''Can we just say that I came to my senses and leave it at that?''

''I guess so.'' He turned up his collar to protect his ears from the cold. ''For what it's worth, Doris, I think this will be good for the kids.''

''You won't mind if I keep hoping Heather comes to *her* senses one of these days?''

''Not a bit—as long as you understand that there's nothing but the kids left between us.''

"I think I can finally accept that. At least, I'll do my best."

"Well, I can't ask for more than that." Beau pushed away from the railing and stretched to work the kinks out of his back. "When did you want to take the kids?"

"I was thinking maybe Brianne this Saturday, and Nicky the next?"

"That sounds fine to me." He still wasn't completely convinced he was talking to Doris—although this woman *did* bear a strong resemblance to the woman Doris had been a handful of years ago. He caught a glimpse of Molly near the sink and shifted the phone to his other ear. "You said something about Molly earlier. *She's* the one who suggested these shopping trips?"

"You're not angry with her, are you?"

"Of course not." He moved so he could see Molly better through the window—the curve of her cheek and the smile that was becoming so familiar. "I just wanted to make sure, that's all. I didn't realize you and Molly were friendly."

"Well, I don't know if you can say we're friendly, exactly." Doris laughed uneasily. "But she was kind enough to talk with me today, and she made sense." Doris paused. "I suppose you could do worse for yourself, Beau."

Her compliment was so backhanded, he almost laughed aloud. "Well, yes," he said. "I suppose I could."

In the house, Molly walked back to the table. She slid an arm around Brianne's shoulders and ruffled Nicky's hair with her free hand, then took her own seat and began to work, still chatting easily with the kids and creating a picture so homey it twisted Beau's heart.

Somehow she'd managed to create the home he'd been craving for years. The happy children. The home-cooked meals. The laundry under reasonable control and only a mild amount of clutter. Laughter and music and happiness. She'd created them all. She'd succeeded where he had failed—and once again, he was relying on someone else.

"I'll have Brianne call so you can set up the details," he said to Doris. "And we need to talk about Thanksgiving. I want to make sure you have time with the kids that day."

"Bless you, Beau. You're a good man."

With her endorsement ringing in his ears, he stuffed the phone back into his pocket and headed for the door again. But his heart sat heavily in his chest, and his future felt like a rock on his shoulder.

Did he love Molly? Or did he love what she'd done for him? The kids. The house. The renewed self-confidence. He just didn't know.

He leaned against the wall, the contentment he'd felt a few minutes ago slipping away from him. He thought he loved her, but what if he didn't? What if someday down the road, he had to look at her and confess that he'd mistaken gratitude for love? Too many people could get hurt if he was acting on feelings that weren't genuine, and he just couldn't do that to Molly or to the kids.

He was going to have to tell her the truth and ask for time. But he had the sick feeling that it was going to be the hardest thing he'd ever had to do.

CHAPTER SIXTEEN

Two hours later, Beau walked slowly across the lawn beside Molly. The evening had dragged on end-lessly, and he'd been dreading this moment ever since he'd walked in the door. Molly and the kids had looked so happy.

Looked? Hell, they *were* happy.

Brianne was herself again after far too long, and he was trying to remember if he'd ever seen Nicky so carefree. So what was wrong with him? Why couldn't he just relax and enjoy Molly's company? Why couldn't he let things keep going the way they were?

Because he knew how it felt to be lied to, that was why. Because he'd been through this once before, and he knew how he'd felt when Heather announced that she'd never really been in love with him. He couldn't let things keep going if there was any chance at all he'd ever say those words to Molly.

As if she could feel him thinking, Molly slid a cu-rious glance at him. "You're awfully quiet tonight. Was there some trouble on the flight?"

He shook his head and resisted the urge to put an arm around her or hold her hand. The contact might make him feel better, but she'd hate him for it when she heard what he had to say. "The flight was fine."

Although he'd tried to sound normal, he must not have succeeded. The smile that had been hovering on her lips faded and her eyes filled with concern. "Is there some other problem?"

"I don't know if you'd call it a problem…" He glanced back at the house and asked himself one last time if he was doing the right thing. He stopped walking. "Yeah, I guess it is a problem."

She touched his arm gently. "What is it?"

Her concern nearly made him change his mind. It had been too long since anyone had looked at him like that, and he liked the way it made him feel. But that was just another part of the problem. He had to look away from her to get the words out. "I think we need to reconsider what's going on here."

He heard her soft, indrawn breath, then, "I'm not sure I understand."

Beau forced himself to look at her again. She deserved that much. "I came home tonight and saw you with the kids, the house smelling wonderful, dinner on the table, laundry done. Brianne's doing great, and Nicky adores you. Even Doris is acting like a new woman. You've worked miracles around here, Molly, and I'm grateful."

Her dark eyes roamed his face. "But?"

"But it also hit me that I haven't been fair to you— or to the kids. I swore I was going to take care of my kids on my own, without help. I swore I was going to get my house in order on my own. Well, the kids are doing great, and the house is in order, but I'm not the one responsible."

"Of course you are."

"No. I haven't learned how to balance. It's still all or nothing for me, and that's not good enough when you have a family. Having you here just makes it easier for me to compound that mistake. If there's anything good going on inside that house, it's your doing, Molly, not mine.'' She shook her head again, but he had to get the rest out. ''You've turned the kids around. You've given me a new lease on life, and you have no idea how grateful I am.''

''But now it's over? Is that what you're trying to say?''

''Not *over*.'' He wanted to reach for her, but he wouldn't let himself. ''I feel things for you I never expected to feel again. But what if it's not real? What if it's a rebound thing, or just bone-deep relief that someone's come along to help me out of the mess that was my life?''

Pain flashed through her eyes an instant before they shuttered. ''I see.''

''I'm not explaining this well.''

''I think you're explaining it perfectly.''

''I don't want this thing between us to be over. I just need some time to figure out what it is.''

''It's friendship, Beau. A few laughs. A kiss here and there. I don't recall ever asking you for a commitment or giving you one in return.'' The coldness in her eyes told him more than the words she spoke.

''But I'm not sure I *don't* want one,'' he said. ''All I'm asking for is time and a little space. I just need a chance to get myself together and figure out what I'm feeling.''

She took two steps backward, but her eyes never left his face. ''You can have all the time you want, Beau. All the space in the world. I never meant to crowd you.''

''But you haven't. That's not what I'm saying. I just…'' He rubbed his face. ''I care about you, Molly. You must know that.''

Her lips formed a hurt smile. "You don't have to say that, Beau. I'm a big girl and I've been rejected before. I think I can survive one more time."

He closed the distance between them and took her hands in his. "I'm making a mash of this, obviously. I *care* about you, Molly. A lot. But I came home tonight and saw you and the kids together looking like a Norman Rockwell painting. And then I talked to Doris and found out that you'd even turned *her* around."

When he felt her getting ready to pull away again, he tightened his grip on her hands and locked eyes with her. "After Heather left, all I wanted was to prove that I could take care of the kids and the house on my own. That's it. And then you came, and I started falling in love with you. You were so beautiful, and I felt young and handsome and worth something again. It was wonderful and exciting and so good for my shattered ego."

Her gaze dropped to their joined hands. "And you think you were alone in that?" She looked back at him, and the raw emotion in her eyes sucked his breath away. "You think my rotten marriage didn't leave a huge hole in *my* self-esteem?"

"I know it did. That's another reason why we can't take this too fast. The kids are another. But honest to God, Molly, if things keep going the way they have been, I'll propose to you before the end of the week. The kids adore you, and I could be a happy man with you in my life and in my bed every night. But I'm not going to ask you for that until I'm absolutely sure of what I'm feeling."

She nodded, and for a split second he thought she truly understood. But then she stepped away from his embrace and looked at him with eyes so cold only a fool could fail to see that he'd lost her.

"Take all the time you need, Beau. I'm leaving Serenity." He tried to reach for her again, but she evaded him easily. "I understand that you're confused, and I understand why. I'm not angry. I knew the risks that came with falling in love with you. It certainly isn't the first time I've been down this road. I want someone who loves *me*, not someone who's trying to convince himself that he does. I love Brianne and Nicky, and it's going to be hell to leave them, but I won't stay just because they like this setup." She picked up her purse and slung it over her shoulder. "In the end, they'll only get hurt—and so will I."

MOLLY ZIPPED the last of her bags closed and told herself to pick them up, but she couldn't move. She stood there, blinking back tears and staring at the bed for probably the hundredth time that morning. She'd only been here six weeks, but already this cabin felt like more of a home than anything else she'd ever known.

She'd let herself get caught up in the fantasy. She'd allowed herself to believe that Beau and his kids could be family. That she could fill the empty places in her heart with someone else's life. And now she was paying the price.

A noise from outside caught her attention, and she flew to the window, foolishly hoping that Beau had changed his mind, that he'd realized he loved her and that he'd come to stop her from leaving. But the blond head she saw near the swing wasn't Beau's.

Nicky stood on the porch, hitting one of the chairs with a stick, and she could tell by the deep scowl on his face that Beau had told him she was leaving. She pulled back sharply and tried to think, but she already knew she wouldn't try to avoid him. No matter what happened between her and Beau, she wouldn't purposely hurt the kids.

She checked out the window again. Nicky had shifted to the edge of the porch, but the stick was still moving, and she knew it wasn't going to get better until she talked to him. Grabbing her sweater, she stepped out into the relatively mild morning. "Nicky? Are you all right?"

He whipped around at the sound of her voice and the eagerness on his little face pummeled her heart. "Are you leaving? Dad says you're leaving, but I think he's lying."

Molly would have given anything not to have this conversation. She sat on one of the chairs and leaned forward so she could look the boy in the eye. "He's not lying, Nicky. I am leaving. I've been here too long, already."

His eyes filled with tears before she stopped speaking. "But I thought you were going to stay. I thought you liked us."

Was it possible to die from heartache? Molly wondered. She drew Nicky onto her lap and kissed the top of his head, but his nearness only made the pain worse. "Oh, Nicky, I *do* like you. You have no idea how much. You're a wonderful boy, and it's not because of you that I'm leaving."

"Then why?"

It was on the tip of her tongue to make up a palatable reason, but she'd spent weeks insisting that children deserved the truth and she couldn't offer this child anything less. "I have to go, Nicky. For a while now, your dad and I have been kind of...playing house and having you and Brianne play along. But we finally realized that it's not fair to you two, and I need to go away before somebody's feelings get hurt.''

"Well, it's too late." Nicky swiped his eyes with a sleeve. "Brianne locked herself in her room after breakfast, and Dad's in a really sad mood. You can't leave. They won't like it.''

She was hopeless. A lost cause. She wanted to be over there, deep in the thick of it, working through the problems with them. She wanted it all, the good and the not-so-good that went along with being part of a family. But she *wasn't* part of their family. Beau couldn't have made that any clearer if he'd written it out for her.

Resting her cheek against the top of Nicky's head, she struggled to speak. "I'm so sorry that Brianne is unhappy, and I wish your dad wasn't sad. But your dad and I aren't in love, and we're not going to be a family. I don't want you and Brianne to think that we are.''

Nicky jerked away from her and slid to the ground. "That's not fair!"

"I know it's not. It wasn't fair of us to let you and Brianne think things were different than they are." No fairer than it had been to let herself get swept up in that old dream. "I'm so sorry, Nicky. I wish I could stay, but I just can't.''

"Well, that stinks!" He jumped from the porch and swung back around to glare at her. "You're just like my mom, and I don't like you anymore.''

With her heart shattered in a million pieces, Molly watched him run across the lawn as fast as his legs could move. She wanted desperately to go after him, to tell him she'd stay and to promise that everything would be okay, but she didn't let herself take a step.

She'd been foolish and foolhardy. She'd been reckless and irresponsible, and not just with her own heart. If she went through hell getting over this, it was no more than she deserved.

MOLLY WAS HALFWAY through town when she realized that, once again, she was running away from the one thing she had come for. She pulled to the side of the road and turned the car around, making her way through quiet neighborhoods toward Louise Duncan's house. After all, what did she have to lose? No matter what she learned about her parents at this point, the pain couldn't be worse than what she felt over losing Beau and the kids.

She parked in Louise's driveway a few minutes later and studied the house as she walked to the front door. Louise had always loved to decorate for the holidays, and that apparently hadn't changed over the years. Uncarved pumpkins perched on bales of hay, sheaves of dried cornstalks tied together with twine leaned against the house, and a garland of silk leaves in autumn colors rimmed the front door.

A shaft of pain lanced her, so deep she thought it might tear her in two. She hadn't let herself think about spending the holidays with Beau and the kids, but on some level she must have been planning to. Thanksgiving wouldn't be so hard, but knowing she wouldn't be with them for Christmas made her almost sick.

She pushed aside those thoughts and replaced them with memories of Ruby and Louise planning trips into Jackson to buy decorations and poring over mail-order catalogs together. She remembered the laughter they'd shared, the phone calls...the secrets? She could only hope.

When she rang the bell, a Thanksgiving tune she

remembered from schooldays began to play. Molly knew that if Ruby had been here still, she'd have used the same tune on her own doorbell. She closed her eyes and sent up a silent prayer that Louise would understand her need to know the truth, and that she'd somehow realize that talking to Molly would not betray her old friend. But after several minutes passed with no answer, she began to lose heart.

Just as she was ready to give up, the door inched open and Louise's narrow face appeared in the opening. She didn't look at all surprised to see Molly standing there, and Molly guessed that she'd been watching from a window. The realization was disappointing but not surprising. After all, the woman had spent the past six weeks avoiding her.

Louise had grown thinner, deep wrinkles lined her brow and bracketed her mouth, and her eyes had lost some of their sparkle. Her once-dark hair was liberally streaked with gray, and a pair of thick glasses perched on her nose.

She looked Molly over without expression and sighed heavily. "So you're here."

Just like that. No shock. No surprise. No defiance. Just resigned acceptance of a moment she'd known was inevitable in spite of her efforts to avoid it. Molly should have realized it would be like this. She could have saved herself a lot of heartache.

"I'm here," she said, "and I need to talk to you."

Louise nodded and pushed open the screen door. "You may as well come in. I guess you're not going to go away until you get what you came for."

Molly stepped into the house, which was at once familiar and strange, and followed Louise into the carefully kept living room. Back when they were kids, this room had been a jumble of toys and books, of crayons and paper. Now, it was devoid of clutter and filled with furniture that looked as if it had never been used.

She perched uncomfortably on one end of a stiff white couch, while Louise settled into a chair covered in pale-cream brocade. "I know you don't want to talk about what happened between my mom and dad, but I hope you can understand why I need to know."

Louise's eyes clouded and she shook her head. "I wish I could, Molly, but I've never understood why your generation needs to look at everything so hard. Some things are better left alone."

"You wouldn't say that if you'd spent half your life wondering."

For a long moment Louise stared at her, then she shrugged and looked away. "Maybe not. We'll never know." She dragged her gaze back to Molly. "Well? Tell me what you want to know."

Molly sat back on the couch and tried to make herself comfortable. "I don't mean to be rude, but six weeks ago you left town to avoid talking to me. Today you're ready to just tell me anything? I don't get it. Why the change of heart?"

"It's not a change of heart, Molly. I still don't want to discuss your mother's tragedy. But all your questions have stirred up curiosity. It's just a matter of choosing the lesser evil. I can tell you what you want to know, or I can leave you out there asking questions and making other people wonder."

The answer disappointed Molly, but she wasn't going to quibble. She set her purse on the floor beside her feet and took a deep breath to steel herself for what was coming. She'd put together much of the puzzle, but there were still missing pieces, and she knew instinctively that finding them would cause more pain and heartache than anything she'd experienced yet.

"I've been told that Mom and Dad argued a lot before Mom's accident. Is that true?"

"You really don't remember?"

"I really don't."

Louise sat back in her chair and linked her hands on her knees. "Yes, it's true. They argued almost constantly."

"But why? That's so unlike what I *do* remember about life at home, I can hardly believe it."

"Oh, it's true, all right." Louise twisted her hands together slowly. "It was a horrible time for both of them—and for anyone who loved them."

"What happened? I thought they were happy."

"They were...until your father found out something he was never meant to know." Louise turned her head and stared out the window, as if she couldn't bear to look at Molly while she talked. "I suppose, in retrospect, it would have been a good thing for your mother to have told him when it happened, but it didn't seem like a good idea at the time. Of course, we were all so young, and what sounds brilliant at twenty doesn't always sound even a little smart at forty." She slid a thin smile toward Molly. "I was as much a part of this decision as your mother was. I regret it now, but I suppose that doesn't count for much."

Molly was ready to jump out of her skin, but she tried hard to remain patient. "What decision?"

After several moments Louise stood and walked to the window, sighing softly as she stared out at the yard. "We were just kids. I hope you can remember that. Your parents had only been married a couple of years, and things weren't going so well. They were young and foolish and selfish—as we all were, I guess.''

She trailed one finger along the windowsill, then studied it as if she'd never seen it before. ''During that time, your parents weren't happy together. Your mother…'' She flicked an uneasy glance at Molly. ''Ruby was disillusioned and miserable. Marriage to Frank wasn't what she thought it was going to be. Frank spent too much time indulging himself, playing pool with friends and doing all those things young men who aren't ready to be married do.''

''I'll have to take your word for it,'' Molly said. ''That doesn't sound like Dad at all.''

''The man you knew *wasn't* that man. He changed when your mother became pregnant. It was so dramatic, it was like someone had flipped a switch.'' Louise smiled sadly. ''If we'd had any idea becoming a father would have affected him that way, we'd have done things differently. We just never expected the marriage to last, and then, when Ruby realized that it could, there never seemed to be a good time to clear the air.'' She ran a hand along her collarbone and turned back to face Molly fully. ''We didn't know, Molly. We didn't think—that's what it boils down to. And by the time we realized what a difference it made in Frank, by the time we realized how much he'd changed…well, it was too late. Or so we thought.''

Cold dread filled Molly, but she couldn't let herself back down now. Voices from the past drifted in and out of her mind as wispy pieces of memory began to surface. So much anger, so much heartache, and all because of her. That was what she remembered most. *She* was the one they'd argued over. She was the one who'd killed their marriage.

She met Louise's gaze helplessly. "It was about me."

"No, dear. Not you. It wasn't your fault. Your mother and I… It was her secret, but I encouraged her. I told her it would be okay. I honestly believed it would be. How were we to know that Frank would turn into such a devoted father? He was so sweet with you, so utterly besotted, neither Ruby nor I had the heart to tell him that he wasn't really your father."

The ice turned to fire, and Molly closed her eyes to block out the pain. But the sudden, clear images of her father's face, hurt and angry, wouldn't go away. And the sounds of her mother's tearful pleas for forgiveness grew louder and louder.

A sob caught in her throat and hot tears spilled onto her cheeks even before she realized she was crying. She'd felt so responsible for the arguments that the accident must have been too much to bear. No wonder she'd locked the truth away for so long.

"I thought I'd killed her."

"That's what I was afraid of." Louise crossed to sit beside Molly and took both her hands lovingly. "I haven't been trying to protect Ruby, sweetheart. She's beyond needing that from me, but you're her daughter, and I couldn't hurt you." She blinked several times and sighed wearily. "Finding out the truth devastated Frank. There were only a few of us who knew about Ruby. Phyllis Graham, and me. Even…the other man never knew. But Frank was certain the story would come out if he stayed here, and he was terrified of losing you. He couldn't have borne that."

Molly almost asked who the other man was, but something stopped her. She didn't want to know. Not right now. Maybe later. She knew where to find the answers when she needed them. "So that's why Dad wanted to divorce Mom."

"He claimed he did, but it was just his hurt talking. He said it so much, though, she finally did something about it. But I don't think Frank would have let the divorce go through. He was hurt and angry, but he also had a heart of gold, and I think eventually they would have worked things out." She patted Molly's hand. "That's what I always tell myself, anyway."

Another wave of memories washed over Molly, and she closed her eyes. Sadness nearly overwhelmed her. She'd come to Serenity to discover the truth, and now she had. But she hadn't expected to lose her identity—and her heart—in the bargain.

CHAPTER SEVENTEEN

MOLLY HELD her breath as her stepmother dangled a pair of jade earrings from her fingers, turning them this way and that to catch the light from the small Christmas tree she'd thrown up at the last minute. Christmas was just a week away, but Molly's heart wasn't in it.

She kept imagining what Beau's house must look like decorated for the holidays. She kept picturing the fun at WinterFest and fantasizing about being there with Beau, Brianne and Nicky. This surprise visit from Cassandra helped distract her a little, and she'd be forever grateful.

Cassandra's eyes glittered with appreciation and she smiled as she lowered the earrings to the coffee table. "Oh, Molly, these are wonderful. I truly think these are my favorites." She glanced at the length of black velvet across the table, where Molly had displayed her most recent creations. "The setting looks almost like lace."

Even though she knew she was still a long way from matching her mother's skill, Molly flushed with pride. She tilted her head to one side and pretended to consider. With Cassandra's rich auburn hair and emerald eyes, the earrings were flattering—as she'd known they would be when she made them.

She picked up a small, red-velvet box, the trademark of Ruby Lane Creations, and put the jade earrings inside. "Take them," she said, holding out the box to her stepmother. "As a Christmas present."

Cassandra's eyes widened, then narrowed speculatively. "That's a lovely gift, Molly. But they're exquisite, and I feel a little selfish."

"Why? You're family. I made them for you." Molly refrained from stating the obvious, but the words echoed in the space between them. *You're the only family I have.* Besides, she hadn't been able to face shopping this year and was having enough trouble acknowledging the holiday at all.

Instead, she'd given up returning to graphic design and had thrown herself into turning Ruby Lane into a viable business. The reaction she'd had so far gave her hope that she'd be able to support herself in time. She'd used hard work, and lots of it, to keep thoughts about Christmas at bay.

The small tree in the window of her St. Louis apartment was her only concession to the holidays. She hadn't had the heart to decorate, to dust off her collection of Christmas CDs or to mail out holiday cards. Next year, she'd promised herself a hundred times. Next year, when her heart wasn't still so sore, when the pain of losing so much wasn't quite as raw.

She realized that Cassandra was watching her, so she forced a smile and held out the box again. "I want you to have them, Cassandra. Please take them."

Cassandra took the box, but Molly could see that she still wasn't convinced. She leaned forward to kiss Molly's cheek, and then cupped her face with one hand. "Oh, sweetheart, I wish there was something I could do to help you get through this."

"I'm fine," Molly insisted. She couldn't allow herself to be anything else. She stood and began straightening the books on her shelf as if there was nothing more important in the world.

"Maybe you should go back to Serenity, Molly. I'm pretty sure that's where your heart is. Besides, there are just too many unresolved issues there for you."

Molly shot a look at her stepmother over her shoulder. "Let's not talk about Serenity tonight, okay?"

"Why not?"

"Because it's nearly Christmas, and because that's a closed chapter in my life."

"Is it?" Cassandra stood and moved toward her. "Molly, honey, it can't be a closed chapter in your life. Not while you're still so angry with your dad. Not while you're still in love with Beau."

Molly pulled away sharply. "Don't, Cassandra. Please."

But her stepmother was relentless. "I know you're angry with me, but I have to say this. If I don't, I'll never be able to live with myself." She stepped in front of Molly and held her so she couldn't get away. "I know you think this is none of my business, but we *are* family. How we got this way doesn't matter, just like it doesn't matter how you and Frank became family. He *was* your father. He will always be your father."

Molly's heart twisted painfully. "He didn't *tell* me. And don't say he died too soon, because he had fifteen years to tell me the truth."

"He made a mistake. A *big* mistake, but still just a mistake. And it was because he loved you so much. Surely you know that."

Molly nodded. She would never deny it, no matter how much his deception hurt.

"I know you'd be happier if he'd never done anything wrong, but he was just a man, sweetheart. Just a man. No better and no worse than anyone else. And certainly not perfect.''

''I never expected him to be perfect,'' Molly protested.

''And yet you can't forgive him? For holding on as tightly as he could to the one person in the world he loved with all his soul? For making sure that he didn't lose his only daughter? He'd already lost your mother. Losing you would have destroyed him.''

''So instead, he chose to destroy *me?*''

Cassandra's eyes narrowed. ''How did he do that? By loving you? Providing a home for you? Sharing holidays and special occasions with you? Really, Molly, how *did* he destroy you?''

''By lying to me. I don't even know who I am anymore.''

Her stepmother's eyes grew hard. ''Shame on you. You're Frank and Ruby Lane's daughter, just as you've always been. That hasn't changed, and it won't change unless you want it to. If that other man had been any kind of a man at all, he would have known about you and he would have fought Frank for the right to be your father.''

She lowered her hand and turned back to the table. Her fingers lingered over the velvet box for a moment as if she couldn't decide whether to take the earrings or leave them. ''This is no different from children who are adopted. The birth parents are in their lives just long enough to get them here. Their *real* parents search until they find them.''

Images of Brianne and Nicky flashed through Molly's head, but that only made her mood worse. ''It's not the same,'' she argued. ''But I'm not surprised you're taking his side. I wouldn't expect anything else.''

"*His* side? Wanting you to stop hurting yourself is taking *his* side?'' Cassandra laughed humorlessly. "It must be nice to think you've never made a decision that's hurt another person.''

"That's not fair,'' Molly shot back.

"Isn't it? Do you think your decision to leave Brianne and Nicky is so very different from your dad's decision to stay with you? You did what you wanted, and you seem to feel your decision was justified.''

Molly gasped in shock. "That's so unfair! I didn't do what I wanted to do. And I never meant to hurt the kids. I left because Beau didn't want me to stay.''

"Really?'' Cassandra trailed one finger along the top of the velvet box. "I thought you said he *asked* you to stay.''

"Yes, while he tried to talk himself into loving me.''

"Are you sure that's what he was doing?''

"You weren't there,'' Molly said flatly. "You don't know.''

Cassandra forced a smile. "Well, you're right about that. And I don't want to argue with you. If you can't go back, you can't go back. I just hate to see you so unhappy. It's been far too long since I saw you smile.''

Molly tried to rectify that, but her lips felt stiff and cold and she knew she failed miserably.

"Are you sure you won't come with me to Florida? We could spend Christmas with my mother and the rest of the week having fun.''

Molly shook her head. "Thanks, but you need to spend time with your family, and I wouldn't be good company, anyway. Besides, I've already committed to spending Christmas Eve at the children's hospital. I can't leave them in the lurch.''

She tried again to smile, and this time thought she was a little more successful. ''I'll be okay, Cassandra. Just give me time.''

But Cassandra didn't look convinced, and Molly wasn't, either. Since she'd been back in St. Louis, she felt worse than she had when she left Serenity. She had an overwhelming longing for home, but she had no idea where that was.

''I AM SO TIRED of watching you mope,'' Gwen said as she handed Beau a wrench. He lay on his sister's kitchen floor with his head under the sink, dodging tiny pieces of hard-water deposit and other gunk that fell from the pipe seam over his face.

He closed his fist around the cold metal and tried to pretend she hadn't said anything.

But his sister wasn't one to let a little thing like being ignored stop her. ''When are you going to do something about it? That's what I want to know.''

Beau fought with the pipe fitting for a minute and sent another shower of dried calcium into his face. He brushed the worst of it away and leaned up just enough to see his sister's knees. ''What *I* want to know is why your damn sink had to act up three days before Christmas. And while we're at it, maybe you could explain again why your husband isn't the one down here getting a faceful of garbage every time he moves.''

Gwen nudged his foot with one of hers. ''You're lucky the sink didn't wait until Christmas morning,'' she said in that no-nonsense tone she used with the kids. ''And what do you want Riley to do? Close the store this close to Christmas? You know what kind of grief people would give him if he did that.''

Beau knew, but it didn't make him feel a whole lot better. He wriggled out from under the sink and stood, brushing dirt and debris from his hair. ''This is going to be a bigger job than I expected. The fitting's shot, and the U-neck doesn't look much better. I can drive over to Hinkley's and pick up the supplies, but you're going to be without water for a couple hours more.''

''Great. I didn't want to cook dinner, anyway. So you and the kids want to join us at the Burger Shack? My treat. We'll stop by Hinkley's afterward.''

He laughed and reached for the sweater he'd left over the back of a chair. ''Your treat? You'd better believe we're coming.''

''Well, it's the least I can do.'' She waved a hand toward a basket on the counter. ''Grab that, would you? I promised Lisa Simms we'd look in on Hazel tonight, and I put together a little basket of goodies for her.''

Grabbing the basket with one hand, Beau swept the other through his hair once more. Hazel Simms had been Beau's fifth-grade teacher, and he'd always had a soft spot in his heart for her. ''I haven't seen Hazel in a while. How's she doing?''

''She's fine. Just a little lonely. This is her first Christmas without Jonathan, and it's hard on her.'' Gwen snagged her keys from a hook by the door and leaned into the family room to tell the kids to get their things and come outside to the driveway. ''I forgot to ask—did you and Aaron get the lights up at the Parkers okay?''

''With a lot of direction from Sheldon.'' Beau closed the cupboard doors, shut off the Christmas lights in the kitchen and followed Gwen to the garage. ''He may have had a heart attack two months ago, but it sure hasn't slowed him down much.''

"That's good news, right?''

He grinned and opened the door for her. "Right. God willing, he'll be raring to go in time for next year's WinterFest, and maybe I'll finally be able to step down.''

Gwen looked at him. "Oh, puh-leeze. You don't want to step down. Don't even give me that load of horse manure. Why don't you just admit that you're like Dad and Grandpa and that you live for your committees?''

"I don't live for them," Beau argued. "I enjoy them, but there's a time and place for everything. This isn't my time to be involved in all that stuff.''

She shot him another look as she headed toward the door of her minivan. "Apparently this isn't the time in your life to be happy, either, is it?''

"Don't go there, Gwen. I don't want to talk about that in front of the kids.''

"Really? Why not?''

Because Brianne had become moody and sad since Molly left, and because Nicky asked about her every day. And because Beau himself had been fighting a horrible empty feeling for weeks. But he didn't want to admit that to his sister. "Because it's almost Christmas, and there's nothing to talk about.''

"Oh, there's plenty to talk about," Gwen said with a laugh. "You just don't like to hear what anybody else has to say.''

Beau put the basket on the floor of the van and climbed inside. "You know what, Gwen? You have a way of making a man wish he was under a sink with a faceful of gunk.''

She laughed as if he'd said something wonderful. "And you have a way of not hearing anything you don't want to hear. Face it, Beau, you blew it."

"You don't get it, do you?"

"I get that you freaked out because you realized you needed Molly in your life." Gwen stuck the key in the ignition, but she didn't turn it. "I get that you're still freaked out by the idea that the great Beau Julander might need a little help now and then. But you're right. I don't get why you'd let a wonderful woman like Molly, a woman who was perfect for you by the way, get away because you're too arrogant to accept a little help from time to time."

"Arrogant?" The word shot out of his mouth and echoed through the garage. "Are you kidding me?"

"Well, aren't you?"

"Hell, no!"

"I see." Wearing an annoyingly superior smile, Gwen pressed the remote to open the garage door and turned the key in the ignition. When a Christmas song came to life on the stereo, she turned down the volume so she could continue railing at him. "So it's perfectly all right for Sheldon Parker to need help, and for Hazel Simms to need help, and for me to need help from my big strong brother, but you're above all that. Is that how it is?"

He opened his mouth to protest, but he couldn't get the words out.

"You don't mind being needed, but God forbid you should ever need anything. If that's not arrogant," she said, putting the car in reverse and turning her attention to the rearview mirror, "I don't know what is."

Twinkling lights from neighboring houses cast a colorful glow on the snow. Gwen's kids bounced excitedly as they waited for her to back out of the garage, but Brianne and Nicky stood a little apart, and their body language sent a pang of guilt through him. He'd brought something wonderful into their lives and then he'd chased it away again.

Out of arrogance? Fear? Sheer stupidity?

He shifted uncomfortably in his seat and fumbled with his seat belt. "I did the right thing, Gwen. I wasn't sure how I felt, and I didn't let myself take advantage of her."

"And now?"

Now he was about as miserable as a man could get, but how could he go to Molly and ask her to forget what he'd said? The back door slid open and kids piled inside. Beau looked away from his sister, grateful that he didn't have to answer her. But he couldn't evade the answer in his heart.

He'd known for weeks that there was only one thing he wanted for Christmas. He didn't care if she never lifted a finger around the house. It wasn't what she'd done that had gotten under his skin, but who she was. The truth was, he loved everything about her. Her laugh. The way she listened. Her warm and generous spirit. He'd been the worst kind of fool. The very worst.

He had no idea if she'd be willing to forgive him, but what kind of chicken-livered nothing would he be if he didn't at least try? Not the kind he could live with, that was for damn sure.

He nudged Gwen with his elbow. "Do you think Mom would mind if we brought another person to dinner on Christmas?"

Gwen's lips curved into a pleased smile. "Mom?

Are you kidding? Besides, I thought Molly was an invited guest.''

Nicky lunged into the front seat with wide, excited eyes. ''Molly? Are we gonna go get Molly?''

Beau turned so he could see Brianne. ''I'd sure like to.''

Brianne rolled her eyes, but her smile spoke a lot louder. ''Well, duh! It's about time. I can't *believe* how long it takes you to figure things out.''

Laughing, Beau turned up the radio and sang along. He didn't even care that he couldn't carry a tune and only knew half the words. A guy couldn't be perfect, after all.

''YES. YES, OF COURSE I'm still planning to be there.'' Working automatically, Molly saved the changes she'd made to the Ruby Lane Creations Web site and glanced at the clock above her desk. ''I said I'd be there at four, and I'm planning to spend the evening in the oncology ward. Did you need me earlier?''

''Four o'clock is fine,'' the hospital's public-relations coordinator assured her. ''It's just that we always get a number of volunteers on a day like today, but too many of them 'forget' and never show up. I'm just following up to make sure you're still planning to be here.''

Molly rubbed her eyes and rotated her head to work the kinks out of her neck. ''I meant to ask when I called the first time. Is there anything special I need to bring with me?''

''Just yourself. We have plenty of books and games. The important thing is to be here. You can imagine how difficult a day like today is on kids who are stuck in the hospital.''

"I'm sure it is."

"If you want to bring a friend, feel free. The more the merrier, I always say."

Molly stood and stretched. "I'll keep that in mind." In case she stumbled across some poor soul with nowhere else to be.

"Just park in the back near the west entrance," the coordinator went on in a voice full of holiday cheer. "Come up to the fourth floor and introduce yourself at the nurses' station. They'll take you where you need to go from there. And thank you, Molly. You won't regret doing this."

"I'm sure I won't." When she hung up, she wondered what the nurse would say if she knew how badly *Molly* needed this. She turned back to the computer, but the sound of voices singing "I'll Be Home for Christmas" caught her attention and kept her from immersing herself back in her work.

She ignored the twinge of melancholy and decided to try for a little Christmas spirit. She was tired of feeling sorry for herself, and she didn't want to show up at the hospital wearing a long face. That wouldn't be fair to the kids.

Going over to the window, she glanced outside, but she couldn't see anyone at the building across the way or even down the road. The voices grew louder. Closer. Almost as if they were coming from her own front porch. A sign, maybe, that she needed to pull out of her funk and get her head on straight.

One of the singers, a man, went wildly off-key and the group broke off in a fit of laughter that sounded too much like Beau and the kids. She must be going crazy.

Settling back in her chair, she reopened the file she'd

been working on, but before it could load completely, the doorbell chimed and the singing began again. Still off-key. Still painfully familiar.

She stood again and realized she was trembling. *Get a grip,* she told herself sternly. It couldn't possibly be them. But as she hurried through her silent apartment her heart lodged in her throat as if it thought there was a chance.

Over and over she told herself not to hope for the impossible, but none of her warnings did a bit of good. Tears blurred her eyes before she could get to the door, and she knew that even if a miracle hadn't happened— even if she spent Christmas alone—she was going to find a way back to Serenity before the new year.

Hoping desperately, she threw open the door. The three most beautiful faces in the world swam into focus, but she still didn't let herself believe. She could just be wishing so hard that she was turning complete strangers into the family her heart ached for.

The singing came to an abrupt halt and Nicky threw himself at her, grabbing her legs so tightly she nearly lost her balance. Brianne didn't move, but the hope on her face filled Molly's heart with love and happiness.

And Beau...

She couldn't see him because her vision was too blurred with tears, but he was there. She could tell, even though she couldn't see his face. She just knew that she was lost. Or maybe she'd been found.

"Molly."

She couldn't breathe. She couldn't speak. She held Nicky's head against her and let the love she'd been hiding from for so long swell within her. She could hear Cassandra's words playing softly in the back of her mind. They were family. She knew it as certainly as she knew her name. It didn't matter how they got that way.

Dashing tears from her eyes, she blinked at Beau. She wanted to tell him…everything. All the things she'd realized about home and family and love. All the things she'd spent so many years running away from. All the things she was finally ready to turn around and embrace.

He came toward her and took her hand. His voice was gentle, but that sense of humor she loved so much was front and center. "Aw, shoot, kids. She's crying! And I was hoping she'd be *glad* to see us."

Molly laughed through her tears, but his little joke was just what she needed to pull herself together. "You're really here? I can't believe it. You're really and truly here? But how…? Did you drive? Fly? How did you manage this?"

"You're forgetting I have friends in high places. Of course, even *they* can't swing airline tickets on Christmas Eve, so we've been driving all night. But it all worked out. I called Heather and let her know we were coming. I offered to let her meet us here if she wanted to, and she agreed. I was hoping maybe you'd let me hang around while she and the kids spend a few hours together."

"She's coming here?"

"Well, not *here*. I'm meeting her at a motel in town. I'd have waited until we got home, but I thought neutral territory might be a good thing—and besides, I didn't know how long it would take to convince you to talk to me again."

"Apparently not long," Molly said with a laugh. She reached for Brianne and pulled her into a hug. The girl melted against her and wrapped her arms around her. Molly knew they'd bridged the final gap.

Beau leaned against one wall and crossed one foot over the other, whistling softly and looking around with exaggerated patience. After a minute he leaned up and tapped Brianne's shoulder. "You'll let me know when it's my turn?"

"Oh, Daddy." Brianne sniffed loudly and loosened her grip on Molly, but she grinned and the light in her eyes was so beautiful it was all Molly could do to keep from crying again. "He's got something he wants to ask you," she whispered to Molly.

"Oh?"

Beau straightened slowly. "So…what are your plans for the rest of the day?"

She laughed in disbelief. "Nothing set in stone, except that I promised to read to some kids at the children's hospital."

"Need some help?"

"That would be nice."

He put one hand in the pocket of his coat and took Molly's hand with the other. But there he stopped and sent a pointed look in Nicky's direction. The boy drew out a sprig of what must have been mistletoe and stood on his toes, trying to hold it over Molly's head.

Molly bit back a smile, but the joy surging through her was so complete it was almost impossible to maintain a serious expression. After his first question, she was prepared for almost anything.

He dropped to one knee and looked up at her. "And what are your plans for the rest of your life?"

"Nothing set in stone."

He grinned and her heart melted. "I've been a fool," he said. "Everybody I know has been telling me so

since you left Serenity, but I knew it all the time. I
don't have much to offer. Just one old farmhouse, a
cabin to run your business out of, two great kids…and
me." He held out a small black box and his eyes
locked on hers. "I love you, Molly. The kids love you.
We want you to come back."

Her heart was so full it hurt. "I love you, too. All
of you."

Nicky nearly dropped his mistletoe. "Then you'll
come home?"

Brianne elbowed him before Molly could answer.
"Let Dad ask her, you dweeb."

Molly was afraid her heart would burst. "Yes, of
course I'll come back."

Nicky let out a whoop and Brianne nudged Beau
with her knee. "You're supposed to kiss her, Dad."

Casting a look of mock exasperation at his daughter,
Beau got to his feet and drew her close. "All this
help… Maybe I should have come alone, but I wanted
to stack the deck in my favor." He kissed her, and the
joy in Molly's heart filled her entire soul. His lips were
warm and his breath slightly minty. He was familiar
and exciting at the same time, and she hoped she'd
never lose this feeling.

Too soon he drew away and gazed down at her, love
in his eyes. "Marry me. Please. Come home where you
belong."

"Yes," she whispered, and the last remaining empty
space in her heart filled. "Let's go home."

HARLEQUIN *Super*ROMANCE®

GOING BACK

What if you discovered that all you ever wanted were the things you left behind?

Past, Present and a Future
by Janice Carter
(Harlequin Superromance #1178)

Gil Harper was Clare Morgan's first love. At Twin Falls High School, they were inseparable—until the murder of a classmate tore their world, and their relationship, apart. Now, years later, Clare returns to her hometown, where she is troubled by thoughts of what might have been. What if she and Gil had stayed together? Would they be living happily ever after or would they let past hurts ruin their future together? Clare is finally getting a chance to find out....

*Available in January 2004
wherever Harlequin books are sold.*

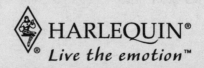

HARLEQUIN®
Live the emotion™

Visit us at www.eHarlequin.com

HSRGBPPF

If you enjoyed what you just read,
then we've got an offer you can't resist!

Take 2 bestselling love stories FREE!

Plus get a FREE surprise gift!

Clip this page and mail it to Harlequin Reader Service®

IN U.S.A.	IN CANADA
3010 Walden Ave.	P.O. Box 609
P.O. Box 1867	Fort Erie, Ontario
Buffalo, N.Y. 14240-1867	L2A 5X3

YES! Please send me 2 free Harlequin Superromance® novels and my free surprise gift. After receiving them, if I don't wish to receive anymore, I can return the shipping statement marked cancel. If I don't cancel, I will receive 6 brand-new novels every month, before they're available in stores. In the U.S.A., bill me at the bargain price of $4.47 plus 25¢ shipping and handling per book and applicable sales tax, if any*. In Canada, bill me at the bargain price of $4.99 plus 25¢ shipping and handling per book and applicable taxes**. That's the complete price, and a savings of at least 10% off the cover prices—what a great deal! I understand that accepting the 2 free books and gift places me under no obligation ever to buy any books. I can always return a shipment and cancel at any time. Even if I never buy another book from Harlequin, the 2 free books and gift are mine to keep forever.

135 HDN DNT3
336 HDN DNT4

Name	(PLEASE PRINT)	
Address	Apt.#	
City	State/Prov.	Zip/Postal Code

* Terms and prices subject to change without notice. Sales tax applicable in N.Y.
** Canadian residents will be charged applicable provincial taxes and GST.
  All orders subject to approval. Offer limited to one per household and not valid to current Harlequin Superromance® subscribers.
  ® is a registered trademark of Harlequin Enterprises Limited.

SUP02   ©1998 Harlequin Enterprises Limited

An offer you can't afford to refuse!

High-valued coupons for upcoming books

**A sneak peek at Harlequin's newest line—
Harlequin Flipside™**

**Send away for a hardcover by *New York Times*
bestselling author Debbie Macomber**

How can you get all this?

Buy four Harlequin or Silhouette books during
October–December 2003, fill out the form below and send
the form and four proofs of purchase (cash register receipts)
to the address below.

I accept this amazing offer!
Send me a coupon booklet:

Name (PLEASE PRINT)

Address   Apt. #

City   State/Prov.   Zip/Postal Code
                                                        098 KIN DXHT

Please send this form, along with your cash register receipts
as proofs of purchase, to:

In the U.S.:
Harlequin Coupon Booklet Offer, P.O. Box 9071, Buffalo, NY 14269-9071

In Canada:
Harlequin Coupon Booklet Offer, P.O. Box 609, Fort Erie, Ontario L2A 5X3

Allow 4–6 weeks for delivery. Offer expires December 31, 2003.
Offer good only while quantities last.

HARLEQUIN®
Live the emotion™

Silhouette®
Where love comes alive™

Visit us at www.eHarlequin.com

Q42003

HARLEQUIN *Super*ROMANCE®

The Rancher's Bride
by Barbara McMahon
(Superromance #1179)

On sale January 2004

Brianna Dawson needs to change her life. And for a Madison Avenue ad exec, life doesn't get more different than a cattle ranch in Wyoming. Which is why she gets in her car and drives for a week to accept the proposal of a cowboy she met once a long time ago. What Brianna doesn't know is that the marriage of convenience comes with a serious stipulation—a child by the end of the year.

Getting Married Again
by Melinda Curtis
(Superromance #1187)

On sale February 2004

To Lexie, Jackson's first priority has always been his job. Eight months ago, she surprised him with a divorce—and a final invitation into her bed. Now Jackson has returned from a foreign assignment fighting fires in Russia and Lexie's got a bigger surprise for him—she's pregnant. Will he be here for her this time, just when she needs him the most?

Available wherever Harlequin books are sold.

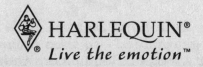

HARLEQUIN®
Live the emotion™

Visit us at www.eHarlequin.com

HSR9MLJ

eHARLEQUIN.com

Looking for today's most popular
books at great prices?
At www.eHarlequin.com, we offer:

- An **extensive selection** of romance
  books by top authors!

- **New** releases, Themed Collections
  and hard-to-find **backlist.**

- A sneak peek at Upcoming books.

- Enticing book **excerpts** and **back
  cover copy!**

- Read recommendations from other
  readers (and post your own)!

- Find out what everybody's reading
  in **Bestsellers.**

- **Save BIG** with everyday discounts
  and exclusive online offers!

- Easy, convenient **24-hour shopping.**

- Our **Romance Legend** will help select
  reading that's *exactly* right for you!

**Your purchases are 100%
guaranteed—so shop online
at www.eHarlequin.com today!**

INTBB1

**Welcome to Koomera Crossing,
a town hidden deep in the Australian Outback.
Let renowned romance novelist Margaret Way
take you there. Let her introduce you to
the people of Koomera Crossing.
Let her tell you their secrets....**

Watch for

Home to Eden,

**available from Harlequin Superromance
in February 2004.**

And don't miss the other Koomera Crossing books:

Sarah's Baby
(Harlequin Superromance #1111, February 2003)

Runaway Wife
(Harlequin Romance, October 2003)

Outback Bridegroom
(Harlequin Romance, November 2003)

Outback Surrender
(Harlequin Romance, December 2003)

Visit us at www.eHarlequin.com   HSRKOOM

COMING NEXT MONTH

#1170 LEAVING ENCHANTMENT • C.J. Carmichael
The Birth Place

Nolan McKinnon is shocked when he's named his niece's guardian. He knows nothing about taking care of a little girl—especially an orphan—but he still would've bet he knew more than Kim Sherman. Kim's a newcomer to Enchantment—one who seems determined not to get involved with anyone. But Nolan can't refuse help, even if it comes from a woman with secrets in her past....

#1171 FOR THE CHILDREN • Tara Taylor Quinn
Twins

Valerie Simms is a juvenile court judge who spends her days helping troubled kids—including her own fatherless twin boys. Through her sons she meets Kirk Chandler, a man who's given up a successful corporate career and dedicated himself to helping the children in his Phoenix community. Valerie and Kirk not only share a commitment to protecting children, they share a deep attraction—and a personal connection that shocks them both.

#1172 MAN IN A MILLION • Muriel Jensen
Men of Maple Hill

Paris O'Hara is determined to avoid the efforts of the town's matchmakers. She's got more important things to worry about—like who her father really is. But paramedic Randy Sandford is determined to show her that the past is not nearly as important as the future.

#1173 THE ROAD TO ECHO POINT • Carrie Weaver

Vi Davis has places to go, people to meet and things to do—and the most important thing of all is getting a promotion. So she's not pleased when a little accident forces her to take time out of her schedule to care for an elderly stranger. She never would have guessed that staying with Daisy Smith and meeting her gorgeous son, Ian, is *exactly* the thing to do.

A great new story from a brand-new author!

#1174 A WOMAN LIKE ANNIE • Inglath Cooper
Hometown U.S.A.

Mayor Annie McCabe cherishes Macon's Point, the town that's become home to her and her son, and she's ready to fight to save it. And that means convincing Jack Corbin to keep Corbin Manufacturing, the town's main employer, in business. Will she be able to make Jack see the true value of his hometown…and its mayor?

#1175 THE FULL STORY • Dawn Stewardson
Risk Control International

Keep Your Client Alive is the mandate of Risk Control International. And RCI operative Dan O'Neill takes his job very seriously. Unfortunately, keeping his foolhardy client safe is a real challenge. And the last thing Dan needs is the distraction of a very attractive—and very nosy—reporter named Micky Westover.